The Death of an Optimist

The Death of an Optimist
a novel about the possible future

Sara Pax

Original cover photo: guildm20
Inside cover art: Piotr Siedlecki
Back cover photo: Jean Beaufort

ISBN-13: 978-2-9565157-0-8

To my heart, Emily
To my soul, Tómas
And my sweet Daisy

*I am an optimist – it does not seem
to be much use to be anything else.*
Winston Churchill

Thank you to my family, friends, and friends of friends, who gave their time to read this story and give me honest and critical feedback that helped make it better than I could have made it alone, including Paul, Lilia, Kim, and Tomas. And a big thank you to Mia Dancey for her thoughtful insight and suggestions.

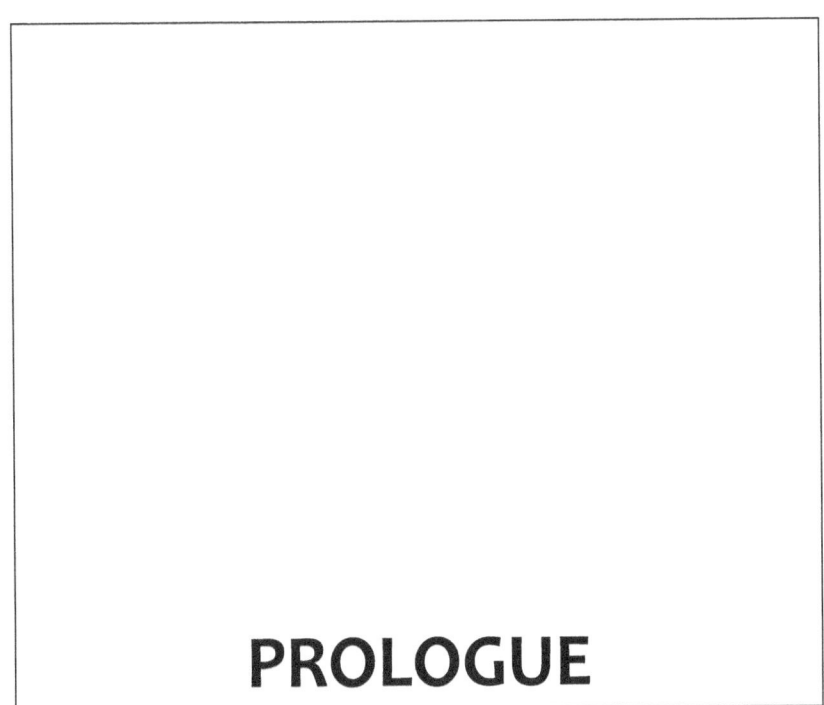

PROLOGUE

Bergen Norway, 17th May 2098

Dammit. I can't sleep. I've never been good at sleeping before a big speech. I wish I could take something and be sure that I would be awake and alert in the morning, but I'm not going to take the risk. I want to be my best tomorrow. It's so important that I'm sharp and intelligent, and reactive in my thoughts and behavior. I can't miss a beat.

Never mind, I'm sure I'll be fine. I'll be fueled by adrenaline, if nothing else. Now, I just wish I could rest a little and relax my brain and my body muscles. I expect that there will be so much to do afterwards that I won't have time – and won't want to – take a break for many weeks, if not months. Exciting times.

Even in the dark, this room is impressive. So many different heads have lain on this pillow. People who I have admired have had this same view of the darkened window, the sea beyond, and the speckled ceiling above. I wonder if they have suffered the same sleeplessness as me. I'm sure they all have their self-doubt, and their feelings of fear and excitement, just like me. Probably. I'm not that special.

I do feel proud though. I feel proud of what I'm about to do and of what we have accomplished in such a short period of time. We'll get things ready over the next few months and launch everything with the turn of the next century. It's hard to believe that's only 18 months from now. So many years of carrying on alone. We've come so far. It's hard to get my head around it sometimes.

What was that noise? Did it come from the street? It reminds me of the sound of my mother's refrigerator door closing. Like a vacuum seal. That door was so heavy when I was a child. The fridge was always full of mysterious things that I wasn't allowed to touch. So many enticing compartments with lights and screens that told her about everything she had stored in there and when to get more. Oh, how times have changed. So many more people have food to eat, even if home-cooked meals like Mum used to make are only remembered in old-fashioned ads that play off our nostalgia.

Those shadows on the ceiling remind me of the speckles of my childhood bedroom. That stuff had been sprayed on and was rough to the touch. I hated it because I wanted to stick those glow-in-the-dark stars to my ceiling, but they always fell off. This ceiling has the same consistency, but I know that it's made of that new paint that's really not paint. It's those new bio-particles that help clean the air in this room. It's actually quite fresh in here but maybe I don't need this comforter. It smells like the edge of a forest on a hot day. Which makes sense of course as these particles are from plants. Genius how they figured out how to use them as air filters. Imagine how worse off the world would be if we hadn't understood the importance of planting those oxygen forests back in the early days. Not that they could counter all the effects and damage that humans had created, but they certainly made a difference.

Dammit. I really have to shut out these thoughts and get some sleep. There'll be plenty of time to remember, to recount, and to relive all our accomplishments. This lovely old hotel has been renovated so well with all these new technologies. Bergen has really thrived over the past 50 years and they've done such a good job preserving their history with these lovely old buildings, while making things comfortable for visitors. There's really nothing stopping me from sleeping but my own busy thoughts.

Deep breaths. Slow deep breaths. In, 2, 3, 4. Out, 2, 3, 4, 5. I wonder if there's any side effects to this plant paint? It makes sense that it can cleanse the air and make the room fresher, even on the hot and humid days up here. But it's still so new that it's hard to be sure that there's no weird side effect that we haven't figured out yet. Two steps forward, one step back. That's how it has always been. No matter who's in charge, and no matter how quickly we wanted to bring change. There was just no way around it. The world just couldn't change that quickly. And sometimes it was two or three steps back before the next step forward could be reached.

Breathe In, 2, 3, 4. Out, 2, 3, 4, 5. I wonder what the reaction is going to be in the room when I finish the speech. Will people will immediately understand, or will they be stunned into silence? What will I do if the room is completely silent. Should I blab on, crack a joke, or just wait for their reaction? What a revolution it will be. So many people will benefit. It will change lives. Dammit. I'm not going to get any sleep, that's for sure.

It's such a shame that Alfie isn't here to experience this with me. We'd be cuddled up under this comforter talking quietly about our ideas. I still miss him so much. It's been over 15 years since he died, but I still feel the hollow in my stomach and the shock of the coolness of his pillow when I roll over in the early hours of the morning to touch him.

No one calls him Alfie anymore. I only hear his name in formal documentaries and historical re-tellings. And they always use his full name, Alfred P. Loughton. He really was a great man, all the way through, and one I admired and loved. But he'd had his failings too, as all men -- as all husbands. He did his best to juggle his work, his public role in the spotlight with some stolen private time. But, ironically, it was only since he had been gone that I have been able to spread my wings and make a name for myself.

Tomorrow will be my day, even though I'll make sure that Alfie's spirit is amongst us. I'm almost embarrassed by all the attention but also so proud of what I'll be representing. He was beloved by so many, and that was what had made it all fit together so well.

What's that? Oh shit. No! What a pity. No one will ever know...

CHAPTER 1

Lynola 2023-2041

As a child, Lynola hadn't really thought of much beyond her own garden gate, her immediate family, and the dreaded days slogging through school work, art camps, theatre groups, weekend get-togethers and picnics. As a child, she probably was quite typical in that way. She didn't have any great insight at a young age and didn't discover some great passion that drove her for the rest of her life. But she was solid, reliable, interested and interesting, and fun. People liked her. Other kids, and even grown-ups, engaged her in conversation, and she went along naturally telling people her opinions and expressing herself freely. She was light-hearted and given the freedom to continue being that way well into early adulthood.

Her face was open and friendly. She didn't turn heads as she walked into a room, but her smile was warm, and her attitude was welcoming. She made friends easily and her hazelnut eyes gleamed when she was excited in conversation. Her hair was thick, wavy, and mousy brown, and she kept it short, tumbling into her eyes over her short forehead. She wasn't overly tall or overly short, but she could hold her own in a crowd. She made a good first impression, even though she didn't stand out from the many. She was average, in looks, in height, and in achievement. But her independent intellect kept her curious and interesting, especially as she grew into her own person.

Lynola's was the third of four children, an usually large family for the times. Her father was a fairly successful lawyer working in a middle-sized corporate law firm handling mergers and acquisitions. Her mother managed a daycare center and stressed much more about her work than her husband, even though she earned less than a third of her husband's salary.

Lynola's older brothers were always in a world of their own, wrestling in the garden or playing in the local Little League baseball tournaments. Her younger brother was a musical prodigy and had been sent off to a specialized music boarding school by the age of 11. He wasn't much of a companion to Lynola anyway as he was always tinkering on his computer and electronic instruments.

Lynola's father was proud of his two eldest sons. They were only 11 months apart and sometimes it seemed like they were biological twins. They played on their high school baseball team, got scholarships to the same university and ended up with the same degree in communications and public relations. One after the other, they were offered contracts with AAA baseball teams and left on the touring life of a minor-league baseball player.

Her mother was preoccupied with her younger brother who, despite - or maybe because of - his musical genius, needed her maternal guidance and care for almost every other aspect of his life. Making the decision to send him to boarding school was difficult for her, but she sacrificed herself to give him the best chance in life.

In the middle, intelligent and quiet, Lynola was largely ignored and left to her own devices. She watched, learned, read, and grew up, and after a relatively calm few teenage years, she was accepted to university and left home without a second thought.

It wasn't until the start of her university days that she started to get glimpses of the realities of the world around her. The turbulent weather had only affected her in arguments with her mother over whether to wear a raincoat to school. The fluctuating food prices were unknown to her; there had always been food on their table and a nice variety all year round. The distinctions in poverty, in culture, in resources were only now starting to show themselves to her. Up until then, although she had travelled and been exposed to different languages and cultures, it had always been in the relative safety of a hotel or with close friends or family, and she'd been blissfully unaware of the deeper differences and inequities that lay around her.

She had been born in a time of deep disappointment. Many of the goals that were laid out at the turn of the century had a 2020 deadline, mostly for poetic symmetry it seemed, as the majority of the proclamations and promises were never achieved. When she was born, 3 years later after this deadline, the world was suffering from a malaise of hopelessness, rampant corruption, and the growing effects of permanent climate change. Upper middle-class families like hers were lucky in that they had safe housing, a largely safe food supply, and relative shelter from the economic turbulence suffered by the lower classes. Her parents made sure that she and her brothers lived as normal and sheltered a life as they could create for them.

When she left home for university at age 18 she was largely unprepared for what awaited her. She was now exposed to a markedly different world, and it shocked her, and excited her. She was challenged by the problems that faced her and her mind, which had always been quick but limited by her exposure, was now continually racing with ideas. Debates with professors frustrated her because they expected her to stay within the lines, but she frequently came to the conversation with a different perspective and interesting new ideas. All the barriers, prejudices and assumptions that were holding humanity back made her crazy. All the untried solutions. All the untapped wealth of intelligence, inventiveness, and ingenuity.

And so, she learned about helplessness. The frustrating inability of one person to make a difference. The immense need versus her ability to contribute. On the flipside, she discovered what people could do collectively and whenever she felt impotent, she would call up that inspiration – the wonder of historic human achievement. From space exploration, to vacuum tubes, to radio waves, to microwaves, to washing machines and irons, to the printing press, to democracy itself, and on and on and on.

She learned about apathy and selfishness and laziness. A majority of her fellow students were there because it was expected of them. Because that was their path, their duty, their blind acceptance of what was laid out for them. She realized of course that she was the same as most of them, as her parents constantly reminded her, but she felt so intensely different inside that she managed to see them through curious and separate eyes.

In her senior year of high school, the first Global President was appointment. Excitement was palpable, in her house, and around the world, as everyone understood that this was the start of a new era of global civilization. There was fear as well as hope, and at the time, hope was the stronger of the two emotions for most. Her parents talked about it over the dinner table as if the messiah had arrived. The new world order was giving hope to people who were feeling that their future, and the future of their children and grandchildren, was in dire jeopardy.

The new order determined that political leaders were no longer to be elected. Elections had been abolished as the vast majority of the world's population became exhausted from the endless corruption and the jockeying for power, the violence, hatred, rhetoric, posturing, punditry, politicking, fundraising, and the whole mess. It had taken 17 years of popular uprisings to permanently contest the status quo and after screaming and yelling and finally, sadly violently in many cases, wielding the power of the masses, a new model of government and leadership had been designed.

It had so radically changed the world that many people were truly stunned. The powerful were eliminated. The weak were empowered. The world as a whole -- seemingly overnight (but of course it had taken many years of serious struggle and fighting) – was transformed beyond people's wildest expectations.

The new world order, which had been unimaginable just a twenty years ago, was based on a way for humans to finally learn from the old adage – "power corrupts" not to mention "absolute power corrupts absolutely". The domino effect started in the early 20s in West Africa and spread rapidly throughout that continent, then into western Asia, then eastern Asia, Australasia, then South America, and then, finally and most reluctantly, to Europe and then North America. And while it ended up taking almost two decades, many forgot about those painful and often frightening years and reveled in what they had achieved and how much such a simple thing had changed the world.

Alfred 2013-2035

Alfred Philip Loughton was the heir to a long political dynasty. He was tall and stately. Handsome in a conventional sense. Dark hair, dark eyes, and a 5-o'clock shadow on his chin at the end of each day. He never grew the thick beard that was fashionable with his peers, opting instead for the more traditional clean-shaven look. His eyes were deep and pensive. When he spoke, he took the time to formulate his thoughts before he opened his mouth. His voice was soft and clear, but he rarely raised it above a normal level. He tended towards silence when in public, opting to listen rather than speak. The irony was that most people thought that he was a really interesting and charming guy, mostly because he listened to their banal stories without judgement or expressing his opinion. At least, that's what it seemed like he was doing. In fact, his judgements were strong, and his opinions were mostly unfavorable, but he preferred to keep them to himself and let people think that he was a compliant and amiable guy. In fact, he was boiling inside at the ignorance and short-sightedness of most people around him. He would pick his battles.

People were naturally drawn to him. He represented the new generation, but also the familiar and comfortable traditions of old. People wanted to be close to him. They felt at ease around him and he fostered that feeling. He was comfortable in his own skin and people were attracted to the feeling of security he gave them. He had descended from a political dynasty that suffered greatly in the worldwide evolutionary step that brought down all political dynasties. And while his ancestors had never been embroiled in any particularly scandalous affairs, Alfie had heard stories whispered among his parents and their friends when he was young. He sensed that it was a big change that was going to affect his family, based on the passion in the raised voices that these conversations often led to, but he was too young to understand how it was going to really affect his future.

The notion that political leaders were no longer going to be elected meant a great change to the Loughton family. The family could easily count back six generations of political figures, some more prominent than others. None had risen to international fame, but nevertheless their influence mattered. They were courted by members of their own political affiliations and their adversaries alike. They raised money effectively. They raised awareness effectively. They were considered reliable allies and solid political statesmen and women.

They were not directly entangled in any of the political uprisings that started in the early 20s and they were able to keep above the fray when their more outspoken political colleagues got swept up in the rhetoric that ultimately was used against them, often in ugly exchanges that never ended well. The Loughtons rode the wave of political changes fairly unscathed and ultimately were able to retire into obscurity without becoming victims to the scrutiny and public backlash that some of their more vocal contemporaries endured.

But Alfie's father and mother were disappointed that their two boys would not get the same opportunities to serve and lead as their father, uncles and aunts, grandmother, and great uncles had done. It had been a privileged existence, being able to stay behind the scenes and coat tails of more powerful – and therefore, more public – peers. They were extended many of the same benefits as their colleagues, but without the same risks. Each of the members of the Loughton family who had held public office, some for decades, had passed along the family's collective intelligence as a legacy to the next generation. Each, in turn, learned how to work the system, play well with others, stay within the lines, benefit from the way things were, avoid public scrutiny, and ultimately enjoy a comfortable and rewarding life for themselves and their family.

Now Alfie and his brother had to forge a new future for themselves. And because the change happened while they were still young, they never realized what they had lost. They never fully understood what their parents were regretful about. And they wholeheartedly bought into the new worldwide system of an unelected political establishment. Ironically, Alfie would have such a huge and important influence on this new world order in his later life, but in the early years of his adult life, he passionately supported and believed in the hope of the new system.

2023-2040

What began in West Africa and eventually spread around the world over 17 years was founded in utopian theory. A theory that great men and women, great leaders, were born not made. That history was full of ideological leaders who were ultimately corrupted by their own ideology, their own ego, their power, and their strength and influence. And modern African history, especially, was filled with such sad and tragic stories of corruption, ego and greed.

One spring, a number of leaders of opposition parties in some of the more democratic West African countries were inspired to come together in a regional conference, originally designed to address some of the more blatant corruption scandals in their countries, and discuss ways to collaborate and win elections. What came out of this three-day conference was revolutionary. An idea that shocked even the participants. An idea that was so powerful but overwhelmingly straightforward that no one could later say who even first proposed it (and no one ever claimed it).

The idea was simple. Anyone who harbored political ambition, anyone who even secretly desired to lead, should be ineligible for a leadership position or a position of power and influence of any kind. A sarcastic version of this idea was not new. There was a common cynical notion that had been voiced hundreds of thousands of times in the modern age that stated that anyone who actually desired to be elected Prime Minister or President was too corruptible to be a good and effective leader. While anyone who was truly qualified, both intellectually and morally, would never want to subject themselves, their families and friends, and their own character to the scrutiny and corrupting process of a political election. And yet, no one had ever thought realistically to implement it.

The idea was crazy and yet so truly liberating that countries which had democratically-elected leaders were able to implement it through their electoral process. The first country to convert was Liberia, whose regime so fully embraced the new philosophy that every member of their democratically-elected leadership agreed to collectively step down in a globally vidded and dramatic weekend of elaborate and formal ceremonies, instating the new government during the same weekend. Within a few weeks, things in the country began to improve and while the world watched and measured, socially, economically and culturally, the country started to witness improvements that quickly became the envy of neighboring countries. Tribal conflicts were being openly discussed in "safe rooms" where mutual respect and trust were nurtured. Corruption was wiped out almost instantly, as members of the new regime were unflappable in their incorruptibility. And finally, deep-rooted historic dysfunctions were being discussed openly and addressed with new perspectives and neutral opinions. Everything from government spending, to infrastructure projects that held value to the widest number of people, to natural resource allocations that benefited most of the people while exploiting the fewest and doing the best to protect for the future, led to a collective optimism that hadn't been seen in decades.

Liberia's courage in taking the first step was celebrated and other countries soon followed. States with more oppressive regimes were able to ride the wave of global discontent to overthrow their governments. It helped, of course, that the global community had been shrinking rapidly in previous decades and that groups of countries like the European Union, the African Union, and the new Asian Union were already used to the idea of collective political and economic leadership, however fragile. And with the lightning speed of information exchange through the vid networks, even in the remotest and poorest areas of the under-developed world, the new power of the people was realized.

One holdout was eastern Siberian, which had become an independent region from the Russian Federation in the nationalist revolution of 2031. Each small city and village was run independently from each other. Since the revolution, they hadn't even bothered to create a collective leadership, and most people lived hand-to-mouth without any time or patience for cooperation. Each village had their council, made up of elders, who had the longest memories and the strongest personalities. They resolved small disputes over land or property. And their power did not extend beyond the village's boundaries. The region had been subjected to a harsher and harsher climate, and the oppressive heat that now smothered the region for a third of the year followed almost immediately by a deep freeze that made it hard for anything to breathe let alone live and grow, required more and more creative farming techniques in order for families to produce just enough to feed themselves. There was no common will or energy to create a collective government, never mind converting to a new unelected system. They just didn't care and didn't have the resources or the will to do the work necessary to collectively implement the new system.

2040-2047

The realities of the idea were eventually standardized by a collective of multi-national and multi-ideological representatives, which, unlike the United Nations and other impotent international institutions, had the tremendous and, unusually united, power of the masses behind them. There were not a lot of difficult issues to resolve. The whole process was very simple and was able to piggyback on existing technology, such as digital birth certificates, that had been implemented globally to track and prevent the spread of global pandemics almost two decades before.

They expanded on these information repositories to classify people based on their character, their behavior, testimonials from friends and neighbors, their achievements, their failures, their ideologies, and their ambitions. As it turned out, when all the information was gathered, and the data was crunched, the number of eligible leaders was a lot fewer that one would have expected – on average, only about 12% of the global population qualified. And so, from there, it was simply a lottery system. In most cases the lottery winners were reluctant, but eventually willing, participants in the political process and after they had served their term, melted easily back into their previous lives. Safeguards were put in place to prevent some of the most obvious corrupting influences, but because the nominated leaders were often mild mannered, moral people of strong character and determination, they were typically quite effective during their term.

The algorithm that went into the lottery system was controversial and caused long and passionate debate among previously elected leaders for a short while. However, the success of the algorithm in choosing appropriate and effective leaders was proven quickly and the naysayers were soon silenced. The international team that initially started the process was put in charge of monitoring the lottery system, but it didn't take much doing as it was built into an open-source software package that was distributed freely to anyone that wanted their own copy. The data collection process was cumbersome at first and required a lot of human intervention, but quite quickly simplified and evolved into surveys that collectors distributed and stored electronically, and which soon became a regular course of people's lives. Filling out a survey on a neighbor or a colleague was a weekly or monthly occurrence and was done easily in a matter of minutes. Surveys were updated regularly, and it became an activity that people were proud to contribute to, as important a societal duty as going to the voting booth had once been. And personal disagreements or vindictiveness that showed up in information that was gathered was, more often than not, identified and eliminated by the program when compared to all the corroborating information gathered about one given individual.

Of course, there were some early problems and algorithm adjustments that needed to be made. The local sheriff of a Romanian town had to be recalled because it later turned out that he had a double life and was attempting, rather feebly, to be a husband and father to two different women and their children on either side of his home town. A state senator from Arkansas was recalled because he had tried to bribe the lottery officials. A council member from Manchester was recalled because she was having an affair with the previously elected council member and had become his puppet in trying to get his previous position reinstated. And of course, a number of other corruption charges and recalls had to be affected. But, in the big picture, the numbers of mishaps and adjustments were minor.

About a year into implementation, there was a huge hacking scandal that threatened to undermine the whole system. People were scared that the reliance on a new automated system that they were so passionately fighting for was subject to sabotage. Of course, it was impossible to please 100% of the people 100% of the time, but the large majority of the world's population came to believe that the lottery was going to rebuild the integrity of their leadership councils and committees and lead to a more just and collective use of scarce resources. The Global Council on Leadership was made up of elder statespeople and their trusted advisors and they led the way in finding ways to easily control the lottery system and resist hacking. The solution ended up being easier than anyone thought. Instead of building higher and higher walls that would never be truly impenetrable, they opened the gates wide and installed a multi-layer verification system that ensured that all data stored was corroborated by dozens, if not hundreds of sources. A form of wiki-verification solved the hacking problems and slowly rebuilt the fragile trust that was so vital.

The more turbulent areas of the globe, especially the ones controlled by dictators, were much harder to stabilize under the new system. The resistance and historical hatred were so infused into these societies that it took more than one generation before the new system was fully accepted and appreciated. The documented success of the lottery system was so powerful in its transformation of political processes around the world, that it was a hard force to fight. And yet some did. And one or two smaller communities succeeded for a while. But soon the world was united under the lottery system.

This is not to say that the world was homogenous all of a sudden. Or had one set of politics. Or one set of cultural beliefs. Or even agreement on many of the traditional issues of strife – country's borders, water resource allocation, immigration, distribution of weapons, religious freedoms, and more. In fact, in many cases, they didn't go away at all. But now, there were leaders whose only purpose was to find compromises and build collaborations and alliances and affect real change. The leaders were not elected because they had the biggest budgets or the biggest egos, but because they had the qualities of a fair, dispassionate and effective leader. And it did make a difference in many cases. Change was underway in cases where positive change was usually slow, if not impossible, to imagine.

Lynola, 2041-2046

During her first days at university, Lynola's world view changed. Of course, it timed perfectly with the new world order currently being built in her name and for her future, but it wasn't that specifically that revolutionized her world. The reality was that she had never been confronted with the world in its barest form. It was true that the university campus didn't totally reflect the real world either, but to Lynola it was shocking. Most of her classmates had never eaten fresh fruit or vegetables, and meat substitutes were everywhere. Fried food substitutes were a student body favorite, and no one seemed to blink an eye at what was being offered in the cafeteria.

Lynola had never really questioned what was given to her at mealtimes. Of course, she'd eaten out with friends and family many times over the years, but she hadn't realized that food substitutes were what most people ate most of the time. She had never truly appreciated the value of the fresh fruit and vegetables that her mother always seemed to have on hand, and the variety of food stored in the oversized refrigerator and freezer she had installed in the kitchen with its fancy and complicated system of lights and screens. At university, Lynola was confronted with the apathy of the masses, their contentment just to exist and accept what was in front of them. To eat what was served without question or care. To learn what was presented to them without analysis or thought. To follow everyone else.

She found it infuriating and vowed to break the mold. She started by talking to her friends about food. Preaching, but in a good way. Most had never questioned the food substitutes they'd grown up with and Lynola was shocked by their indifference. Surely, at least their parents should have known better as they had grown up with real vegetables and real meat. It wasn't that she wanted to lord over her peers, it was just so truly shocking to her that they were so accepting of the status quo and trusted in the corporations' propaganda.

Lynola found herself advocating for healthy food alternatives and against the processed foods that they all ate. She surprised even herself that she even cared about it so much. She was amazed at her own passion about the issue. She'd never consciously considered it before.

She tried to start a gardening club, convincing the school to give them a patch of dry ground behind the dorm on the edge of campus. It was a pathetic little patch, and she tried desperately to get things to grow there and get her fellow students involved. Neither were easy, and she didn't get very far, but she did develop a reputation for doggedness and persistence, even though she never managed to get any edible vegetables out of that dreary frozen patch.

She was nothing if not passionate, and she drove some people away with her persistence. But she didn't give up and she talked about her ideas whenever she got a chance. She was surprised that Alfie listened. He was the TA in her Intro to Sociology class, and she was one of 150 freshmen and women in a big lecture hall. But he had noticed her through her writing that he was in charge of grading for the professor. Even though they weren't really friends, she had made an impression on him with her intellect and quick wit. They ran into each other on campus from time to time and he was the first to really engage with her and brainstorm about solutions to her garden club problems. They were both well-schooled in history - him through his own family history and his doctoral thesis on the effects of climate change on indigenous people, and her because history had always been one of her favorite subjects, like reading a good novel but during school time. Their conversations became intense and stimulating and they started to see each other through more appreciative eyes.

They didn't run in the same social circles. He was with the more entitled children of alumni, an up-and-coming professor with a quiet intelligence that she was attracted to, and she was just one of the new freshmen. He was almost 10 years older than her and was clearly establishing himself in the university world, while she was just starting out, all wide eyed and fascinated by it all. They ran into each other at guest lecturing events or alumni meet-and-greets and stimulated each other intellectually when discussing the subject at hand. But socially, they weren't in the same league. Lynola had a few good friends, and some casual boyfriends throughout her college days, but she knew that none of them were lifers. And that was fine by her. There were so many other things to explore and discover that she didn't have the patience to nurture anything else.

Her studies focused on history, as it related to modern day. She was surprised by all the devastating failures in history, especially recent history. And the selfishness; the short-sighted selfishness of so many people. Redirecting rivers from one population to another instead of addressing the core problems of water waste and conservation. So many decisions that led to lose-lose situations. And, of course, the biggest farce of human's capacity to rule themselves was evident during the last 150 years in dealing with the changing climate, the failing free capitalist model, and all that they implied.

It wasn't that human beings were incapable, of that she was sure. It was just that they were inherently selfish and that the political structures of the past 200 years had fed into that ever-growing selfishness and prevented any other method of rule. By understanding this, she truly got what an amazing feat of human ingenuity - together with the power of the masses - it had been to change the way leaders were elected. It was a huge step-change in human evolution and one she had great hopes for. And of course, she wasn't the only one. But it was a surprise to her that she seemed like one of the few of her generation who grasped its immense importance.

Alfred, 2035-2037

Alfie came from a very different world and his social circles were poles apart from Lynola's. He had a solid and loyal group of friends, many of whom he'd known since his childhood. His group was tight and enclosed, and he rarely went out with women from outside his social class. It wasn't that he was bigoted or racist, but it was just more comfortable to stay within the confines of what was familiar. Through friends' encouragement, he finally asked Serena out after knowing her for most of his teenage years and having a crush on her for as long as he could remember. Serena was the daughter of one of his father's political collaborators and they had spent a lot of time together as children. She had grown into a beautiful woman, and as her name suggested, was serene in her beauty. Her life plan was laid out before her and she was completely confident and happy with that. Alfie was one of the crowd and he wasn't bad looking or controversial. He fit her image perfectly.

Together Alfie and Serena became the It couple. Alfie was doing well at the university and had potential in rising to the top of a renowned institution. Serena was tall and stunning and knew how to work a room. She kept her hair long, blond, and straight, and it swayed gently with whenever she moved. Alfie loved how they looked together. Handsome and refined. Serena's taste in clothes, jewelry, restaurants and even vacations, was consistent with his taste - or at least the taste of his family – and he was sure that they were the right choices for him.

After two respectable years of dating Alfie decided that the time was right to get married and settle down. He went the traditional way and spoke to her about it first, then spoke to her father, and then popped the question with an heirloom ring that had been in his family for generations. Unsurprisingly she said yes to his proposal and they started planning the wedding. Everything was falling into place nicely and Alfie was satisfied that his life was exactly how it was supposed to be.

That was, until two weeks before the wedding. He came home from class one day, smiling and whistling, expecting to see Serena there with her flower arranging group or charity planning committee. Instead he found her in their bed with a stranger. A swarthy stranger, clearly not from the neighborhood, who was obviously giving her pleasure. Her face was contorted in ecstasy but immediately changed to horror when he walked into the room and gasped. She flung herself out of the bed and ran to him apologizing and begging him to listen. He was frozen. It was if he had walked through a looking glass and his reality was shattering and lay in shards around his feet. He stumbled and held himself steady against a wall. Within seconds he ran through a series of intense reactions. He was horrified by what he had witnessed, then horrified by what Serena had been doing, then horrified at his own stupidity, and finally heart-broken that his perfect life was crushed. He lurched out of the bedroom, and out of his perfect life forever. It would be years before he was able to trust again. And when he did, it was Lynola whom he put his trust in.

Everything changed for him after his wedding was called off. His life plan had been to settle down, start a family with the woman he loved, and work on his budding career. His plan had imploded the instant he walked into that bedroom and he suddenly had options he'd never considered before. He was young, unattached, educated, and eager to rediscover the world and himself.

He started recklessly. Heading out to places that were known for their fun, lively and carefree lifestyles. He was a little older than the rest but blended into the crowd of young kids of privilege enjoying what different cultures had to offer. Sex, drugs, and rock and roll were the basic themes of his existence. In his later years he was thankful that he'd been spared some of the dangers that had befallen other random partygoers. Too much sex, too many drugs, not enough sense. Luckily, he came out unscathed and reborn in many ways.

Inadvertently during this time in his life, he was exposed to some of the more critical issues of his generation. He witnessed poverty so profound that he could barely look at it in comparison to his own good fortune. He saw the devastating effects of too much rain, not enough rain, and overpopulation in many of the cities. In what had once been Russia, he saw desperate families fleeing, slowly, in endless lines down muddy roads searching for a better life. In Asia, as he drove past city centers to get to the bars and the beaches, he saw deformities and destruction. And even though he wouldn't consciously register them at the time, these memories stuck and would drive him in his later years.

When he came home, he was reluctant to simply pick up his old life, as even where his old friendships were mostly intact they were reminders of the broken life he left behind. He dated women in his circle but the memories of Serena's face contorted in pleasure never left him. These women were clones of Serena and he had to find a different mold. He started his doctorate studies and started going back to some of his old university haunts. One night he happened upon a poetry slam and was taken in by the energy and ferocity being expressed by the young creative people loudly proclaiming their passions on stage. He was fascinated, and started attending the slams regularly, although never participating. He was invigorated by their vigor and carried by the waves of their convictions.

He became a regular at these events. He found them both stimulating and mesmerizing in their diversity and power. He didn't know these people. They weren't part of his familiar lifestyle and that both pleased him and excited his sense of adventure. One night a new poet tentatively stepped onto the stage. He recognized her from one of his classes. She started reading her poem. Screaming it really. The force of her passion made him uncomfortable, but he couldn't look away. After the event he waited to find her in the crowd and introduced himself as her sociology TA. Of course she recognized him and they easily picked up the subject of their classroom debates. They made plans to meet up and the intellectual spark that had glimmered in their early conversations was nurtured and truly ignited.

Alfred, 2037-2041

January 27, 2037

I can't believe it· My life is over, my dreams are over· Serena has broken me, stolen my dreams· Who is she? I loved her!! Who did I love? I dot understand· We had everything and she's thrown it all away· How could she have done this? I'll never forgive her· I'll never see her or talk to her again· How could I have been such a fool? How could I have trusted her? Did she ever love me? What was I thinking???

July 12, 2037

These Groeners are amazing· Just think that 20 years ago this landscape was ice and rock· Greenland is green again· And blue, and full of gorgeous blond Danes· The beaches, the women, the men, the drugs· This is the life I'm going to dedicate myself to for a while· Goodbye world·

November 24, 2037

The weather is the same day after day· The water is clear and warm enough to swim· The nightlife rocks –

lots of kids – from all four corners of the world. Making tons of friends. I never want this to end.

March 11, 2038

M&D getting on my case. It's true I'm starting to get too old for this scene, but they don't need to know that. The natives are getting a bit tired of me, maybe I should go home. I'm not sure I'm ready to get back to "adult life". I wonder if that teaching position with Prof Margil is still on the table. I liked her style and she liked me. I could see myself back in that world again. Am I ready? Yes, probably soon....

June 28, 2038

Heading out tomorrow. Can't say I'm taking too much of this place with me except some scarred lungs and luckily (!!) a clean bill of health. I'll miss the beaches and the sunshine and the distractions. It's been paradise. I won't forget this place in a hurry. Decided to take the long way home so I can visit a few more places before I "settle down". Not sure what awaits...

August 12, 2039

Geez, I feel so guilty and disgusted with myself. I spent so much time satisfying my own shallow desires and wallowing in my own self-pity. The world is so complex and struggling on so many levels. I'm grateful to have these months to explore and see it firsthand. This first stop in Nepal has been so eye-opening. It's beautiful, and confusing, and rich with culture, and poor in so many ways. The people need for so much but aren't sad. But I'm sad for them, which doesn't make any sense. It's stimulating and enlightening and my brain is firing on more cylinders than it has for quite a while. I'm invigorated again. I'm looking forward to the rest of the trip, before I head home to reality and the daily work grind.

April 17, 2039

No words... Nepal, India, Mongolia, Siberia, Bulgaria, Italy, Morocco, Kenya, Zanzibar. Next Namibia, Brazil, Argentina, Uruguay, Panama and Mexico. So many stories. So much density and history and tragedy and joy. I'm overwhelmed and I'm full of love, and fascination, and ideas, and deep sadness. So much that can be done, but isn't. I need my 'small' life again to put things into perspective.

September 25, 2039

Prof Margil loves me!! I'm ready to get my head into something other than myself, a decadent lifestyle, and other people's stories. School starts in a week – I will have time to rediscover the campus and check out the new students. I wonder if any of my classmates are around. Most of them think I'm mad, but it feels right somehow. Feels weird but not too weird. M&D pleased.

December 5, 2039

Been a whirlwind few weeks. Hardly any time to breathe. Lots of class world, lots of teaching work (mostly grunt work – why did I think anything different?). I'm definitely here for my brawn and not much of my brains. Hardly any time to socialize or meet people. Met up with some old school mates who are still here doing research, etc. Been thinking a lot about the Groeners. What a mess they're in.

June 26, 2040

Recovering from a totally crazy year. Work, work, and more work. Got another month to go and then back at it. At least this time I know what I'm in for. Prof M says I should look into Green Corps. M&D not totally thrilled about that idea. Interesting program. Could be something! Given what I've seen, I feel the tug of wanting to help somehow.

September 7, 2040

Back to the grindstone· Not so slammed this time around – I'm better at anticipating now· More time to breathe and think· Met a couple of alum who did Green Corps· Amazing stories· One was in the Sahara, reseeding the pine forests· Another in Mexico, trying to counter desertification – sounds like a losing battle· Very sad·

October 17, 2040

Ran into an old pal from Greenland· Sounds like life there hasn't changed, at least for the tourists· Townies lives are getting tougher· He couldn't tell me too many details as he didn't pay much attention (kinda like me when I was there)· Makes me curious though· I'd like to go back and see for myself one of these days·

January 11, 2041

Talked to Prof M about the Groeners· She's pushing me to talk to Green Corps to see if any projects underway in the region· Got to think through it carefully though· Don't want to make a fool of myself·

March 23, 2041

Met a woman at one of the poetry slams· She was so fired up· Totally mad but interesting, intriguing· Actually I'm pretty sure I know her from sociology class· Her writing is good. I was impressed by her ability to create arguments in her writing. And now I've seen her live on stage. Took my breath away...a little.

> *May 17, 2041*

Spoke to the Green Corps. They don't have anything going on with the Groeners. The Danes won't allow it. Prof M going to support me and my hypothesis. Seems rather a long shot that I'll get to take this on.

> *October 27, 2041*

Green Corps deadline approaching. Not sure I'm going to get this off the ground right now. Hanging out a lot with Lynola. She really gets me thinking. I think I might be falling for her. She's definitely keeping me on my toes. She's a wild one, crazy and inspiring and we make a good pair. Hope M&D like her.

Alfred & Lynola, 2041-2048

It certainly wasn't a done deal. For the first time in Alfie's life he had met someone who challenged him. Someone who challenged the status quo that he had never really questioned. Someone who demanded that he express himself, intellectually and emotionally. Lynola was skeptical of him. This privileged man who was older than her and who had so seldom questioned the world around him. Despite herself, she was flattered by his attention and stimulated by their interactions, and slowly their love bloomed.

Their relationship was one of mutual support and challenges. It wasn't as easy to love Lynola as it had been Serena. Lynola didn't let him get away with not speaking his mind and not standing up for his opinions. Lynola made him consider new situations and figure out which side of the fence he sat on. She made him quantify his commitments by taking action whenever possible. In all, she made him a better version of himself.

She also had plans and a vision for herself. She wasn't going to quit school and follow him around like a puppy. She was just starting her intellectual pursuits and she had plans. She wanted to study politics, history, collective governance, cooperatives, unions, and other community organization structures. It fascinated her how they were sometimes successful, sometimes not, but always slow moving. Why were people so hard to motivate and energize? What made the difference between the successes and the failures? Alfie was caught up in her fascination, and in his own doctoral research that he shared with her during their long nights of debate and conversation, playing off each other's interests and passions.

For Lynola, Alfie was an angel (not that she would ever had admitted that to anyone, especially not to Alfie). It was true that he was privileged, but he rose to her every challenge. Every opinion was strong enough for her to respect, even when she disagreed. He didn't just tolerate her passions, he inspired them and encouraged them. And he did it with a calmness that she could never muster. A confidence that she was never able to feel. She fell in love with that confidence, that calmness, and the inner passion that she could incite with her prodding.

Together they were a formidable team. Lynola hadn't travelled as much as Alfie, but she was certainly well-read and didn't miss out on anything that was going on in the world, even if she'd only witnessed it on the newssites. He projected an air of knowledge even when he didn't really have a complete understanding of a situation. He was building a good reputation at the university and she was writing furiously and getting recognition for her insight and opinions on a wide range of global maladies.

Their families were happy with the union, even though each family was foreign to the other. Ironic really since the roots of each family were within 200 kilometers of each other. And so, in the winter of 2048 when Alfie was 35 and Lynola was 26, they got married in a civil ceremony with their friends and family around them. It was a happy time. They honeymooned on a small Caribbean island, off the beaten path, picnicking on beaches that had been villages just a decade before, but were now deserted as they could no longer sustain a permanent population, watching the sunset over the endless horizon, basking in the warm winter sun and each other's company.

Alfred, 2047

He stroked her cheek as a final goodbye and slipped out the sliding door. He shouldn't have stayed. He should have walked away as soon as she had started talking. But his compassion made him weak. He didn't want to create any more hurt. He just wanted everyone to live in peace and harmony, even though it had been her who had shattered their life. But he felt compassion anyway. Even guilt, that maybe he had been somewhat to blame, not for the cheating, of course, that was all her. But maybe for a reason that she had cheated at all. Maybe he hadn't given her everything she needed. Maybe he could have listened to her better, paid more attention to her, experimented and had more adventures with her, like she wanted. He knew he couldn't stay. Their time was over. It was over a while ago, and it had been her fault. He would have worked hard to create their perfect life, but she had thrown it all away. But her guilt and regret at the pain she had caused herself, and him, of course, was clear in her face, in her words, begging him to forgive her, to take her back, to go back to their perfect lives. It had been almost 10 years, but he needed to consciously close this chapter of his life before he fully committed to the next one. He smiled inside at the thought of his new life.

He had allowed her to touch him, to cry on him, and to kiss him. Their embraces were familiar and comfortable. He knew every curve of her body and how every muscle and tendon moved when she was hugging him. He felt disconnected. He was in his head, not in his heart. He was doing this for her, not for him. Maybe he could ease some of her pain and guilt. Give her closure, when she really didn't deserve any of it. But he knew he had the power to help her, and he wanted to use the power for good, and not to create more hurt. She had to know that he was behaving out of compassion, and not love. He had moved on, it wasn't a secret. She had to move on too. So, he let her seduce him. She knew his body too and knew what he responded to. He let her kiss him like she used to. He reacted predictably and responded to her touch. Their movement together was familiar and easy. He knew that he could settle in this life if he wanted. But he didn't want to. Just this one last time for her. Then it would be goodbye forever. She knew it. He knew it. It was their farewell.

It was only three weeks later that Serena realized she was pregnant. Her body felt strange and she immediately thought back to that last night with Alfie, before he slipped quietly away. It was almost unbelievable to think that her plan had worked. She knew she had been ovulating and she knew that he would come to her out of compassion. And now she knew that he couldn't leave her. Not with his child growing inside her. Despite all her indiscretions, which, but the way, she had apologized and apologized for, he was going to have to forgive her now and they would restart their charmed life together. People got over these things all the time. She knew he could forgive her and forget. She just knew it.

She rang him on his vid, but he was out of service range. Where could he be? There weren't many places left in the world that were out of service range. Either deep underground or in a remote village somewhere in Siberia. Or maybe he'd just cloaked his line for a few hours. He was prone to doing that when he was sleeping or wanting to work on something uninterrupted. She'd try again tomorrow.

Serena, 2047

Serena had a difficult pregnancy. Alfie had blocked her from all his comm channels and eventually she gave up trying to get through. She felt too sick most days to try hard anyway. She desperately chewed on the seaweed supplements that her nutritionist had given her and drank ginger tea like it was her life's blood. In this day and age, how come they hadn't cured morning sickness? Or "all-day" sickness as she was having.

Everyone said it was a good sign for a healthy baby, and all the scans were good. The baby - she - had round cheeks and a mischievous smile on the last scan. But Serena didn't really pay much attention. She knew she wasn't going to keep her. Alfie was clearly done with her and she didn't want him anymore anyway. He obviously was going to ruin his life by living below the status that was rightfully his. She didn't want anything to do with that. And she certainly wasn't going to raise his unwanted daughter alone. She was ready to move on. As soon as this interminable pregnancy was over she was going back to her old life. The potential parents - sterile, each and every one - were lining up at her door ready to take the load off her hands. And thank goodness for that. She couldn't even be bothered to pick a potential parent. She let her agent handle that. She spent all her free time watching vids on how to get her body back after pregnancy and talking to treatment specialists on how soon after the birth she could come in for the necessary work. She was going to break a record for bouncing back to her real life. And no one would ever be the wiser.

Alfred & Lynola, 2047-2059

They hadn't planned on having children right away. Lynola wanted to spend some years traveling and working on community-based change, to go to some of the places that Alfie had seen and talked about so passionately – especially Greenland – to get more involved in grass roots advocacy and community issues and explore different career paths and lifestyle options. She was 10 years his junior and had every intention of visiting Nepal and Mexico and the other places that Alfie told her about. There was no reason to rush into anything. But the fates disagreed with her timeline and she was pregnant within 3 years of the wedding. They had barely had enough time to settle into a routine of work, research, travel, and community development before they met their first child, Amelia.

When Amelia was born, their life changed forever. For all her philosophizing, Lynola knew instantly that she was going to be unable to work full-time and leave the baby in the care of the community. It surprised her, this overwhelming nurturing instinct that took her over. Less than a year ago she would have laid money on the fact that she would have put the baby in care and go back to work. She was a huge advocate of the care centers and knew that they were a critical part of a woman's ability to have a fully fleshed-out career. But she realized very quickly that she wasn't going to be one of them.

Alfie was a great dad in the way that society asked him to be a dad. He shared the night-time feelings and daily care of the baby until he went back to work -- to rest, he said, half-jokingly and Lynola was left to forge her own way. Mothering didn't come completely naturally to her, but she soon got into a rhythm and her confidence grew. She met few other mothers, women like her who were bucking society's trends and staying home to raise their children. To most, it was old-fashioned and backward. But she just couldn't imagine herself doing what other women did, and she had nightmares about being forced to leave her baby behind. She had to follow her instincts. She didn't care how it looked to others.

Living on one salary was practically impossible. Alfie's job at the university was stable and his upward mobility was encouraging, but one salary was not enough to feed a growing family. But despite Lynola's training and part-time apprenticeship as a community organizer, she felt ostracized by the society who couldn't accept her choice to stay home to raise her child. As a consequence, she spent a lot of time on her own with the baby. She worked their community garden with vigor and compensated for her lack of income by supplementing the family's diet with fresh fruit and vegetables. She read a lot. It was her window to the world. She commented on the newssites and added her opinion to debates on every subject - from homeland security to baby rash to the newest fad in food supplements. On that, she had plenty of opinions.

Two years later she was pregnant again, and she felt happy. She knew she was swimming against the tide in many ways, but she filled her days with the activities of raising her children, taking care of their little house, and tending her garden. By the time Drake was born, she had all her comebacks down pat. All the stares at her walking down the streets with the three children who were so obviously hers. The sideways comments about her "laziness" in not going back to work. The whispers as she took care of her abundant garden and carried armfuls of fresh vegetables home. She knew society held different things in higher value - contributing to social networks for example - but she was strong enough not to care too much.

Lynola, 2059

Look at me now. I can barely recognize myself. A stay-at-home mother with three children under 8. I would have scoffed in the face of anyone suggesting that was my future just a few years ago. Big dreams and no reality. But I just couldn't leave these kiddies and concentrate on anything else. Ironic isn't it. These little pests, who I'm annoyed with 95% of the time, take up so much of my brain power that there's just so little room for anything else. Alfie does his best, but it's never good enough - yes, according to me - so why bother to burden him. He has his work. He has to have quiet time and space to think, to prepare his classes, to grade his papers, to participate in his research projects. I'm so damned conventional - in a turn-of-the-last-century kind of way. I didn't know that this was me. But it turns out it is. My mothering instinct, to keep these kids in one piece, fed, clothed, relatively clean, and educated, has overtaken me and any other interests that I had. Nothing else seems quite so important. Even though they truly drive me crazy. The two girls constantly waking up the baby, and the endless laundry and picky eating habits of all three of them. Can't wait until schools starts again in September. Amelia and Charlotte will be outta here from 8 to 4:30 four days a week. Bliss. God, I hope no one ever reads this. I'd be hanged in the town square for my blasphemy. Children are supposed to be joy and laughter and hope for the future. And they are, at least 5% of the time HAHAHAHAHAHA. The other 95% is drudgery, but drudgery that I can't seem to pull myself away from. I guess. My catholic guilt gene is still intact after so many generations of agnostics in the family. HAHAHAHAHA I'm even cracking jokes for myself now. I'm really going bonkers. Alfie will be home soon....time to get these critters cleaned and fed and ready for bed (yes, I even rhyme without thinking about it HAHAHAHAHAHAHA).

Alfred & Lynola, 2059

When Alfie first got the notice of his lottery nomination they were stunned. He wasn't even 50 yet. How could the council think that he was the right candidate? It was incredible that the algorithm had identified him as a good candidate for political office. He could hardly get his head around it.

Deep down, Lynola knew he was perfect for a position in government, but the disruption to their family life was something that terrified her. She was used to her routine. The kids were all in school now and mostly doing well and she busied herself with her homemaking and food growing. They talked about declining the nomination. It wasn't a common practice, but it had been done before. Alfie's sense of duty and pride in being nominated eventually won out and he began the vetting process.

At first, they weren't told what position he'd been nominated for. Just "public service" which could mean anything from local school counselor, a county judge, a state or regional representative, or on a more global scale. But when he found out where he was being asked to travel to, he knew immediately that it wasn't a local position.

The vetting process was done by interviews. Lots and lots of interviews. These were mostly done in person, rather than by vidcam or virtually, so Alfie started traveling. To Nepal first, home of the Global Council on Leadership who started the vetting process for all nominees to be placed in a global role. He'd been to Nepal before, during another life, but now he spent much of his time in conference rooms being watched and judged. Alfie was flattered and excited and overwhelmed. The questions that were asked of him were so varied that in many ways it was very off-putting. It wasn't like an exam when you knew the material was going to be about a certain subject. These questions were about everything.

Some of the questions stumped him completely. Things like who to choose between when deciding the fate of two sides of an argument, when he could empathize with both sides. How to decide where to put a new dam when all the choices required displacing millions of people from their homes and communities? Also, why he had chosen the job he had? And the woman he had married? And the number of children he had? Most of the questions had no right answer. The vetting panels were as much interested in his facial expressions and body language as he heard the questions, and the readouts on the emotsensors as he thought through the answers, as they were the words that came out of his mouth.

Sometimes the questions seemed so off-track and absurd that he wanted to laugh out loud. What was his favorite color, his favorite meal, the place he most wanted to visit in the universe? How did he choose the names of his children? What music didn't he like and why? What was his most vivid memory from childhood? How would he describe his feelings towards Serena? What God did he believe in? What does he think of his wife's opinions? And her cooking? If he were a tree, what kind of tree would he be? If he were Noah and could only save 50 species from the flood, which 50 would they be and why?

He actually enjoyed the process, mostly. In some ways it was grueling and invasive, but it was also stimulating and thought provoking. The longer it went on, the more curious he got about the position he was being vetted for. He spoke to Lynola every day and talked to the kids via vidcam every night before bed. He told Lynola about the questions of the day and their conversations were interesting and varied as they laughed at some of them, and further discussed the more serious topics.

At the end of the almost three-week process he was flown back home, and they waited. They went back to their normal lives, mostly, and really only spoke about the possibilities late at night after the house was all quiet and they were half asleep. They were more curious than excited, more intrigued than hopeful. They waited.

Alfred, 2060

I should tell her. It's the only real secret I've ever kept from her and with all this scrutiny, I feel like she might find out another way, and that would be devastating to her, and to us, to our family. It's not something I've ever felt like I needed to tell her. It's only the guilty who feel unburdened by confessing their sins. The victims are hurt even more by the reality. But I think that I should tell her, even if it doesn't become public knowledge.

I don't really feel guilty. In my heart of hearts I always felt like it was an act of charity, of kindness. It didn't mean anything to me, but it meant a lot to Serena. I wanted to set her free and give her forgiveness and closure. I assume that I succeeded as I didn't give her any more openings after that night. I cloaked her from my vid and moved on with my life with Lynola. This is the life I was supposed to have, and all the ease and familiarity that Serena offered didn't appeal to me anymore. I really wanted that night to be the manifestation of my forgiveness. And actually, if I'm truly honest, I wanted to thank her in a way, for liberating me from the conventional life that had been planned for us, and free me for this new life, of love and passion, of challenge and inspiration, of open mindedness and adventure. This is where I thrive and it's mostly due to Serena that I ended up finding my way to Lynola. It was an act of kindness and gratitude and, even if she didn't understand it as such, that was what I knew in my heart.

I should tell Lynola. It's been a bunch of years. I don't know if she'll really understand. Woman are not very logical when it comes to matters of the flesh, but given my - our - potential path ahead, she should know everything. I wouldn't feel right telling the committee and not telling Lynola. And for sure I will tell the committee. I am laying myself bare in every other sense, so that should be included too. Even if it derails my candidacy, so be it.

Alfred & Lynola, 2061

When Alfie had first got the call, Lynola was skeptical and unbelieving of the whole thing. Could it be true that Alife was the lottery winner? How ironic that his family history was in politics, and now, in a system of true randomness, it was he who was selected to be Global President for 5 years. It was the irony of it that threw her. Not her faith in Alfie. She actually believed he was completely suitable to be Global President because he had so many of the characteristics of a natural born leader – which, of course, she had known about him for many years. So strange how the fates worked.

He couldn't believe it either. After all the disappointments his parents had faced after the Electoral Revolution, to have been chosen by random for this role was so ironic. It was a shame his parents hadn't been around to enjoy the moment. He had done well for himself despite their skepticism. He had fully embraced the new electoral system and never aspired to any political position, locally, nationally or internationally. He believed whole-heartedly in the new philosophy of political leadership and, truth be told, was relieved to have that particular family burden taken off his shoulders. However, unknowingly he exhibited a lot of the characteristics of a good leader in his life and work.

Initially, like many young people, he was idealistic and wanted to help the world. He had wanted to join the Green Corps to work with the native people – the Groeners – in Greenland, to plant crops in areas that had been covered in ice for so long that they had lost the ability to farm and harvest their own food. He had had the opportunity to travel the world and experience different cultures and perspectives on life. He grew to respect many different cultures and belief systems and especially enjoyed the calmness of the Eastern Buddhist-influenced societies that embraced their lives wholeheartedly.

He had witnessed the extreme climates of many parts of the world and volunteered with the World Food Distribution program to first help give out their food to villagers, then to towns and cities, and then gave input on their plan to ensure that food was shared among nations and communities. And after returning home to settle down and build a career for himself, first as an assistant to a university professor and then as an adjunct professor, and then as a full professor and administrator specializing in global programs. He enjoyed the daily details of the work and found a way to manage a small side consulting business with a global perspective. He brought his personal philosophy of fairness and awareness of others into work and was admired and respected by many in the organization. He often referred to his time abroad and the things he had witnessed, but he rarely tried to rock the boat or make any large or significant changes that would upset the management or shareholders.

Inadvertently his family heritage of leadership and diplomacy had seeped into his blood and was reflected in his ability to run his business and the university. He kept the board happy. He kept his clients happy, and he managed to create a work-life balance that kept him sane and entertained. He was a calming influence and the university benefitted greatly from his leadership. He was ambitious, not overly so, but enough to push to get promotions and eventually was offered tenure. Once he was a full professor, he pushed harder for change even while staying within strong ethical boundaries. The university thrived and benefitted from his contribution, and his consulting clients were likewise recipients of his good advice and strong commitment to global and ethical standards.

Alfred & Lynola, 2061

After he was sworn into office, life was a bit of a whirlwind. Even before the swearing-in ceremony their life changed dramatically. Even though they didn't have to relocate or move the children (thankfully), they did have to have bodyguards and their daily life was scrutinized for unnecessary security risks. Vidcalls and congratulatory messages streamed in from everyone they had ever known, and then some. The university had to make arrangements for his leave of absence, and Lynola's peaceful gardening routine turned into a photo-op on steroids. Viddrones followed them everywhere and they had to keep install mirrored blackout film on their windows at home in order to avoid prying eyes.

But the honor and recognition were amazing. It was flattering and exciting and filled with possibility. The fact that Alfie had been selected by the algorithms, and then cleared by all the interviews was a mind-boggling achievement in and of itself, and that was even before the global presidential duties started. The algorithm required that all nominees be of able mind and reasonably able body, have had some experience in business or academia, with some success, but not too much, be a solid and trustworthy citizen, have no warrants/arrests/legal violations, have some family, and never had any public ambition (or privately harbored any) for politics. After selection, the nominee must endure an in-depth background check including interviews with friends and neighbors, coworkers, and anyone else who'd crossed paths with him. Not to mention the obligatory DNA and intense health tests. It seemed that Alfie had passed them all, to the highest degree.

It took them a while to get their head around the concept and adjust their daily routines as much as they could in order to get their feet under themselves again. As it finally started to sink it, reality struck. Alfie started traveling. Traveling a lot. And while most nights he was home, he was exhausted and not much of a husband or a father. Lynola and the kids' lives slipped back into the routine of school, homework, bathing, eating and sleeping. Lynola's daily gardening activities grew old and too boring for the newssites to cover each day, and she lost her following fairly quickly. Besides, most people couldn't understand why (a) she didn't haven't career of her own and (b) why was she bothering with the dirt and weeds and the time it took when she could get nutritious supplements at every corner mart.

After the first few months, Lynola realized that she and Alfie were starting to drift away from each other. And while some distance was to be expected, she wasn't going to let a little thing like the Global Presidency ruin her relationship with the man she loved most in the world and who she couldn't stomach the thought of being without.

She also saw the toll it was taking on Alfie. He wasn't naturally a quick thinker. He was a slow and deliberate scholar. He considered all the options, he heard all the different points of view, and then he noodled on things for a while, sometimes a long while. He was well-suited for smiling and charming the crowds, visiting foreign dignitaries and leading diplomatic negotiations, but absorbing and sifting through the continuous feed of information was not his strong suit.

Lynola on the other hand could sift and skim with the best of them. She was the ultimate quick thinker. Too quick many times, but quick nonetheless. So, to be of help, she started skimming through the briefs that came through to his vid each morning. In a matter of 15 to 20 minutes she was able to tell him what was important enough for him to know more details about and what he could ignore. She was able to help him sort through 50 or more briefs and whittle it down to usually less than a dozen that needed his thought and input. She usually did it while he was in the shower and over the course of a few weeks they had started talking in more depth about some of the more interesting things that she had picked up for him. It was a rekindling of their intellectual spark, and Lynola planned to keep that spark alive, if only to keep a strong connection with her husband.

Alfred & Lynola, 2061

At first the security detail was unnerving. There was always a bodyguard nearby and someone following Lynola and the kids wherever they went. The Global President had natural enemies, whoever he or she was, and their families were targets too. Nationalists, supremacists of all kind, cult leaders, religious extremists, and more. But for some reason Alfie seemed to get more than his fair share of threats. There were some conspiracy theorists who thought that his nomination was somehow rigged because of his family background, some who resented Lynola for not "contributing" to society, some who vehemently disagreed with his policies and weren't afraid to express themselves, and some who were just nut-cases.

Alfred spent the first few months putting together his advisory council and meeting with past directors and advisors to create his official administration. There were directors, associate directors, and support teams for every aspect of global affairs. And Alfie wanted to have a close relationship with all the directors. He had always believed that leading by example was the most effective form of leadership. An organization with an authoritarian, dishonest, and scheming leader, will have these qualities reflected in every action and position down to the lowest assistant. While an organization with an open minded, honest leader with integrity and compassion, will have those qualities reflected. As a result, within a few months, Alfred had built an administration with excellent credentials and integrity at every level. He was proud of his team and almost immediately laid out his ideas for projects that they will collaborate on for the next seven years.

As Alfie's administration started coming up with new global directives and policies, the number of his detractors grew. One of his earliest directives was to prohibit financial subsidies to any company in any industry who turned a profit. This policy was something that he and Lynola had conceived of over breakfast one Sunday morning. The kids had eaten and were off playing or vidding with friends and Alfie was enjoying a couple of hours of rest before he had to leave for diplomatic talks in Istanbul. He and Lynola were talking about her garden and thinking back over the historical lessons of the agricultural industry over the previous 200 years.

These days, the industrial farms were even larger than they had been just 50 years before and all the while food was generated with even fewer natural ingredients and more modified ones. It was true that genetically modified crops had finally been proven safe for humans (although Lynola remained stubbornly unconvinced) and so GM crop production had skyrocketed around the world. With the shifting climate patterns, this was a godsend to many communities who had struggled with droughts, floods and food shortages for decades, and it was also a boon for industrial farms. There were crops that could withstand the worst flooding, weeks of drought, new and old pests, and still produce abundantly. So why did these farms, these corporations need subsidies? And for that matter, what about the fossil fuel industry, still going strong even after cleaner fuels were well developed and the dirtiest fuels were running out of easily accessible extraction points. Or the auto industry, well, really, all the sectors of the transport industry, including the new personal helipod manufacturers who were doing so well. And steel, and mining, and on and on. Any industry that collectively turned a profit for three consecutive quarters had their subsidies stopped by the fourth quarter. Clearly, this didn't earn Alfie any new friends.

Another of their early morning brainstorms that he later turned into a directive, created an even greater class of passionate enemies. It was his proposal to overhaul the tax system. While nation states still controlled their own internal tax structures, Alfie had the power to create an international standard that could be voted on by referendum and adopted by any country. The proposal that his administration developed ended up being adopted by 83% of countries, essentially making it the global standard in taxation. Once again, Alfie wasn't making friends, but he was able to distance himself from their wrath mostly because, unlike before the lottery process, he wasn't under any obligation to any group or party. He was his own man, with his integrity and morality still intact, which was still a point of great pride for him, and for most of the global community.

He was especially proud of his taxation policy. It leveled the playing field for so many, made redundant thousands of tax accountants and attorneys, and made taxation easy to understand to every 18-year-old of sound mind. Everyone paid their fair share, everyone benefitted, and there were no loopholes. The rich could still get richer, but the poor didn't get any poorer. This program was a great source of pride for Alfie and that it had been approved by more than 80% of the world's population, ensured his legacy would live on for lifetimes to come.

Alfred & Lynola, 2067

By the time the tax policy was worked out, voted on, and adopted, Alfie's seven-year term was almost over. It wasn't common knowledge - as everything was so new, there were many details that weren't common knowledge - that the new system had a built-in contingency for keeping on leaders who were thriving in their position and making a measurable difference. It hadn't happened since the new system had been put in place over 20 years ago, so it was certainly unexpected and besides Alfie was just happy to return to his quite family life and university and consulting again (especially now as he had a bunch of new ideas to expand his client's global best practices in a variety of areas).

When the Global Council on Leadership invited him back to Nepal for more interviews, he first thought that these were some sort of exit interviews - what lessons could he pass along to his successor? And when he found out that the Council had unanimously voted to re-nominate him to a second term, his immediate instinct was to say no. He hadn't even considered the possibility. But, less than a second after his head screamed NO at the possibility of staying in the position, he knew he wouldn't turn down the honor of serving again and doing more good. Lynola was stunned but supportive. She had also been looking forward to returning to their family life, but she knew that the opportunity to build even better communities was something that neither of them would ever walk away from.

The re-nomination was unpopular in with some loud and influential constituents, and Lynola's influence and her lack of "societal contribution" came under scrutiny again. Lynola tried to shy away from the spotlight and keep the focus on Alfred and his successes to date. The newssites were cruel and delved into every available crevice. They published the children's school reports. They interviewed everyone associated with any of their social media accounts. They even spoke to the children's teachers, their classmates and the parents of their classmates.

After the initial newssite flurry, life went back to the normal that they understood. The children had their school life, their friends, their camps, their school trips, and the usual rounds of exams and holidays. They didn't see their dad very often, but they'd had gotten used to that and so they didn't much care about the re-nomination. Some of their friends, and the parents of their friends, whispered in corners during birthday parties or picnics, but mostly the children were oblivious. However, Alfie's detractors weren't happy at all. They considered him too socialist in his views and were continuously trying to find dirt on him to implode his presidency, but to no avail.

His views were not really socialist, at least he wouldn't call them that. He felt that he was motivated most by fairness. Fair competition, if he had to label it. He wanted people and businesses to have an equal stake, but also reward those who work hardest and were the most passionate. His policies reflected these views, and he was continually surprised, in fact flattered and often bemused, by how much support he got for his policies and directives. The majority of the people were with him, even if there were small groups of disparagers, he could fend them off easily, especially with the overwhelming support and encouragement that he got from his enthusiasts.

And he must be doing something right. Global poverty had shrunk during his first term and agricultural production yields had increased. Infrastructure spending was up slightly around the world and while there were still wars and disease and inequities, there were also improvements. Measurable improvements in people's quality of life and standards of living. For that he was proud. And Lynola was proud too. Of her husband and of his accomplishments. And of herself, since she knew she had a great deal of input and influence, even if the rest of the world remained unaware.

Alfie & Lynola, 2069

Lynola watched Alfie get dressed. He was still a handsome specimen. And still all natural. Strong jaw. A good head of hair, turning grey on the sides. Good muscle definition, not too much, not too little. Tall, but not too tall. Good shoulders, good proportions – all over – and a beautiful winning smile. His eyes smiled as much as his mouth. And the warmth in them reached down into her stomach, her heart, and her soul. Every time he smiled at her, with those eyes, she melted. She was afraid of how vulnerable she felt in that smile. She would do anything for him. She believed in his goodness. In his integrity. How did she get so lucky?

He was puzzling over something, she could tell. After the nomination, she had worried that he would become so dedicated to the challenges ahead of him that he would lose himself in his duties. But she had found a way to stay connected to him and build the collaborative relationship that she had always wanted. She got to stimulate her own mind, as well as strengthen their relationship on a continuous daily basis.

What was he puzzling over this morning? She had already scanned the newssites and nothing huge had happened overnight, luckily. Their proposal to eliminate farm subsidies was receiving huge blowback, but they had expected it. Alfie's job was now to go out and sell it to the people. That was what he was good at. That was his forte, his métier, his calling. She did the paperwork, the heavy lifting, in terms of policy and implementation details, and he was the front man. What a great team. She smiled at him and lifted herself up for a kiss. For his warm hands on her neck and face. She was truly blessed by the universe.

He left after their usual hearty breakfast of the eggs her chickens had given them this morning, a muesli of grains and goat's milk yoghurt, and a bowl of berries. She got down to business. The details of the farm subsidy elimination protocol had to be carefully planned to avoid future retraction. The resistance was strong with this one, but so were the benefits to everyone when - if - they managed to get it imbedded into the long term corporate and societal assumptions. Alfie was doing a good job of making the case across the newssites and at all the events she had encouraged him to attend. She was working in the nitty gritty. How and when to scale back corn subsidies, the one that was most engrained in the international psyche of industrial agriculture. Already, during Alfie's first term as president, they had tackled subsidies in many industries, oil being one of the easiest as the industry was on its last legs anyway and the infighting had meant that the coalition was weak and ineffective against their global campaign. But corn was going to be a doozy. The agricultural sector had been propped up for so long that they barely knew how to run a farm profitably. They were going to have to learn a great many things, and Lynola was going to have to make sure that there were no loopholes that would derail their work. She loved this. This was her true place in the world. This was where she could excel. Her quick, thorough, and logical mind was at its best.

Alfred & Lynola, 2069

It had been a sunny day, the day the protests started outside their home. There was no longer a 'White House' or an 'Elysée Palace'. Those symbols of corrupt wealth and singular power had been given back to the people decades ago. They lived comfortably, in their townhouse convenient to public transportation, which is how Alfie preferred to travel. He always stayed close to the people, having frank and unscripted conversations whenever he had the chance, which undoubtedly fed his popularity and his re-nomination. He never changed. He didn't even consider a full-time security detail or a personal driver until the protests started, and even then, it was only at the insistence of Lynola who cited the children as her main concern.

The signs read 'Farmers Feed the World' and 'Farmers Rights are Everyone's Rights'. Some were more explicit saying 'No Subsidies, No Crops' and 'Keep Your Eyes on My Corn' with a clever image of eyes instead of 'ears' of corn. These protests seemed remarkably more insistent than any previous resistance they had seen to policies they had introduced. Obviously, taking money out of people's hands was not going to be popular, but the bigger picture made so much sense that Alfie and Lynola hadn't anticipated the depth of passion and violence of the resistance. Of course, resistance was slightly too strong a word for this group. More like the one percent of the one percent. But they were loud, and they were angry. For the first time since his nomination, Alfie felt an instinctive need to protect his family.

Their logic was simple. There was too much food in some places in the world, and not enough food in others. People could blame the changing climate or other out-of-their-hands conditions, but in Lynola's mind, it was simply a question of proper motivation. Technology existed to make water out of air, to create crops resistant to the inconsistencies of a too hot or too cold climate, and many of the other conditions that people couldn't control 100 years ago. If you added up all the potential agriculture and related side-industries, there was more than enough to feed and clothe the entire world's population, and then some.

It was a just a matter of redistribution, which required some clever techniques of motivation. Alfie and Lynola never believed in forcing the world into a quasi-communist state. They knew from the lessons of history that it would never work. People lose incentive to produce and work if they can't benefit personally from their efforts. Humans are selfish and egotistical creatures who have evolved with a need to horde and be greedy. Fair enough. Nothing was going to change this inherent human need for survival and selfishness. All the global government could do was modify the barriers to encourage certain types of behavior. Motivation, not imposition, that was the goal.

When she took the time to study the history of commercial farming, starting at the dawn of the Industrial Age and followed it up to the Great Depression in the United States in the early 1930s, Lynola understood the logic that had been in place when farming subsidies began. It made sense for the government at the time to create programs to offset where the capitalist model couldn't control - the supply and demand of farm crops. Of course, farmers should be helped in the event that they overproduced and couldn't sell their crops. And of course, they should be helped when their crops failed, and they didn't have enough to sell to support themselves. But so much had changed in these past two centuries. Why were they hanging on to the vestiges of the past that had such immense impacts around the world, just because a small group of people couldn't be persuaded to willingly give up their safety net? She had no intention of leaving them out in the cold, so to speak, but she also knew, that by looking at this issue through new eyes, there were solutions that would address so many of the serious issues the overpopulated world was facing. And it was her responsibility, and Alfie's, to address them.

First off, a true examination of worldwide needs. They developed a 'basket of goods' approach, generalized to a year's supply for a family of 5 in different communities around the world. They had over 50 categories of families and communities. Lynola loved this part. She and Alfie got to travel all over the world and visit with families in their homes. What were their basic needs for food and water? What were their traditional foods for nutrition, for medical treatment, for celebrations? A family of 5 in rural Mongolia unsurprisingly had a different lifestyle than a family of 5 in Dakar, Senegal. But the remarkable differences could be flattened out if you looked at categories such as water, protein, carbs, fiber, and broke down foods into groups of ingredients and nutrients. The multicultural, multilingual group of scientists and researching were fascinating in their own right and were fed by the inspiration they got from the goals they were working towards. The study took more than two years, but the results were in-depth, comprehensive, and set a clear path ahead for food distribution reform.

Alfred & Lynola, 2075-2077

After 14 years in office, Alfie was offered a seat on the Global Council on Leadership, which he humbly accepted. He wanted to support his successor in his or her work as much as keep an eye on the programs that he and Lynola had already started. His last year in office was a series of honors and awards. Global and regional awards poured in from every agency in every country. Alfie's tenure embodied the success of the lottery system. He had been fair, humble, and strong when necessary, passionate when appropriate, and above all open-minded and diplomatic.

Lynola had stayed home and raised the children, keeping a low profile during almost his two terms. The children were now old enough to run their own lives, and although there were no weddings or grandchildren yet, Lynola had high hopes that soon that would change. But for now, she had her husband back and they took the opportunity to spend lots of quiet quality time together. Alfie deferred all the vid offers, speaking engagements, and teaching positions. Instead they booked a series of cruises. A North Pole one to revisit the communities where Alfie was first inspired by traditional farming practices. Then down south to Australasia to see the last remaining live coral reef, passing by the incredible Oxygen Forests in South America along the way. Then to the moon villages and the international TriCities. And then finally they decided on an old-fashioned RV trip around the African National Parks.

All in all, they were gone for 14 months. They kept in touch with the kids and Alfie managed to squeeze in a couple of conferences with the Global Council on Leadership. But mostly they just enjoyed each other's company and reminisced about their amazing work. Many of their projects were in the nascent stages but all indications were that they were being well received and had a positive future.

The healthcare pyramid system that was first tested by Doctors Without Borders in Northeast Asia and that later adopted by the World Health Organization was up-and-running and was boosted by its ability to curtail the pandemics of 2077 and 2081. The retirement plan for people living in the poorest areas of Central America that was inspired by Lynola's quilting group - everyone making a little, even a tiny bit, building something bigger than themselves. The taxation system that was fairer and helped redistribute resources without uninspiring the most ambitious capitalists to work hard to fulfill their own greed.

They were both proud of their work, but Alfie was starting to get more and more spooked by the threats that still kept coming in. He wasn't even in office anymore and the threats continued. He didn't have the full-time security detail that he used to have, and although he was fairly off-the-beaten-path these days, he still felt shaken from time to time. The ones that cited specific policies that they opposed were less scary than the ones that came in from the crazies. The vid messages with spooky lighting and crazy looking faces. Especially the eyes, the crazy eyes freaked him out the most. He didn't share most of them with Lynola. It upset him that there were still people who he hadn't been able to help, and who were still suffering from effects of climate change or poverty or disease. However, there was no point in scaring Lynola even if sometimes he was truly shaken.

Alfred & Lynola, 2079-2082

After they returned from their adventures, their lives settled into new routines. Alfie travelled and taught and spoke and worked on his memoirs. Lynola went back to gardening and quilting and catching up with the children. Her new granddaughter was a delight and a distraction, and she was proud that Amelia had grown into a competent and well-rounded adult. Charlotte seemed to be enjoying the highlife and wasn't quite ready to settle down yet. While Drake still sought their approval and support, which of course they gave whenever it seemed like he needed it. Their life seemed fairly humdrum, which suited them both quite well.

On the second anniversary of Alfie's "retirement" from office, GN, the Global Newssite, aired a piece that reviewed his work and time in office, specifically contrasting Alfie's style with the new president, a woman from Malaysia who was quieter, more cerebral, and much less personable that Alfie. In doing the piece, the GN reporters started to speculate about Alfie's many innovations, even implying that Lynola played a significant role in developing them. And while some of that was true, neither Alfie nor Lynola had ever divulged the nature of their working relationship around new policy development. It was always assumed that the spouse played a supportive role to any politician, but the extent of Lynola's ability to influence was above and beyond most people's expectation. Instinctively Alfie and Lynola knew this and so never said anything out loud about this aspect of their relationship and had always contributed their work to the committees of the Global Council.

It was reported as a scandal, and Alfie and Lynola weren't quite sure how to respond. The Global Council wasn't all that helpful. It would be a huge embarrassment to them if one of their vetted nominees turned out not be the source of his or her own policies and directives. And yet, as most public opinion held, it was natural that a spouse should support his or her partner. But it was the level of support and influence that Lynola had provided that bordered on scandalous. Lynola and Alfie knew that if they kept a united front, a front that didn't divulge the intimacies of their relationship that it would blow over. And so that's what they resolved to do. And did, until Alfie died suddenly in the summer of 2082.

Lynola, 2084

Alfie's memoire was a bestseller the minute it hit the wires. Whether it had anything to do with the so-called-almost-scandal, no one would ever be able to say for sure. What was certain was the success of his leadership. His two terms were the only time that a Global President had been re-nominated. His healthcare pyramid directive proved to be a revolutionary step-change in a nation-state's ability to provide healthcare services for its citizens. His taxation policy was a success almost instantly and never soured. And among his other great achievements, his influence on agricultural practices was far reaching, decades after his death, even more than his work on the fair distribution of wealth.

He died unexpectedly at a young age, only 69, when the average life expectancy of a man of his social and economic class was closer to 90 in the Northern Hemisphere. Lynola and a few of his closest security detail were the only ones who knew his genetic profile, and this thankfully was by law. If genetic profiles were made public, all sorts of prejudices and profiling would inevitably occur skewing so much of people's daily decisions. So, it was only his wife and his security detail that knew of his genetic blood markers. The ones that said he was more likely than most to develop an embolism or have a stroke. This information had been shared, of course, with the Global Council on Leadership, but by law they were not allowed to consider any details of his genetic profile in their decision process. And in this case, they certainly hadn't held it against Alfie.

It wasn't a violent death, but unfortunately it was a very public one. One that was vidded from more than one angle and those vids were played over and over again worldwide whenever Alfie was spoken about. It was one of Lynola's biggest frustrations that she could never suppress the vids of Alfie getting ready to stand as the keynote speaker at the Alliance for World Reconciliation's annual banquet and then seeming to hear something off-stage just before he slumped with his eyes open in his chair. It was a grim and morbid few seconds that were aired thousands of times after his death, and then repeated whenever a newssite did a profile of him or any of his policies.

She hated that the children were exposed to these images over and over again and that she couldn't protect them from the depressing sight of their father slumped in the chair staring out slack-faced above the heads of the crowd. But that was the age they were living in, and it was just another burden of the family's fame that they had to endure. And of course, it greatly delayed her ability to mourn. To mourn her husband, her partner, the father of her children, to mourn the future quiet life of travel and retirement that they would never enjoy. To reminisce and enjoy the memories they shared. It took Lynola a full year before she felt fully strong enough again to venture onto the world stage.

Lynola, 2086

Reading his journals felt like a betrayal, even to her. Obviously, she knew most of what was in them, and he had even read occasional sections to her over the years. But mostly, it was an activity that he did alone, often at night or in the early morning while she was still sleeping or getting the kids ready for school.

He loved writing. He would use an old-fashioned ballpoint or ink pen that could be refilled with cartridges. He had a quaint fascination with real paper and real ink, and the smudges that came with them. He didn't use any erasers or whiteout when he made errors or wanted to rewrite sections. He just crossed them out or scribbled notes above, below, or in the margins. It was a throw-back to an earlier time and a nostalgia that he indulged, even while he looked continuously to the future.

The journals themselves were of different sizes, shapes and colors. There must have been more than 20 in the box, ranging from cheap imitation leather with logos and touristic designs, to beautiful rich and weathered brown cow leather. Each one was full, from cover to cover, of pages and pages in his handwriting. There were occasional papers and clippings stuck in or tucked into a page. And they were mostly in good condition, despite the occasional smudges or coffee stains.

It was the intimacy that felt weird to her. Alfie hadn't been gone that long, but he had already faded from her daily reality. In some ways he had evolved to a mythic creature that she shared with an adoring public. The soul of her Alfie, the man she loved dearly, admired beyond reproach, and would have followed to the ends of the earth, was present in her heart every minute of every day. But the one who was writing these journals was the Alfie she shared with the world. The one who pondered over big and small societal problems and solutions. The one who was intelligent, and sophisticated, and calm in the face of every storm. The one who was a good father, a good husband, had no (or very few) flaws, and who had the faith of the world behind him.

Her Alfie had been quiet whispers on a Sunday morning through still-sleeping eyelids. Her Alfie had been the one who laughed at himself and questioned everything. Her Alfie had been the brave one who indulged his adoring public and gave them what they wanted, even when he felt unsure and insecure in his own beliefs. But this Alfie wasn't in these journals. He was only in her memories and in her heart. And now, sometimes, she had a hard time summoning him to her mind.

She always thought that she would find him within the pages of his leather-bound books when she finally had the courage to look in them. But she was disappointed, and then saddened, to discover that her Alfie wasn't really there. She wasn't sure why she had taken so long to read them. Maybe she was still trying to respect his privacy, even after all these years. Or maybe she was a little afraid of what she would see written on the linen colored sheets.

Either way, she didn't find what she had expected. Instead, she found an Alfie who was writing for posterity, for the adoring public of the future, and to defend his (and her) positions in the face of potential future challenges. He wrote mostly to clarify the details and persuade the unconvinced. To argue every angle of every point. There were a few sections interspersed throughout that were more intimate and reminiscent of her Alfie, but mostly, it was clear that he was writing to be transparent and thorough in his arguments and opinions, and not for any need for intimacy or even disclosure.

In some ways, after the shock had worn off, she recognized the positive side. Obviously, he hadn't felt the need for an outlet. He didn't require a valve to release pressure or a vent for his frustrations. That was a good thing, she decided, as he obviously had all the support he needed from her and his closest advisors. But, the disappointment of finally getting the strength to sit down with his journals, craving for glimpses of her Alfie, and being faced only with the public Alfie, was initially crushing.

Lynola, 2086

She wanted to start at the beginning and read through every word. But he had been young and impetuous and hadn't put any structure into his thoughts at first. They started with the ramblings of a young man, with passion and conviction, but driven by emotion and not a lot of substance. But as he grew into his university role, his thoughts became clearer and his theories more academic.

His style and his purpose came fully into focus after he had been nominated. For each topic he started by meandering through the different aspects of the issue, often writing in detail and from multiple angles, debating every point, even if they were contradictory. Then, at some point, he got intense with his perspective and arguments, morphing into definite and clear lists of key opinions, and then back to speech and lecture drafts, all on the same subject. She could see his thoughts form, and then be challenged, and then form again. It was both a fascinating view and made her worry that she hadn't been aware of how much he had been tormented by the conflicting thoughts battling in his head. And after he had convinced himself of every angle of an argument, he would close the chapter completely, and move onto the next without looking back.

Lynola decided that she needed to separate the two Alfies in these writings. Over ninety percent of the journals were in Alfie's adult handwriting and focused on the experiences around his work as Global President. She would take out the ten percent and keep it close and private. No one needed to pry into these intimacies. These were the last pieces of her Alfie that she could hold onto, and she certainly wasn't going to share any of it with anyone.

She found references to his experiences and passions early in the writings. There were references to her and her effect on him. She smiled at his reactions to some of their most compelling intellectual debates, not too soon after they had met. She remembered them too.

She smiled at the image of a tousled-headed Alfie, high on life, on drugs, on sun and youth, hanging around the beaches in Sweden or Thailand, or in Greenland where he had spent so much of that year. She felt his pain when he wrote about Serena and what she had done to him and his dreams, but smiled again, through tear-filled eyes, when he wrote about how she, Lynola, had helped him rebuild his spirit and reignited him.

There were some passages that found incongruous with what Alfie seemed to be accomplishing with these writings. They were excerpts about their life, their kids, their arguments, and even their love-making. Intertwined with notes about upcoming debates about climate change and territorial disputes. She wavered in her thinking that he was writing for an outside audience. Maybe he had been just writing for himself after all. It certainly didn't look or feel like he had a particular goal in mind. But then, she would get pulled back into sections that were clearly modeled after academic briefs and debate notes.

In some ways she was discovering a new side of Alfie. One that had never been fully clear to her before. He had been conflicted and haunted by indecision and fear. He had played a role for her – as well as for the public. She was both mad, and also more in love with him for that. He had always tried to do the right thing, no matter for whom. She had no doubt that he had loved her with all his heart. And he wanted to protect her from himself and his fears. But obviously, he had loved the world and his responsibility to it, almost equally.

After weeks of reading, parsing, making notes, and organizing the pages within the books, she had finally decided that she would put them back in the attic and let them age for the next generation. She didn't have the strength or the will to light fires or start revolutions at this point. She didn't want to ignite debate or doubt in Alfie and his legacy. She didn't want the scrutiny herself either. So, she lovingly boxed them up again, a multicolored stack of beautiful memories and deep thoughts, and archived her index and her notes.

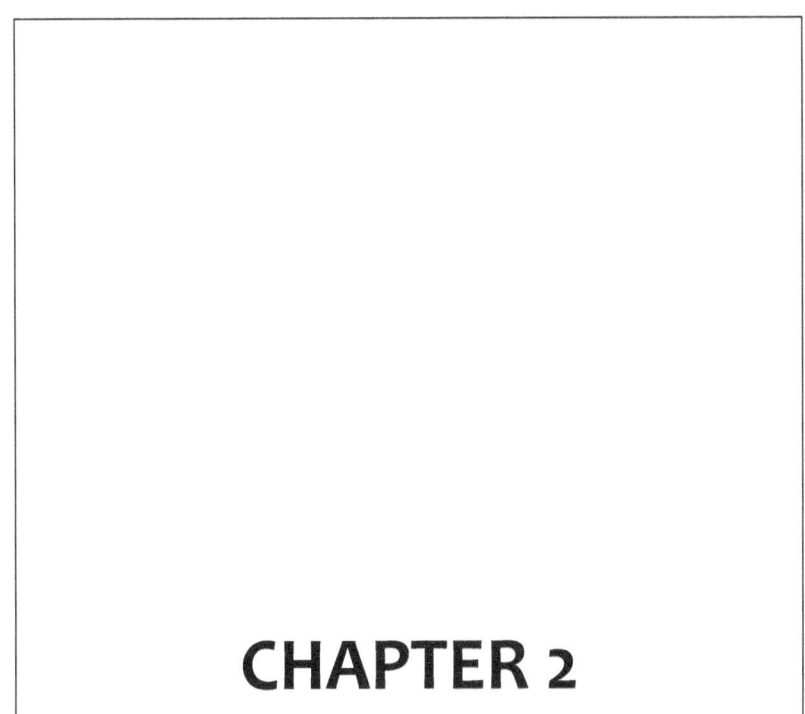

CHAPTER 2

Sean, 2077

Sienna and Dorothy were planning their next move. Sean and the two younger boys were playing in the surf outside their camp site. The sea was calm, but still cold, so the women knew that they didn't have to worry about the kids drowning. No one was swimming today. Even with the warming seas, the far northern Atlantic was still too cold to swim in early spring. Sienna wanted to head south. Maybe do some farming in southern France for the summer? But Dot was struggling to find a working farm in the region that was still productive enough to need seasonal labor. If they really wanted to be farmers this summer, they should stay in Norway. But Si was restless. She wanted to move onto new horizons. They'd been here for almost 6 months. She couldn't stand a single place much longer than that. Dot watched the boys. What a world they were growing up in. Such turmoil. Such corruption. And yet, such community spirit and collaboration. Change was coming, she could sense it.

Sean wasn't very good with his younger brothers. He tolerated them. He didn't seem to feel any closeness with them, which puzzled Dorothy. He should be happy to have an expanded family like this. When it had just been the two of them, it had been really hard. Really hard for Dot, but maybe Sean hadn't felt the hardship. Maybe she had done that right, at least. But now he was clearly jealous and resentful of his younger siblings. At 12 years old, she wanted him to feel a sense of responsibility for the younger boys and, perhaps, the confidence of a role model. She'd hoped he would grow out of the brooding that he'd fallen into when she and Sienna had got together almost 5 years ago, and fully integrate into the new wonderful family that she and Sienna had created.

The restlessness in Sienna's spirit was deeply ingrained. She rationalized it by thinking of all the wonderful experiences the kids were having and what a rich and diverse childhood they would always carry with them. She knew, if she was totally honest, that the disruption was sometimes hard for the kids, especially Sean who seemed to withdraw even further each time they moved. She loved him as one of her own, and was convinced, that in the end he would have more opportunity for success and love in his adult life with this patchwork of experiences. It was all about the experience after all. Not the stuff they acquired, not the people they knew, but the experiences. The changing landscape, the diversity of the communities and their rituals of food, celebration, and even child-rearing, and the people, the individuals who shared their lives, their stories, and even their homes with them.

Dot was pushing her to stay in Norway and farm over the long summer. But she wanted to go south. Try a new place. Southern Europe was getting too depressing, with struggling farms and dying crops. Maybe further south. Maybe central Africa where the jungle was still productive. They could learn the ancient arts of hunting and gathering in the woods. Maybe they could work on one of the new biomimicry projects, turning ancient medicines into modern cures. She looked over at Dot and asked her to search for communities and job opportunities in the jungles of Congo. Dot raised an eyebrow, but dutifully started the research.

Celia, 2077

Celia was pissed off. The guy left without paying. Seriously! Usually she got payment before starting, but she felt sorry for this guy for some reason. He looked so pathetic, and she gave him all she could. It wasn't her fault that after 20 minutes of her best moves, he couldn't get it up. Come on! What a waste of time. She ran after him for a while, but she didn't want to draw too much attention, so she slid back into another alley to calm down and regroup. Shit! What a day. She had to try again in order to get one decent meal today. Damn! She'd better straighten herself up and get back out there!

Wasn't that hotel nearby here? The one with all the herds of sheep tourists, and the bored businessmen (or women, she didn't care). The one with air-con and the cute bartender. She wondered if she could slip past the security guard again.

Celia straightened her skirt and twisted her ripped stockings so that the ladder didn't show too much. She spat on her hand and straightened her hair as best she could. She glanced at herself in the dirty reflection of a warehouse window. Not too bad. She hadn't lost her looks completely. Unlike some of her "colleagues" who were washed up before they hit 40, Celia still had some good years left. She had the shelter where she could wash up and catch a few hours of sleep each day, even under the judgmental gaze of the nuns who made her wash the dishes of the 200 sheltered women as her penance for her evening's activities.

She wasn't bad looking. In better days and in better circumstances, she had been a bit of a head-turner, but she was already weathered and rough around the edges at only age 30. Her brown hair had turned the consistency of straw with all the cheap treatments she had subjected it to. Her face was clear and unlined when she could afford the better creams and treatments. When she couldn't, she noticed the puffiness below her eyes and the rosiness around her nose. And her blue eyes, which had always been her most eye-catching feature, were weary-looking, mostly a side-effect of the life she led. But it was her hands that gave her away. They were always cracked and torn. Her nails were bitten or split, and she had little cuts or scabs all over her hands. The soapy water from the dishes that she washed on an almost daily basis, didn't help, and her rough living showed up in the condition of her hands. No fancy cream or laser treatment could fix this, and she never had enough time in a safe place to give her hands time to heal and rejuvenate. They were a dead giveaway of her social standing and she was ashamed of them.

She walked past the hotel on the opposite side of the street. Traffic was heavy during rush hour, so she was fairly sure the security guard didn't notice her. She walked slowly and scanned the entrance area. The pickets were up, but she didn't think the electrical charges were turned on yet because there were too many people going in and out making it impractical to keep turning the charge on and off all the time. She walked another 50 meters and then crossed over the street. As she walked back towards the hotel, she peeked down the side alley just in case she got lucky and there was a shift change going on. If there was, she was fairly sure she could slip in with one of the maids. But no such luck.

As she walked closer to the front entrance, the security guard was still preoccupied with guests and didn't notice her. And then, her luck turned. A bus full of sheep-like tourists pulled up. What amazing timing! This was turning into her lucky day after all. She slowed down to be absorbed by the chaos of passengers getting off the bus and suitcases being unloaded. Once it was well underway, she slipped past the electric pickets, dutifully turned off, past the security guard, 2 baggage boys, and the concierge, and walked slowly into the shadows along the back wall of the great entrance hall. This was going to be a good day – and night – for her!

Celia, 2077

Celia's good night had turned into a good week. Slipping past that group of tourists had been her lucky break. She'd managed to get picked up quickly at the bar, and the guy wasn't a pervert or even too demanding. He seemed happy for the company and she was certainly thrilled with the situation. He left for his conference each morning and she relaxed in the room, watching vids, eating leftover room service from the night before, and luxuriating in long hot and steamy baths. When he came back each night, she was waiting, smiling to greet him and study his every desire. He was only in town for the week, and she knew this wasn't going to lead to any long-term proposition like in those old-fashioned fairy tales, but she would make the most of it while it lasted. She thought about robbing him just before he left, but she'd developed a soft spot for his sweet and unassuming demeanor, and she didn't want to get him in trouble with his wife. So, she contended herself with living in the comfort of the moment and enjoying her few days of stress-free living.

But Celia's good week turned into a bad month, a really bad month. She couldn't even seem to entice anyone, male or female, to a hand job, in between the conference halls. She'd never dealt with such a long drought before and she was starting to get worried. This was bad, really bad. She stole some food from the trays going back to the kitchen after one rubber-chicken conference, and immediately felt sick at the thought of eating someone's leftover meat-substitutes. The half-eaten deserts weren't bad, and the mediocre wine lessened the guilt, but what life was this. She had never had truly big dreams for herself, but this was getting beyond her lowest expectations.

She thought about going home for a spell. Her step-monster still lived in that horrible cookie-cutter house in that horrible cookie-cutter suburb of Cleveland. She could hop on a magtrain and be there in just a few hours. But how long could she really stomach that life. She had never fit in. Her step-monster was truly a monster, married to the only dad she had ever known.

She had found out that she was adopted early in her teen years and after the initial shock wore off, a lot more things actually made more sense. She understood why she didn't look or feel or act anything like her dad or her mum, even though at that point, her mum had been gone now for a few years. She had always tried to find the commonalities between them, but now she looked at their relationship more objectively and realized that they truly were just apples and oranges. Not much in common after all.

She often wondered about her birth parents. Under what circumstances did they decide they didn't want her? Was it when she was born? After she was a few days old? And what could have led them to such an extreme decision. She had a hard time getting her head around it, and an even harder time convincing herself that it didn't change her worth.

Her dad's new wife, her step-monster, hated her. The jealousy in the room was palpable every time they found themselves sharing the same air. Celia hated the new distraction in her father's life, and the older woman clearly couldn't tolerate the affection that he shared with his daughter – only his adopted daughter after all.

Her step-monster had used the knowledge of her adoption to make her feel even further separated from her father, whom Celia genuinely loved. And it worked. She felt more and more apart from the happy couple, especially after they started producing babies of their own. A few times she tried to reach out to her mother – her biological mother – but she was long gone and shielded from identification. She was told that her mother had been a socialite and had she tried to trap her partner by getting pregnant and forcing him into marrying her, but that her plan had failed and she couldn't wait for the pregnancy to end so she could return to her highlife. Celia was blocked at every avenue from trying to find out who she actually was, and eventually gave up. Obviously, she didn't want to be found, which should tell Celia enough about her.

Her dad tried to appease the two women in his life. He made an effort to spend time with each of them individually and at the same time tried to find commonalities between them. But the truth of it was that he was too infatuated with that fake woman, with her fake hair and fake boobs and fake smile, to see anything clearly. Their life was clearly perfect, and Celia was only getting in the way.

Celia's sense of family was tenuous. She had been adopted as a baby by two loving parents who were infertile but desperate to raise a child of their own. Despite all the love she had felt in her earlier years, Celia was always curious about her biological parents and wondered why they hadn't wanted her. When her adoptive mother died of ovarian cancer, a direct side-effect of her fertility treatments early in her marriage, Celia was shaken to her core and her ties to her family were further endangered. After her mother's death, Celia and her father lived in a fog, going through their daily lives automatically, and trying to love and support each other. And when her father remarried, he fell easily back into the routine of married life, but Celia was left out.

By the time she was 15, she already had one foot out the door. Her dad tried harder and harder to integrate her into their life, but the more he tried, the more fake it felt and the more she felt apart from him, his new wife, their new baby and the one on the way. Nothing felt right, and nothing made sense. Their comfort made her even more uncomfortable and she started spending more and more time with the rebel crowd at her youth camp. They broke the rules - small ones at first, like smoking old fashioned cigarettes behind the garage shed, or stealing candy bars from the corner store. Then their rule-breaking got even more exciting.

At least twice a week, Celia snuck out through her bedroom window and dropped down quietly while everyone was sleeping. She jumped on her electric scooter and raced over to the empty town hall, a huge monolithic building that had once been a fine image of a prosperous and hopeful future, and now was being rehabilitated to be a school for the physically challenged. Celia and Buck - her man of the moment - snuck through the construction site into the back entrance and down into the basement. Nothing much had been disturbed here for at least 100 years. It was still painted an institutional beige over cinder block with grey vinyl tiles. The empty offices were strewn with old documents that meant nothing to the teens. They only wanted a quiet corner where they could explore each other and experiment with different substances that Buck had picked up through his vid contacts.

By 17, Celia found herself hanging on only weakly to her life in the suburban house with her father - her adoptive father, as she was constantly reminded - her step-monster and their 2 intolerable brats. She knew it was time to go, even though it hurt her heart to think of leaving her sweet, kindhearted, but feeble father. He would recover quickly, she was sure. He had enough to handle with his job, his house, his wife and his real kids. She packed her belongings into a hiking backpack that she had found in the basement – probably a leftover from when her parents used to enjoy the outdoors, before they had adopted her – and wrote and rewrote a note to her father. She couldn't decide what would hurt him less... knowing that his new wife had driven Celia out of the house or thinking that Celia had just rebelled herself away.

She finally stuck to the truth and admitted that it was a mix of the two. She was ready to go out on her own, and she couldn't stand being there anymore. She loved him, she would try to keep in touch, and she wished him happiness, forever. She flung the backpack out of the window, dropped quietly down, jumped on her fully charged electric scooter, and left without looking back.

Celia, 2064

Celia headed east towards the sunrise. The roads were quiet and the bike lane where she rode her scooter was smooth and well-lit with bioluminescence that indicated cross streets and curves in the lane. By the time the sun was above her, she was hungry and sore from standing on the scooter and gripping the handles so tightly. Her shoulders and back were complaining about the heavy backpack and she realized she had been tensing her whole body since she had pulled out of her father's driveway. Her dyed hair felt stringy and greasy and her face, which was usually pale and pouty, was shiny with sweat and starting to get red from the sun. She turned off the lane and stepped into a diner to have a late breakfast. She set her scooter to charge and sat down at a clean and bright booth, modelled after the old-fashioned diners of the 1950s and 60s.

She ordered a "rock and roll" plate. Scrambled powdered eggs, meat substitute colored and flavored to look and taste like old-fashioned bacon strips, fresh tomatoes that were a little spongy, and toast. She devoured her meal quickly and gulped down 3 or 4 glasses of water, before sitting back in the booth and looking around.

There weren't many people in the small diner. The glass was shaded against the heat of the sun and the fans rotated above, moving the air and keeping it fresher inside. There were two waitresses who had clearly been there for a few decades. Their faded pink uniform dresses were stained and worn. They sat behind the counter, shoulder to shoulder, in deep conversation. In another booth, a mother was trying to ignore her two children who were fighting over the catsup bottle, while she tried to sip her coffee in peace.

A business man in the corner with ear buds and his vidglasses clearly keeping him occupied while he went through a huge stack of pancakes. And another man, with slicked-backed hair across from Celia was eyeing her with interest. She quickly looked down at her plate and blushed gently. She glanced up again and this time he was smiling at her and seemed eager to catch her eye.

She quickly got up, swiped her vid to pay, swung her backpack onto her shoulders, unplugged her scooter from the entrance, and got back to her journey. She wasn't ready to talk to anyone, never mind fend off the curiosity of a greasy man like that. She pulled a sunhat out of the top of her pack and covered her head and shoulders. No point getting burned to a crisp on her first day of freedom. She had an idea of where she wanted to end up tonight and so she had to keep moving.

Celia stayed to the bike lane that followed the old highway. Cyclist and electromotos passed her in both directions, but no one got in her way. Oases of shade and water stops were scattered along the right side of the path, so she had ample options to stop and rest and recharge. At one stop, she went over the bridge to the truck stop to grab a few snacks. The truck drivers were a rough sort and eyed her from head to toe as she slipped through the crowd to pay for her items. She hurried back to the shade of the camping area by the bike lane and sat on a bench while eating her sandwich and wafers. She filled up her water bottles and didn't wait long to get back on the lane.

She was heading to the Susquehanna River and a small town called Lock Haven. She'd heard, from one of her old boy-toys, that a teen-house was there, on the edge of town. She was hoping that she could find friends there and try to stay for a few days. Not too long, because the big city, New York City, was calling her.

She had cloaked her vid when she had left the house this morning, but curiosity got the best of her and she checked to see if he had tried to reach her. 14 missed calls from him immediately pulled up on her screen, 2 from the step-monster, 2 from one of her friends, and 1 from the school. She swallowed hard and set the vid to cloak again.

Celia, 2064

Just after dark, she pulled up to the address she had for the teen-house. It was clearly a house without adult supervision. The gravel in front was a disaster, small rocks everywhere, littered with bits of rags, old toys, torn up papers, and general rubbish, up until the sidewalk where the morning street cleaners were obviously keeping the mess limited to the front yard. The house was tall and wide, old-fashioned in style and clearly unkempt. But lights were shining in all the windows and Celia smiled at the thought of her new independent life.

She plugged her scooter into the sidewalk post, propping it up against 3 others that were there, and walked up the front steps. The wooden porch was in need of maintenance and repair, and there were clearly signs of daily use. Empty food containers, a small pile of clothes in one corner, and a pipe of some kind balanced on the window sill. She knocked hard on the door. Music was blaring out of the one of the upper floor windows and she tried to peer through the cracked glass at the top the door. She jumped when the door opened abruptly and took a step back in surprise. A tall boy, about 19 or 20 years old, stood in front of her. He didn't have a shirt on and his skinny body barely kept his shorts from fall down. He wore several necklaces of string and beads, and his hair was long and dirty blond. He smiled and welcomed her inside. She smiled shyly and stepped in through the door.

Celia, 2067

Celia ended up staying in the teen house for almost two years. The boy who had answered the door – Evan – was an immediate attraction for her and within a few days she was sharing a room with him. He had been on his own since he was 13. He hated his old family, hated school, hated society and everything it stood for. He survived as a day laborer. Working the fields during harvest, moving heavy boxes at the docks, cleaning the streets after a sandstorm, and so on. It wasn't much, but it was enough to keep himself fed and cover his share of the expenses of the teen house.

Celia was inspired by his strength and independence. And, of course, his body. Oooh, what he could do with that body. He was creative and had the stamina of a stallion and was generous and gentle too. The perfect lover. Up until then, she had only had one-hour-stands behind the school or in the renovation site of the old Town Hall. They were typically uncomfortable and lasted just a few minutes. The boy was usually embarrassed and awkward and immensely grateful. She craved the attention and wanted nothing more than to stay cuddled in someone's arms for a night. But the boys were rarely interested – despite what they promised before they got undressed.

Evan on the other hand was generous and caring. His life had been challenging and he had had a lot of unsavory experiences that he didn't talk much about. He was more mature than other boys of his age, and he was gentle with Celia and seemed to care about her needs and desires as much as his own. She fell for him completely and was putty in his hands within the week. The other girls in the house weren't friendly, and tittered behind her back, while the boys in the house mostly ignored her.

Celia was Evan's property, and no one else should be interested in her. She didn't care. Evan was her whole life now and she was completely enamored.

Each morning Evan dropped Celia at the grocery mart from the back of his electromoto. Her job was to help parents with their children, load bags into the backs of cars, or offer to watch one child while the parent took the other to the bathroom, and so on. She got to know the employees and the regular customers over a matter of weeks and was soon earning enough tips to save up some money on her vidaccount. She also benefitted from being able to bring home day-old food from the deli section. Sliced meat substitutes, potato salad –that was more oleo than potatoes – fried tofu wings, bruised fruit and vegetables, and milk and juice that was recently expired. She stocked the fridge of the house with these treasures, and the teens ate well.

There were the typical fights among them. 12 teens in one house without adult supervision tempted a lot of fate in terms of power struggles and tantrums, but they seemed to manage. Every once in a while, a new kid showed up, like Celia had done, and the other kids let him or her in. They didn't always stay, and some of the ones who'd been there when Celia had first arrived had already left.

Celia was happy. She had even vidded her dad a couple of times, just to let him know that she was safe and doing okay. He was relieved and thankful and stopped asking her to come home once he knew she was safe and well. Her work at the mart was consistent and good. She even got offered a job doing part-time work in the storage room, breaking down boxes and putting them in the composting vat. Each night she came home from work and waited for Evan. Sometimes he was there before her, but mostly he came home hot and dusty just as she was starting to fall asleep.

Until the day he didn't. She had fallen asleep on the porch hammock waiting for him. The wind was dry and hot, and she was tired from her long day waiting around in the parking area of the mart in the hot sun. When she woke up, the sun was starting to come up and the air had stilled. She immediately wondered where he was. It wasn't like her to leave her on the porch and go to bed alone. She started to get angry and she walked up the two flights to their room, but he wasn't there either. She popped her head in the bathroom, no one. And then ran down to the kitchen, hoping he was there. He wasn't. Where could he be?

She took a quick shower and headed out to work. She couldn't afford to miss a day at work, but her head wasn't in it. She broke down boxes for most of the morning, until the compost vat was full. Then helped a couple of her regulars with their youngest children while they shopped for their weekly supplies. Then she grabbed some day-old bread from the deli and headed back home on her scooter. He still wasn't there. But the house was buzzing with rumors.

There had been a raid. At the farm where he had been working, picking oranges in the hot sun. Police had arrested him and some of his coworkers around their lunch break. But why? Why had he been arrested? Surely picking oranges wasn't a crime. That's when she started to hear the stories of his former life. At 12, he had been a runner for a middle-level drug manager in Chicago for a few months. After escaping the clutches of the gang, he had gone up to Wisconsin and had been a regular pickpocket along the strip of new luxury beach resorts beside the

Green Bay-Lake Michigan coastline. At the Bay Beach Amusement Park, he had worked at one of the rides until he had been caught stealing out of people's bags. He was well known to the authorities in the upper lakes so he stowed away on a cruise liner that went from Green Bay to Niagara. He had kept a low profile on the boat and managed to escape detection, while thoroughly enjoying himself on the boat with endless food, entertainment and gullible girls. From Niagara, he made his way to Pittsburgh and finally to Lock Haven to hook up with one of the girls he'd met on the cruise. He stayed in her dorm at the university for a few weeks, enjoying himself to no end. After she finally kicked him out, he wound up at the teen house, and like everyone there, was finding a way to make a living and feed himself, as legitimately as possible as he'd had enough fast living to last him a lifetime. But, like everything else in life, the consequences of his actions had finally caught up with him and he had been arrested for petty theft and larceny.

Sean, 2083

The morning air was heating up quickly. Four months of continuous heat, hazy and suffocating. Sean remembered his grandpa telling stories of when Dubliners complained about the rain and grey skies. What he - and most of Northern Europe - would give for a few weeks of rain and grey skies. After four months of sweltering heat, the potato industry had no hope left, and most of the farmers were struggling to find reasonable alternatives to the centuries-old traditions of their long-held family farms. Pistachios were growing in popularity these days. Easy to grow in dry and dusty conditions, and rich in protein and flavor. Cashews too. But who could live on those? Whereas before, in desperate times, Irish families managed to survive on their potato harvest, no one could live completely on pistachios and cashews.

Sean knew that the regional government supported most old farming families. It was expected of them. No shame in their circumstance, just a societal expectation of support and then moving onto to greener pastures, so to speak. He was conflicted by gratitude that society supported those who could have been his neighbors, and revulsion that society had allowed these circumstances to occur. He felt an innate instinct to contribute. But, because Sean was Sean, his contribution couldn't just be a few days of putting together food crates to be sent out to needy families. That was paltry and kind of pathetic considering what he was capable of. Sean was going to make a name for himself. He was going to make a difference. A real difference in the world. One that would bring about real changes. Not just this week's dinner for a struggling family of four. Anyone could do that. But not anyone could do what he had in mind.

EF's outreach was growing, but Sean knew they were still weak and ineffectual. From the frozen inner villages of what had been the great and powerful China not so very long ago, to the ever-warming plains of Siberia, Earth First (EF for short) was getting better at distributing posters and recruiting new members, but it was tough going. Sean was constantly in fear of being discovered (even though he was protected by strong free speech laws) and insisted on moving the servers every two weeks so that their signal would keep being be reset making them very difficult to trace. They didn't need face-to-face contact with their members and they didn't need a fixed address, but they did need a consistent message and to grow their base support.

Sean knew that he was not going to be suspected, at least without any real proof. He was young and single, lived a standard middle-class life, and managed to maintain a small social circle where he made sure to be seen regularly at normal events. He never mentioned his side project to anyone in his circle. They would never understand. They would condemn him, try to dissuade him, and maybe even turn him into the authorities if they suspected his plans.

What no one knew, and what Sean kept as his most closely guarded secret, was that he didn't grow up in the comfortable suburbs of Dublin as most of his friends thought. He had, in fact, been the child of nomadic neo-hippies who travelled around from country to country, town to town, experiencing local culture, local food, and local traditions. Dorothy, Sean's biological mother, and Sienna, Sean's other mother and Dorothy's partner, started travelling after they met and fell in love, just after Sean turned seven. Sienna was beautiful and headstrong, while Dorothy was reliable and plodding. Together, they were a formidable team. Sienna dreaming up their next adventure and Dorothy took care of all the details to make it happen. Sean and his younger brothers, Duncan and Ian, were byproducts of their imaginations and dreams. Dot and Si loved life to the fullest and didn't always follow the rules. And as a result of his rebellion against them, Sean developed a strong admiration for societal rules, but wasn't ever fully able to leave behind his roots in the rebellious nature of his two mums.

And Sean believed that EF, the group that he had inherited from some ineffectual do-gooders who couldn't properly organize a rally or raise any real money, was going to help him expose the REAL world. The one that was hidden behind the curtain maintained by the newssites, and the Global Council on Leadership. The real one that he had witnessed with Dot and Si. The diversity of cultures, the suffering of its ordinary people, and the pain of all those broken, and now long forgotten, promises. EF was going to be his mouthpiece, his triumph over the sterilized world they lived in, the 'perfect' society that everyone was so proud of. EF would force the curtain open. It would be his contribution to the world. His contribution to society that would never be forgotten. His gift to all those villagers and strangers who took him and his family in when he was young, gave them food and shelter, and warmth and kindness, even though they never stayed more than one season and never paid back all the generosity they received.

Sean believed that the Council wanted to make the world a better place, for real. But he knew, because he had witnessed it time and time again, that saving people from the outside just didn't work. You couldn't impose eastern principles on western society, and you couldn't set the rules from a centralized global power, because people lived their lives locally. There was no one solution for every world problem, and the arrogance that permeated from every Council directive, irritated him more and more. What narcissism led them to believe that they could create the perfect standardized school model around the world, down to every tiny town and village? True, all children were now guaranteed an education, and true, boys and girls were treated equally and without prejudice in every classroom. And also true, that in every village or city that they passed through, he and his younger brothers received a consistent and effective education.

But how narrow their viewpoint was to think that every classroom should function in exactly the same way. The Maasai preferred to sing, as did the Amazonian tribes of Brazil, while the Germanic towns in Central Europe preferred clean white walls and orderly lessons. Sean knew. He'd seen these things. His job, his calling, was to expose the antiseptic, modular society that the world had become and if he had to resort to dramatic and explosive means, he wouldn't shy away. He wasn't afraid. He was driven in his passion, his chosen mission in life. His job was to release the world from its blandness. He would flood the world with color and light, and his name would be remembered forever!

Celia, 2083

Celia's life had gotten considerably worse with the inconsistencies of her "career". Some weeks and months were good, and she was fairly comfortable and could sleep easily at night. Some were terrible and the uncertainty of where she would lay her head or find her next meal was unbearable. She'd been using synthetics for a while – a welcome escape – but it was hard on her body and got in the way of her making ends meet.

She'd made her way to the higher-end hotel district of southern Virginia on the buck of a business man who'd she'd met in NYC and who had taken her there for a 3-day conference. He was rough, bordering on violent, and he liked to dominate and treat her badly. She'd seen worse and could handle anything he dished out. He was only a stupid middle manager suburbanite. He didn't pose any real threat to her.

She reveled in the luxury of the hotel room while he was out, busy promoting his industrial lubricants or something. Soft towels, soft sheets, hotel shampoo and hair conditioner, leftovers from room service, secure vid signal, and the safety of peace and quiet that could only be found in a hotel. She stayed away from the hotel staff and took a quiet walk around the hotel grounds while the maid was cleaning. She didn't want to cause a stir.

She needed a few more touch-ups, and pretty quick. She was bordering on 35 now and the touch-ups were going to become more of a necessity if she was going to get anywhere in this decrepit life. She didn't have any way of knowing that in comparison to her birth mother, she looked old and haggard. Her life choices had given her a much rougher time than her mother had ever had, and she was starting to fray at a much younger age.

She stopped by the hotel spa the evening before she was going to leave, just to check out their menu and see if could afford a little touchup. There was a good selection of treatments in a carefully crafted environment of soft candlelight and gentle aromas. A woman passed her as she stood by the window. She was tall and lovely, clearly very adept at keeping up her regime. It was impossible to know her age. Her long blond hair was straight and waved gently as she walked, her back was straight, and her skin was pale and clear. Celia looked at her longingly. The ease of the stranger's life drew envy from her.

The next morning the rough client paid her for her time and she bundled up her bag to head out. At least she was clean, her clothes were clean, she had a fully belly and she had some credits. She sighed. For her, that was a measure of a good week. She stopped by the restroom in the lobby, staying out of sight while he paid the hotel bill and left. She fussed with her hair, examined the crow's feet that were becoming visible again, and the slight droop in her round cheeks. This wasn't going to get any better.

As she started to leave, the woman who had passed her at the salon the day before, stepped into the restroom and acknowledged her with a slight nod. She nodded back and turned to go. The woman asked her if she knew what time the salon opened as she wanted to get one last refresher before leaving. Celia shrugged and looked at the ground mumbling that she'd used up all her credits at the spa. The woman looked at Celia closely. Celia knew that her crows' feet, barely visible in the soft yellow light of the bathroom, were exposing her lie. Celia looked at her reflection in the mirror, not wanting to catch the woman's eye, feeling intimidated by all the ways she didn't measure up. The woman scanned Celia from toe to head and asked her gently if she wanted to keep her company at the salon. She needed to get her face refreshed one more time before going back up to the Newfoundland coast with her friends.

Celia immediately shook her head and blushed slightly, ashamed and embarrassed. No, no, thanks. She had someplace she had to be. She fake-looked at the time on her vid and turned to go. Really? the woman asked. She was sure the salon could squeeze her in and they could charge it to her male companion who wouldn't pay attention to the bill anyway.

Something in her voice made Celia stop and turn and looked at the woman carefully. Her slender figure, her dark eyes, her clear skin and gorgeous hair. She hesitated again and looked at the ground and wondered what the lady wanted. Almost nothing was beneath her these days, and so she had nothing to lose by taking her up on her offer and almost everything to gain. She was used to doing 'favors' in return for gifts and money. How was this any different? Celia looked up and smiled. Sure, that would be great! Thanks. The woman stretched out her hand. I'm Charlotte, she said with a big smile with white, even teeth. I'm Celia, said Celia, dropping her bag gently on the ground and shyly grasped Charlotte's hand.

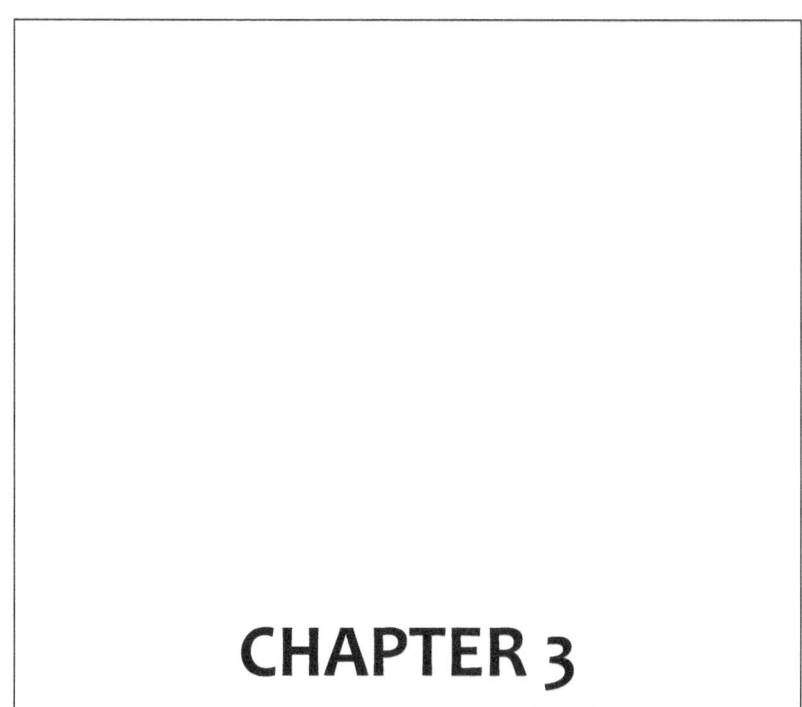

CHAPTER 3

Lynola, 2092

To mark the 10th anniversary of his death, GN ran a multi-part series on Alfie's life. His privileged upbringing, his university years, his time in the Arctic, meeting Lynola and starting a family. Then a short piece on his career as a professor, moving straight into his nomination, the interview process and then the major focus on his world-changing policies. During their development of the series, the producers requested interviews with Lynola and the children. The children's interviews were fairly cursory, but Lynola's were quite revealing. It had never been her in front of the cameras. It was always her as a proxy or stand-in for Alfie. Now of course he wasn't there and Lynola stood alone.

It was during these interviews that the extent of Lynola's role in many of Alfie's work came more into focus. And this time, whether it was because he was already dead, or that she was still working on her causes, or that the scandal was over and done with, or maybe just a sign of the times, but this time she was celebrated. The spotlight, kind and flattering this time, turned on Lynola and she, although tentative at first, started to enjoy it.

She gave interview after interview. She wrote articles, accepted speaking engagements, and was honored at dinners and banquets around the world. She always spoke of Alfie, of their partnership, of his strengths in diplomacy and negotiation, and always credited him for implementing the ideas they developed together. Their innovative ideas that had so shaped the last 30 years were popular and successful because of him, and also her. The world craved for more so Lynola was invited to join think-tanks and focus groups, to meet with national, regional, and global councils, and to brainstorm with specialized committees dealing with the toughest global issues of the day.

It was exhausting and inspiring work. She was exhilarated, flattered, excited, and inspired. And it wasn't long before Lynola Loughton was known as much for her own ideas as Alfie's. It was the breathtaking pinnacle of her success when she was notified of her nomination for the Universal Peace Award of 2098. She was overwhelmed with the honor and the pride that came with it. She wanted her children around her, and she wanted to honor and respect Alfie's memory too. She was clear about how she was going to address the world that morning when she made her acceptance speech. She knew what she would say and how it would be received. And she was happy.

17th May 2098

17 MAY 2098 - OBITUARY (global edition)

Lynola Loughton died late yesterday in an explosion in Bergen, Norway's prestigious Clarion Hotel. Ms. Loughton was in Norway to accept her nomination for this year's Universal Peace Award. Ms. Loughton is survived by her children Amelia, Charlotte, and Drake.

Lynola Loughton was the wife of the former Global President Alfred Loughton (died 2082). It is well known that Ms. Loughton was a hugely influential figure during her husband's presidency and is widely attributed for many of the successful policies that Mr. Loughton implemented. *More on her life and achievements*.

The cause of the explosion at the Clarion Hotel is under investigation. There is no immediate claim of terrorism, however authorities are not ruling out any theories. One other guest, a hotel security guard, and another hotel employee were also killed, while 7 other guests were injured. Ms. Loughton's staff and family were not at the hotel when the explosion occurred.

Brandon, 17th May 2098

Brandon heard the faint boom over the loud and raucous chatter at the restaurant-slash-pub where they had all chosen to go, but he was really too far gone to have only a fleeting and vague curiosity about it. He had spent the majority of the past three decades jumping at every click, whir, boom, and shadow, and now he just wanted to drink, and laugh, and forget all his troubles. It wasn't that his life was so bad, it was just exhausting, and he was tired. And he knew everyone was safe here, so he didn't have to be on guard.

He'd grown up in the big city and for the majority of his life had lived within its confines. He'd had a number of careers (if one could call them that), but the one that he'd finally settled on was taxi driver before he was recruited by Alfred and Lynola. His hair was now battleship grey with white edges, and he had no intention of dying it despite the latest trends in men's fashion. His hairline had receded a bit, but he was lucky that still had a full head and he kept it cut short in a flat-top, imitating the military styles of old. His eyes were dark, small and always alert. He was constantly scanning the areas and constantly challenged himself to notice every tiny detail. His face was square, matching his hairstyle, and his shoulders were broad. He was a big man and he knew that he could intimidated people just by looking at them. He was okay with that. He'd been told to smile more and be warmer in his expressions, but that just wasn't him. He was gruff, he felt gruff, and he didn't take well to being told not be gruff.

He was mad at Lynola. She was getting this great award, she'd been successful in so many things, and yet all she seemed to do was nag him all the time. It was his job to be diligent and gruff. And he certainly wasn't going to relax. So why was she always on his case? Always asking about his feelings and his opinion on her policy ideas. Like it mattered. Like anyone but her really cared. Brandon was fine with this fact. Why couldn't Lynola just leave him be? Tonight he would let it all hang out, but tomorrow, he'd be back to his rightful place, at her side, protecting her and their legacy with a frown on his face.

He'd met Alfred – Mr. Loughton –a few years before he was hired to be his driver. They'd met on a construction site when Alfred was doing a photo-op for the new environmental requirements for office buildings. Brandon had been on one of the construction teams – one of his many previous careers - and had been chosen as a spokesperson for the event. He was young and tidy in his uniform and hardhat. Alfred was impressive with his entourage and intelligent face. He had asked Brandon some perfunctory questions about the building site which he had clearly been prepped for and while the cameras rolled and clicked, they played their roles to perfection.

Brandon had been surprised at how accessible Alfred had seemed. Emotionally that is. He didn't seem haughty or aloof or even too fake. He seemed to genuinely care about the reduced environmental impact of the new watercycle system, and how the layers of window glazing worked with the sun's angle.

Brandon wasn't an expert in these things, but he managed to answer them satisfactorily, and together they were printed on the front page of newssites all over the world.

He didn't think much of the incident after his 15 minutes of fame had subsided. So, it was just a huge coincidence when Alfred's wife and kids flagged him down as he was driving his cab through the city a few years later. One of them, the 10-year-old boy Drake, recognized him from those old newssites photos and they started talking.

Lynola was especially interested in Brandon background and "careers". Military service, construction, driving, among the more acceptable ones mentioned. Lynola took his contact information and 4 months later he got a call to come and interview for the position as driver. From there it was just a few years before he was put in charge of all the transportation and security needs of Alfred, Lynola, and the children.

He liked his job. He knew he'd caught a break or two in getting where he was. He took pride in the trust they had in him. But man, they were annoying, and he was mad at Lynola for always trying to "better" him. Why couldn't she just butt out and leave him be. For the majority of the past two decades, she had been on his case. His personal life was none of her business and while he knew that she meant well, he really would prefer it if she just let him ruin his marriages and his relationships with his children and stay gruff.

And besides, he was just as happy sitting here with the crew, drinking, and checking out the ladies in the restaurant-slash-pub, many of whom were already checking him out. He was gonna advantage of the fact that he didn't have to be back on duty until 0800 and really have some fun tonight. There was nothing stopping him. He caught the eye of the buxom redhead across the bar, flashed her his winning half-smile, and when it was returned, he got off his stool and walked over to her.

Drake, 17th May 2098

Her boobs were completely fake, that was obvious. And her hair looked more like straw with all that color and treatment in it. But she was a great distraction. He couldn't believe that Brandon got there first. What did that stupid jerk have that he didn't have? Maybe just the balls to make the first move.

He glanced over at his two sisters. They were deep in conversation – something obviously important to only them – he had been left out, again! Those two never included him. What could they possibly be going on about at this late hour when they had nothing to do for the next two days but smile for the cameras and support their mother? Mother! She was tucked up safely in the hotel getting her beauty rest no doubt. As she had gotten older she had developed this look of serenity that everyone thought reflected her inner peace. But he knew better. Her inner peace was a fake. She was never happy with anything. With the world, with the house, with his sisters, and especially with him. He could never please her so why is he still trying.

Inner peace, my ass! He supposed as people got older, they did become wiser, but wisdom didn't always help. Now that he was in his mid-30s he was certainly wiser than he had been a decade before, but no more successful at controlling his passions or his excesses. His father, the great and powerful Alfred P. Loughton, had been absent most of his childhood and his mother, while present, too present, was much more interested in solving the world's problems than worrying about his little life.

She trusted him, she said. That's bullshit. If she trusted him, why was she always nitpicking about his life? His job, his girlfriend(s), his apartment, even his clothes? He was almost 40 years old for god's sake! She didn't trust him to make good decisions. But she wasn't that interested in guiding him either. Then again, he wasn't too interested in her guidance, so he guessed that actually worked out in the end.

He snickered into his drink. Was this number three or four? No way! Brandon was actually leaving with that stupid redhead. Well, good for him. At least someone was going to get some tonight. He looked around. Anyone else a possibility? Well, maybe that brunette in the corner, how old was she? She couldn't have been older than 19 or so. Although with today's technology, how could one really know? She looked fairly good. Nothing that another couple of drinks couldn't transform into something appealing. Barkeep!

Amelia, 17th May 2098

Drake was definitely getting drunk again! Stupid boy. He was going to have to smile and be pleasant for all the newssite interviews and cameras tomorrow. But it probably wouldn't matter anyway. It was planned out and scripted for them, as usual. Charlotte was the only person who understood how she felt about these things. She and Charlotte were a team. Although Charlotte didn't completely get the responsibility she felt at being the eldest, married, with kids, she at least had grown up in the same house, with the same parents, with the same stupid younger brother.

People looking at them wouldn't have guessed that they were sisters. Amelia with her short, rust-colored thick hair, slightly crooked nose and asymmetrical face. Next to Charlotte with her long blond straight her and her clear green eyes. Her peacock-colored dress clinging flawlessly to her curves without giving too much detail away. Her skin was flawless, her eyelashes were long and perfectly curled, and her cheeks had the perfect amount of rosiness to them. Amelia's skin was more weathered and tinged towards grey around the edges. Her sensible pantsuit was a clingy around her hips and slightly too short at the ankles. And even though they were both tall, Charlotte beat out Amelia by almost a centimeter, not counting the heels she seemed perfectly comfortable standing in. While Amelia was slightly hunched and seemed uncomfortable, even in her sensible camel-colored shoes.

Amelia wasn't drinking tonight. She had to be on top of her game for the next two days. She wanted her father's legacy and her mother's achievements to be center-stage. She didn't want any drama or distractions from the main event. She didn't want her, Charlotte, or Drake to take away from the newssite's focus on her parents, and she especially didn't want anyone to focus on, and ultimately be absorbed and amused by, her follies.

Her marriage was in trouble, she knew it and she was telling Charlotte about it. But she thought she could save it. If only no one got wind of anything. So, he'd had an affair. That she could live with. That was forgivable. He seemed contrite. He seemed genuinely interested and anxious about saving their marriage. He wanted to talk about it, work through it all, do the counseling and the therapy, and she did too. But she knew that all that would go to hell if any of the newssites got wind of even a tiniest hint that there was trouble in paradise. She really couldn't let that happen.

Charlotte knew all the gory details. Charlotte always knew everything. She couldn't keep any secrets from her younger sister and it was nice to have someone to trust with them. She did trust Charlotte. She had moments of fear that perhaps she shouldn't, but who could you really trust if not your own sister. Charlotte was always there with the right words and the right inflections. Although she wasn't married, she seemed to understand all the pressures and conflicts that Amelia felt, and that felt good – to have someone who had her back, even when her husband didn't. She wished Charlotte would find someone for herself. Someone substantial, unlike the playboys or playgirls that she usually went out with.

She knew she could save her marriage, she just knew it. If only her secrets could stay secret, just for a little while longer. Mother didn't suspect anything, and Drake was completely self-absorbed, as usual. So, with only Charlotte in the inner circle, she should be fine. She hoped the next few days would go by quickly without any hiccups, all the focus on her mother and her achievements and then home to face reality again.

Charlotte, 17th May 2098

Drone, drone, drone. Charlotte's face was frozen into her very-well-practiced-look-of-concern interspersed with appropriate mumblings of "of course" and "you're right" and "I know". God, her sister did go on. Like she was the only daughter of a famous person whose husband had cheated on her. Yes, yes, she wanted to save the marriage, take him back, blah blah blah.

Charlotte amused herself by intermittently picturing the hard bodies that she had got to play with last night on the yacht. She'd been with that body before and, and usual, it was always tantalizing and good for her ego. He was hot. He was sexy. And, more importantly, he made her feel sexy. Sexy and hot. Mmmm. They had had a lot of fun together. Until she had to run to catch her helipod, so she wouldn't miss the family's liftoff time. She hoped she would get to see him again soon. He was fun. And the woman he'd brought along for their amusement was a nice touch. She'd been hot too. Hot and dumb, just how she liked them. Fun, fun, fun!

Poor Amelia. Taking life so seriously when they were rich, they were famous, and they had the world at their fingertips. Why settle down? Why get burdened with all the emotional baggage of marriage, or children, even a relationship, when you could go from hotel to yacht to penthouse and back to resort again with so many willing partners. Who needed all that baggage and that stress when you could be having so much fun?

And poor Drake. Look at him. Drunk again, silly bastard. Why was he so sensitive all the time? He was good looking (for a younger brother), single (definitely) and had all the wealth and advantages that she had had, so why couldn't he enjoy it too. Stupid to get so worked up over petty jealousies and insignificant conversations. Stand up for yourself little brother and get a life. Enjoy yourself. Travel. Pick up women – check out that redhead there with the huge fake boobs. Even Brandon has bigger balls than you. Come on already!

Charlotte was bored already with Bergen. They'd only been there a few hours, but the hotel was same-old same-old, and this restaurant-slash-pub didn't seem to cater to her sort of taste. Nevertheless, she guessed she could use the opportunity to rack up some good-little-sister-listening points with Amelia which she'd probably need to cash in at some point. Amelia was so concerned about the newssites catching wind of her little marital hiccup. Oh please! Like anyone really cared. She, Charlotte, was always of interest to the newssites – with another sex symbol on her arm – that was much juicier stuff. Of course, this week it'll all be about their mother. OK, she could deal with that. Charlotte could use a couple of days off anyway. She could check out the spa and see what openings they had for massages and touch-ups for the next two days. No time like the present to keep everything glowing and firm.

I wonder how Alice is doing these days. It's been a while since I've seen her, and she was always a good spa-mate, even if I paid for everything. Who cares anyway? There's always more where that came from given the right companion-du-jour. I should look her up and see if we can meet up at one of the new resorts in the Shetlands after this shindig is over. I've heard they're really happening this time of year.

Jeez Amelia. "Poor you" "I know" "Of course you're right".

Brandon, 17th May 2098

Brandon was pleased that he'd hit up the redhead sooner rather than later. He was going to have plenty of time to play with her before he had to be back on duty. He was going to make the most of the next 8 hours. They had left the bar out the back (no need to draw too much attention) and they'd hurriedly walked up two blocks through the back alley and across a street before she indicated that they'd arrived at her building. Her apartment was in the back and so they went down the alley between the buildings, up the fire escape and through the back door. It was a little dingy, but nothing as bad as some of his own living quarters had sometimes been.

She turned on a soft light in her living room and then motioned to ask him if he wanted a drink. *Bring it on baby, keep in coming.* He knew her boobs were fake, but he didn't care, and he was sure there were other less-obvious parts of her that were fake too. So what! He was horny, and she was willing. He glanced around her place. Normal stuff. Nothing to indicate she was anything but another drone, another boring global citizen trying to find something interesting to do on a weeknight. A few photos on the wall – must be her and her family, her sisters or friends maybe. Looks like they were camping or something. A vase with fake flowers. Her vidwall was off but it was a good size, not too small and not too indulgent. The air smelled a little stale, probably as a result of living over the alley and garbage chutes.

She came back with his beer and she'd changed. Mmmm. The beer was nice and cold, and she was smoking hot. She'd changed into a loose tank top and little pajama shorts. She was making this easy for him. She dimmed the lights and he took a long swig. She hit the vidwall and jazz poured out of the speakers and she started to sway a little and move her hips. Man, he had picked a good one tonight. He was getting excited just watching her. He took another swig of his beer. Life was good tonight!

She smiled and slowly walked to the kitchen, glancing back at him seductively over her shoulder. Her heart-shaped ass swinging from side to side. It was firm and round, and really gorgeous. He wondered vaguely how old she was. Not young, that was for sure, but her age was hard to pin down. She'd had some high-quality treatments, that was for sure. Who cares anyway, she was ready for him and he was most certainly ready for her.

She came back with another cold beer and she sat across his lap. She opened the second beer and handed it to him. He took a long swig. Then another. They smiled at each other and he kissed her neck and then rested his head on the back of the futon. She was straddling him, and he loved the fact that they couldn't even speak the same language. It didn't seem to bother her. No need for all that chit chat and sweet talk. This was going to be a great night.

He kissed her, and she started to slowly unbutton his shirt. He was excited, but also tired. He was relaxed and warm, and strangely, he felt his eyes closing. She was unbuttoning his shirt slowly. His eyes were closed as he kissed her, and then he gently broke away and laid his head back on her futon. He felt so relaxed and calm and was just enjoying her hands on him. Later, he wouldn't be able to say how long he'd been asleep for when he felt her gently pull away, but he did remember falling back slowly onto the futon before succumbing to a deep sleep.

Drake, 17th May 2098

Again!! Here I am sitting on the floor of the men's room, hugging the fucking porcelain god and thinking about what a screw-up I am. I'm almost 40 fucking years old. It's all mum's fault. She never believed in me. She smothered me and never let me stand on my own feet. She had never believed I could make it on my own. Her expectations of me were so low that I believed them myself. One of these days, I'm gonna show her! He closed his eyes as another wave of nausea wafted over him.

If only she would take a leap of faith. After all, I am his father's son, and I know– they all knew – how much she admired him. Why did she have to always make me feel like shit? Always feel like I'm not measuring up. It was her fault that I have no self-confidence and am always screwing things up. In fact, if she had had more faith in me, I would have more faith in myself. Like last week, when I was kinda losing at that private high-stakes poker game. I'm sure that I would have been able to turn it around if only I had more confidence in myself. If she believed in me more, I would have been able to make smarter calls and would have walked away from the table a winner instead of a fucking loser, again. It was all her damn fault.

How was he going to tell her that he needed more money? He hated asking her for money, but he'd lost so badly at that game. And truth be told, had lost at the last 4 games. He just needed a little help to get over this slump and then he was sure his luck would turn. She would understand. Maybe she'd be so distracted by the award and the interviews and the latest surge of fame, that she wouldn't even pay much attention and just send him the wire. If she asked about his job, he'd just continue with the lie that he was still working hard on that big deal and that the prospects were looking very good. He could sweet talk her into a little short-term loan. He'd done it before, many times. She was fooled by his sincerity and his eagerness. He'd gotten that act down long ago.

It was the look he couldn't stand. Occasionally, she would get the look that made it seem like she could see right through him. He was sure that he was fooling her, but every now and again he caught that look which gave him shivers of doubt. But he was her little boy, her youngest, the last best hope to carry on his father's legacy of honesty, integrity and public service. That was his legacy, he knew, and he would get to that, as soon as he got over this last losing streak and started getting back into the black. It wouldn't take long. One game, two or three at the outside. He just needed a little loan to get there.

Charlotte, 17th May

She was tuned out. Amelia was still going on and on. Drake had left, stumbling in the direction of the men's room. Her thoughts were drifting off, back to her father. She had loved her father, completely and without any reserve. But he had been busy. Off saving the world, introducing new programs, making speeches, and christening new technological advancements. She'd hardly ever seen him and when he was home, he was usually preoccupied with the next photo op, or huddled up with their mother going over the details of his next speech.

She was just a young girl craving her father's attention. Her mother gave her plenty, but most of it was unwelcome. She knew her mother thought her frivolous and stupid. But her father hardly even noticed her. She tried to make herself as pretty as possible, spending hours choosing clothes, carefully applying makeup, and doing her hair in the hopes that he would pay some attention to her and notice all her hard work. But he didn't. He only had eyes for her mother and his work. Her mother! Who hardly ever dressed up and was always discussing boring ideas about how to fix this, or how to change that. She wanted her father to herself, without her mother's interference and distractions. But she rarely got it.

As she got older, she realized that there were plenty of men who would pay attention to her. And the more she worked at looking pretty, the more attention she could get. She learned how to flip her hair just so, and to walk with a slight shimmy and shake that the boys seemed to like. She read about the latest fashions, the latest lip color, the latest hair styles, and she kept up with all the new trends. She giggled and flipped her hair, and wiggled and shimmied, and became the center of all the boys' attention. They asked her out. They bought her presents. They wanted to take her to the dance and out afterwards. She found that if she teased them a little bit more with kisses behind the school and quick feels in the back of the car, she could get even more attention. She learned how to get all the things she wanted and still remain in control.

In her twenties, things got even more exciting. She was invited out on private yachts, on private moon-landers, to private islands. She hobnobbed with all the rich and famous and was in great demand. She touched up her skin tone, whitened her teeth, and colored her hair. She got her boobs perked up a little, and her ass trimmed down a little. She got her calves strengthened just a touch, and her face rounded a little. She dated sexy rock stars, steaming actors, and sizzling models. She found out that some of them were gay, some were sadly endowed, some had strange sexual requests, and most had childhood baggage of their own. She discovered that she hardly needed to speak and certainly didn't need to share her own baggage, just continue to smile and giggle at the right times, wear the right clothes and makeup, and keep up with her beauty perfection regimens in order to stay on the hot list. She travelled the world, and then some, and enjoyed herself immensely. She managed to keep family embarrassment to a minimum, and therefore avoided the wrath of her mother and much of anything from her father. It took great determination, ambition, and intelligence to balance the two sides of herself. And she felt happy. Excited and fulfilled by her lifestyle.

And now she was as popular as ever. Her father had died without ever truly recognizing how good at this she was, and that was his loss. She was the center of attention. On the front page of all the social newssites. The most cherished guest. In highest demand. She was seen with the hottest stars and had influence over who was in and who was not. She was asked her opinion and was a style leader. She had her own perfume line, her own opinion newssite, and her own line of makeup accessories. Her approval was coveted, and she was often quoted on the fashion newssites. She was hip, she was hot, she was relevant, and she had a loyal staff to take care of all the boring details. But right now, they couldn't take care of this boring moment. Poor Amelia. She had absolutely no idea what fun could be had out there in the world.

Drake, 17th May 2098

Drake knew he had humiliated himself again. He was trashed, completely, blind drunk. He was furious at himself and furious at the world. Another shitty night in another shithole talking to no one and being noticed by no one. Just another shitty day in his shitty life. He tripped as he left the bar to go back to the hotel and, in his disorientation, didn't notice all the lights and noise. At first, he just assumed it was all in his own head.

When he stood up he saw that there were people in uniform running in the same direction. He went along with them wondering what was going on. He stumbled again and this time when he looked up he noticed smoke coming from a nearby building. He looked behind him to the bar, then in front of him again, as if to orient himself. That was their hotel. Wasn't it? The reflection in the harbor water made the view even more disorienting. He was almost sure that was where they were all staying. That was where he'd left his suitcase. His vids. His drugs. His mother.

Holy shit! His mother!!! He ran a few steps towards the building, then stopped suddenly and turned around and ran back into the bar. He burst through the doors and starting yelling, for his sisters, for anyone to listen. There'd been a bomb, an accident, a fire, in the building where Mum was. They all need to go there, now!!!

Charlotte looked over at him with lidded eyes, uninterested in his rantings, and then back at Amelia. Where was Brandon? The bartender looked at him for a moment or two, and then went to serve his customers. He tried again. Mum! Hotel! Fire! Accident! Terrorism! Bomb! He lurched over to his sisters. It was like he was in one of those dreams when you're trying to yell at people, but no noise comes out of your mouth. But he could hear his voice, so it wasn't one of those dreams. They just weren't listening.

Amelia looked at him with disgust and frustration. *What is it Drake? It's Mum! Well, the hotel! I mean the hotel and Mum. I mean the hotel had an accident! I mean a fire! Or a bomb! It's Mum. She's there! The hotel!!*

He slumped against the barstool. He couldn't seem to say anything properly. Amelia was looking at him directly, trying to decipher his incoherent words, but she wasn't moving.

Now!! He yelled. Now!! The hotel where Mum is!! Now!! Amelia looked at Charlotte and stood up, scanning the bar around them. Charlotte looked at Drake. What was he saying? Charlotte looked up at Amelia and stood up too. She turned towards the door and saw the on-and-off shadows of the emergency vehicle lights. Her mind focused on the sirens and the lights. She looked at Amelia, her eyes widening, and then grabbed her coat and vid and ran for the door. Amelia and Drake were right behind her.

Amelia, 17th May 2098

When Charlotte started for the door Amelia's brain clicked. *Oh my God! Something's happened! Something bad!* Racing up the street, inches behind Charlotte, she could see the fire and smoke across the harbor. Amelia's brain just kept screaming *No! No! No! No!* She saw the smoke, the ambulances, and the responders with their laser extinguishers and water cannons. She saw a crowd of uniformed hotel employees. She saw crowds of people everywhere and she started scanning for her mother's face. *No! No! No!* Then she turned to *Please! Please! Please!*

Oh God, Mum. The newssite lenses were on them like wasps. Buzzing around, their vid lenses blocking her view. *Oh God, they were going to run stories on the family. They were going to be doing interviews with the whole family. They would talk to her husband, maybe even his girlfriend. Oh God, everyone would know. Everyone would find out about her personal failings. Mum! Where are you? Mum! Please! Please! Please!*

Amelia ran from group to group. She lost track of Charlotte and she couldn't see Drake anywhere. *Where was Brandon? Shouldn't he be here? Who was in charge? Mum? Mum? Where are you?*

She looked up and saw that the whole side of the building had gone. What floor had they been on? It seemed liked weeks ago since they checked in. Was it 5? Or 7? Wait, it was the top floor. She looked up again. Where was the top floor? There wasn't any top floor. *Oh God, Mum! She must be here somewhere.* Her family, her marriage depended on finding her mother. She searched the crowds frantically.

Who was in charge? What chaos! There! Charlotte was talking to someone who looked official. The noise was deafening. The sirens. The loud speakers. The laser extinguishers. The water cannons. The lenses in her face. Everyone talking, crying, shouting. All made worse by the reflection in the water doubling all the images, making everything seem bigger, wider, scarier. Where was her mother? She ran over to Charlotte and as she got closer she saw her sister's face. *Oh God, Mum!*

Charlotte, 17th May 2098

The lenses were all pointing at her. Her first instinct was to smile, her infamous wide white-toothed smile, but less than a split-second later she realized that smiling wasn't appropriate given what she was looking at. Lucky that she remembered. Lucky that her brain hadn't choked up completely. What a disaster that would have been.

The vid lenses were whirring and clicking, and people were yelling questions at her. She knew that she should look frantic, harried, worried, ruffled, and generally not her usual poised self. She played the role well, looking up, looking around, and trying to find Amelia and Drake. The responder had told her that the top floor had exploded and everything that had been there was instantly gone. Her suitcase, her travel gear, Mum! *Oh God, Mum.*

This was going to instantly stir up the media. They would rehash her mother and father's lives, the children's lives, when they were young. That infernal vegetable garden that she had been dragged to so many thousands of times. Even with the chaos, the noise, the smells, the voices yelling at her, Charlotte was acutely aware of every lens pointed at her. She knew that her every movement would be scrutinized, judged, complimented or criticized. This was what she was good at. This make-or-break moment was important, and she knew it. Amelia and Drake were a disaster, but Charlotte was on top of things.

She started quietly talking to the lenses shoved in her face. She had been informed that her mother was missing and presumed dead. There had been an explosion, possibly a terrorist attack. Her lip quivered appropriately, and her hair had unraveling over her eyes just perfectly. She thanked the first responders. She asked the media for respect while she and her siblings tried to find out more information. She thanked the security services for their work in finding the perpetrators of this shocking crime. She looked dutifully shocked, forlorn, upset, and appropriately ruffled. It was the performance of her life, and she was nailing it.

Amelia broke through the crowd and shoved the lenses aside. She half-fell, half-fainted into Charlotte's arms. Charlotte dutifully held her and bowed her head to her sister's, while she looked around for her brother. Where was that insufferable man-boy? Didn't he understand the photo-op that they had in front of them? Come on! She couldn't stand there forever. She slowly starting walking towards the first-responders tent, encompassing Amelia in her arms as she worked on a combination of glamour, grief, and poise. *Oh, I'm good. Really good!*

Drake, 18th May 2098

Drake couldn't get himself up on his feet. He couldn't decide if what he had seen and heard was real or simply a figment of his brain spinning out of control. He heard the sirens, didn't he? Or was that just ringing in his ears.

God, he hated himself. Why must he be such a loser, such a wasted loser? He resolved, for the thousandth time to change his life, once and for all. He'll get that money from his mother and turn his life around. He'll pay off his debts. He'll never play again. He'll relaunch his career by calling in some favors from family friends and loyalists. Someone will have a job for him. A proper job that pays a normal salary. He'll even agree to start at a low level, the mail room, the tech room, whatever. He'll make his mother proud. Wait… his mother. Had something happened to her? Were those sirens still going? What had they got to do with his mother?

He lowered his head to the cold, filthy pavement and it felt so good. He looked up at the sides of the colorful buildings around him. The alley was dark in comparison but that's what he needed right now, just for a few minutes. He felt a bit better. Almost good enough to sit up again. But no, back to the pavement. He'll close his eyes for a few minutes and then clean himself up and go and see his mother. Did something happen to his mother? He'll figure it out in a few minutes.

Brandon, 18th May 2098

He opened his eyes and looked around. His shirt was unbuttoned but his pants were on. His neck felt sore from being in an awkward position, half off the futon and half on. He moved slowly. Shit, his head pounded. *Where am I? Oh, yes, the red-head.*

He smiled. *Did we do it? We must have, but why can't I remember? And why do I have my clothes on? Did I get dressed again? Probably ready to leave right after, but then why am I still here? Did I fall asleep on the futon? Really? That's not like me? And where is she anyway?*

He got up slowly. Something was strange. The lights were off. There were no sounds from the apartment, except his breathing. She was definitely gone. There was a strange orange flickering repeating itself throughout the apartment. For a second, he thought it was coming from the vidwall, but slowly he realized that it was a reflection from lights outside. He looked out the window and saw lots of flickering orange, red, and white lights. They were coming from a few blocks away, but he didn't have a direct sightline. Maybe there's some sort of party going on at the harbor.

He checked the small kitchen, bathroom, and bedroom and confirmed that he was alone. Then he glanced around once more. This apartment seemed strange to him. Something was off. His heart started beating a little stronger. His hackles raised, and his gut soured. Something felt very wrong. He checked the cupboards and drawers in the bedroom. They had a few odds and ends in them - a bottle top, a broken zipper, a few salt and pepper packets -but mostly they were empty. He looked in the bathroom, one dirty grey towel bunched on the back of the toilet. In the kitchen, there were all the basics, but no food. Only a few beers in the fridge.

Back in the living room, he took a closer look at the family photos. He couldn't clearly remember in which picture he had noticed his redhead and her sisters. Now, he realized that the people in the photos seemed unrelated. He didn't see his redhead. In fact, all the people in the photos looked like they were happy and smiling, but more like models than families. Camping on the beach, at some kind of party, but no redhead.

Then he noticed that the vase, the one on the table with the obviously fake flowers, was gone. He looked on the floor. Behind the futon. Under the furniture. But there was no vase. Where was it? He couldn't see any broken pieces? Anything to indicate that it had fallen. Why would the vase be missing? Why would a bunch of obviously fake flowers be taken? He visualized the vase again. At least part of his memory was still intact. He remembered the vase – a kind of iridescent blue. And he visualized the flowers – plastic yellow daisies and other red flowers he couldn't name. With colors a little too bright and leaves a little too green.

Suddenly his heart started pounding furiously and his knees got weak. His stomach cramped, and he felt dizzy. Oh God! He suddenly knew what they were and why his brain had registered them at all. They were those new devices that date-rapists were using. The ones that diffused an opiate in gas form that made victims drowsy enough to relax and be raped. He'd read about them a few months on one of his security newssites. He didn't focus on this a threat for the family as the children were all old enough to avoid situations like this. And so, he didn't file it away in his checklist of credible threats to the family. This wouldn't be a risk that he needed to worry about.

The diffusing flowers were the new hot thing on college campuses and young female co-eds were being warned to look out for obviously-fake flowers in Frat houses or in drab college campus dorm rooms. The future-rapist would take the neutralizing compound a few hours before luring the unsuspecting female to his chosen lair, and the diffusing aromas would lull the victim to sleep while the perp would be unaffected by the drug for at least 8 hours. Plenty of time to have a little fun before the victim woke. Obviously, the designs of the flowers had got better, and less fake and so victims were still being lured. The flowers that Brandon had seen were clearly some of the early models. So obviously fake that they would only last once. But that's all the time that the redhead had needed.

Amelia, 18th May 2098

Amelia was staring. It was shock, she knew. She was staring at one of the medics, watching his fast hands grab supplies, wrap wounds, talk gently to victims, smile and provide solace and warmth. He looked like a nice guy. She felt such an attraction towards him. His gentle touch. His kind eyes. His capability and efficiency. It was all she wanted. A reliable shoulder to lean on and some intimate kindness. She watched his face. His easy smile. His eyes, showing concern, but also intelligence and quickness. She wanted to walk over there and pull him away from his patients. Have him take her in his arms and both of them fade away into an alternate reality. One where none of this was happening. Her mother was safely asleep in her bed. Her husband was waiting for her at home. And everything was as it should be.

She felt her heart starting to pump again. She felt an energy returning to her body and her thoughts. Enough of this self-pity. She was unharmed. She was privileged. She was capable and intelligent. She needed to stand up and do something. She slowly stood up and starting walking towards the entrance of the tent. In front of her, through the opening, she could see strong lights, flashing orange, red, and white. She could hear voices, yelling, shouting orders, calling out instructions. And she could see debris lying on the ground and dust hanging in the air. She walked through the controlled movements inside the tent and emerged into the chaos all around the building, lying half crumbled and smoldering.

She looked around and tried to figure out what was going on. Clearly the medic tents were busy. The wounded had all been taken away and were being treated, she presumed. The dead had also been taken, she couldn't say where. She could see people in uniform climbing through the rubble. There were dogs. There were lots of lights, helmets, and ladders. Everything reflecting off the water and the brightly colored historical buildings along the quay. Obviously one of their top concerns was to make sure the fire didn't spread beyond the hotel corner. She saw the logic, clearly and dispassionately as she looked around, overwhelmed.

Newssites were being kept off to one side, their viddrones overheard whirring. And then she saw Brandon. Stumbling, confused, looking drunk or high, but definitely panicked at the scene that he had found. She moved towards him, fast as he was turning around almost as if he didn't know where to look first. His disbelief was clear. His confusion was all over his face, and his pain was obvious. She didn't know what he knew, but she was going to find out.

Brandon, 18th May 2098

Oh my god. Oh my god. Nothing he was seeing with his eyes was making sense. What was going on? What happened? Where was everyone? Lynola? *Where's Lynola? Where's the fucking hotel?* His head was spinning. His brain wasn't firing properly. *Lynola, where are you?* He turned around and around, his eyes and brain barely registering what was in front of him. He spotted Amelia and was flooded with relief. She would know. She was coming towards him, and he righted himself and stared towards her. They met amongst a crowd of yellow-jacketed responders, and she pulled him off to the side without breaking eye contact. They couldn't hear each other. The sirens, the viddrones, and the helipods with floodlights flying overhead. Everything was loud and confusing.

She pulled him behind a tent. *Where have you been? What's wrong with you? Look at me! LOOK AT ME!!* He was having a hard time. She frowned and shouted, but it wasn't making sense to him. *Was it war? Was it real?* She hooked an arm in his and pulled him in the direction she wanted. He went, willingly, almost gratefully. She seemed to know what she was doing, and he followed her without hesitation.

He remembered when they first met. She, a high-strung privileged white girl with a snobbishness that came from being sheltered. He, rough around the edges, resentful almost to the point of anger, with various and sundry life-experiences under his belt. Immediately he knew that he could love her. He knew that he could devote himself to taking care of this young and innocent girl, giving her space to shine and grow, and share beautiful moments with her. Ridiculous, he knew. But it was a stirring and visceral feeling that stuck with him. And even though he suppressed it long ago, the seeds were still there, easy to reignite.

The moment when he had buried his feelings came just a few months after he had started working for Alfred and Lynola. Amelia was in the kitchen, bubbling over her new beau, full of energy and life. She was talking about the new guy in her life, handsome and educated. Climbing the corporate ladders and hobnobbing with all the right people. Of course, being the daughter of Alfred P. Loughton opened a lot of doors for her and attracted a lot of attention with the up-and-coming jet-set elite. Ironically, Alfred was immune to all those influences. That's what made him such a good and successful leader. But his kids were another story. They loved the privileges they received, and he didn't resent them for it. He just stayed out of those relationships and listened politely to their stories. In no way was he going to be influenced by a bratty hotshot who was wooing his daughter. And while he certainly didn't want her to get hurt, he knew that all three of his kids were smart and could take care of themselves. Lynola had taken care of that, and Lynola was the smartest and toughest one of all of them.

Amelia was radiant with excitement. Alfie looked on with a slight smile, enjoying his daughter's youthful exuberance. Lynola watched carefully over her daughter, giving advice, urging caution, and providing calm in the whirlwind of energy that Amelia was producing. At 18, she was tall, dark, and beautiful. Not in a model, classic sort of way. Her face was a little too long and her nose was a little too wide. She had a good shape, clearly athletic and light on her feet, but you could see the beginning of her widening hips and slightly drooping shoulders. Brandon loved her even more for these flaws. It seemed to make her more accessible. And her seeming disregard for her flaws, and her confidence despite them, were intoxicating to him.

He was supposed to be taking Alfie to an opening of a new oxygen forest and farm. The farm that was made possible by the policies that Alfie had dreamed up and convinced the public to support. The forest was unique in that it was reintroducing species that had recently become extinct in the area due to deforestation and soil erosion, but now, in collaboration with the new farm, its chances of success was bright. The farm was one of the first of its kind. Organic-based, of course, with vertical features, a water preservation system, and an army of community urban farmers who would reap what they sowed. It wasn't a long drive, and traffic would be light now that public transport carried more than 90% of city and suburban dwellers to their jobs, so no one was in a particular hurry to interrupt Amelia's stories of parties and romance.

Suddenly Brandon's ear focused on the details of the story she was telling. Amongst the details of sparkling lights, beautiful people, and amazing spectacles, he heard a spitefulness he hadn't noticed before. His gaze sputtered slightly as he listened to her tale of girlfriends who were urging her towards the new love-interest, despite the fact that the boy already was in a long-term relationship. She seemed completely indifferent to the hurt she was causing the other girl. It shocked him back to reality. He could never keep up with her. Never appreciate the things that she loved. Never treat people that way. And never close his mind to the hatefulness and greed that had led the world to the brink of disaster almost 20 years ago.

He made eye contact with Alfie who nodded slightly, leaned into his daughter brushing his lips along her cheek, barely interrupting her breathless stories. He gave Lynola a gentle kiss and walked quietly towards Brandon who opened the front door for him. His small smile stayed on his lips, blinded by his love for his family, oblivious to the undercurrent that Brandon had just now glimpsed in Amelia.

The irony was that the guy did eventually leave his girlfriend, but only after initiating a steamy affair with Amelia. And, as she later grew to understand, once a cheater, always a cheater. Leaving her on the verge of her 40th birthday with an empty marriage, a teenage daughter of her own who was sullen and resentful, and a circle of friends who were as shallow and opportunistic as they had been back when they were all just 18 years old.

Brandon, 18th May 2098

Brandon followed Amelia as she led him away from the crazy lights and noises. Across the harbor, a few blocks away, they stepped into a lobby of another hotel, the Bergen Harbor Hotel, a nice-looking place, more modern and brighter than theirs. Guests and employees were staring out of the glass walls, and the vids were playing scenes on a loop with narrators at a loss for words. No one paid much attention to Amelia and Brandon, as she led him to the back of the reception area and sat him down gently in a small round armchair with a high back. She pulled up a footstool and sat down, leaning into him and staring inquisitively into his eyes. He couldn't hold her gaze. *What happened*, he asked in a whisper. She told him what she knew. The explosion. The futile search for Lynola. The wounded and the dead. There wasn't much that she knew, and she finished quickly. She took his hand. He looked fragile. *What happened to you?* He was overcome by shame and embarrassed and stared at the floor. He didn't want to tell her the truth. He mumbled something about being drugged. The after-effects were obvious, so he didn't have to explain too much. She nodded and looked into his eyes with genuine concern. *Stay here. I'm going to go back and try* and find out more. She was also going to find Charlotte and Drake and bring them here. He should stay. *Do you want water or anything? There's a bathroom just behind there.* He nodded slightly, realizing that his tongue was stuck to the roof of his mouth and his lips were cracked. An aftereffect of the diffusion toxin, he knew.

She brought a glass of water and set it on the table next to him. *Promise me you'll stay here. I'll come back as soon as I can.* She gave him a quick squeeze on the shoulder and then slipped through the staring crowds back to the chaos on the streets. Watching her go, he was overwhelmed with admiration, and hung his head with shame and fear of what was coming. The truth would come out and she would hate him. They would all hate him. Big tears started rolling down his cheeks. He was grateful she wasn't there to see them.

Amelia, 18th May 2098

This time she had a goal. She would find Charlotte and Drake and get them to where she had left Brandon. They would debrief to figure out what each of them knew about anything. From there, she would find whoever was in charge. Should she call Desmond? Maybe he had already been called and was already on his way? She would manage her family and team. And she would craft the right message for the media and public. She would get ahead of this and handle it well. She could do this!

Moving quickly from cluster to cluster with her slim scarf over her head to protect her identity from the eyes in the sky, she searched for her brother and sister. She spotted Charlotte in the lights of a newssite reporter. Her makeup was appropriately smeared, but only enough for effect, not in the ugly way that desperation looks like. Her hair was slightly ruffled, with a perfect wisp felling over her unlined forehead. Her teeth were pearly white. Her clothes were rumbled, but not dirty or torn. She looked like a caricature of a shocked and grieving victim. Exactly as she was supposed to. The masses didn't want to see real grief. It made them uncomfortable with their own luck and relief at being spared the disaster that they were watching, glued to every image, judging every detail. And they couldn't tear themselves away from the sight of damage, destruction, despair, and pain. Charlotte had a real gift. She instinctively knew what would fascinate and captivate the masses. Not too much, not too little. She always got it just right.

Amelia ignored Charlotte for now. It was going to be hard to drag her away from the spotlight. She focused on finding Drake. He was probably drunk too. She quickly searched the shadows, in between the tents and buildings and in the alleyways. She remembered seeing him at the bar. Had he left when she did. She hadn't seen him since. She circled back and walked quickly, in the shadow of the other buildings, in the direction of the bar. Before she got there, she saw him slumped just inside the alley next to the bar. God, he was a disaster. Poor kid. He had never found his footing out of the shadow of the great Lynola and Alfred P. Loughton. Always too much to live up to. Falling short with everything he tried.

She grabbed him by the scruff of his jacket. Get up Drake. He worked better with direct and unambiguous orders. He opened his eyes and struggled to his feet. He clearly wasn't all there, but he recognized Amelia, recognized the authority in her voice and went willingly as she walked him the few blocks to the Bergen Harbor Hotel to sit with Brandon. What a pathetic bunch they were. For a moment Amelia panicked that they would be headlined looking like this. She had to hurry and get Charlotte so they could figure out their next steps.

She had a flash of an idea and grabbed one of the hotel staff who was in the uniform of a front desk clerk. The young man looked at her, first with irritation at being dragged away from the fascinating scene across the harbor, and then with recognition and awe. He started asking a bunch of questions at once. Tripping over his own tongue, not really making any sense. She shook her head and glared at him to silence him. Get her the keys to a room. The biggest suite they had free. He started typing, nervously as he was fairly sure they had been fully booked because of the award ceremony tomorrow. Yes, as he suspected, nothing was free. Although, one of the suites was reserved for an official who had never checked in. He had been marked for late arrival, so it was probable that with the happenings, he and his entourage had never made it. The clerk made the immediate decision to give it to Amelia. He was 99% certain it was the right move, and he loved his first taste of making a decision without having to ask the boss. He handed Amelia the keycard and then asked if he could help. She was unsure. Anything could be turned into a story for the newssites these days. Even just a few minutes of an encounter with a bunch of famous drugged, drunk, and shell-shocked almost-victims of a horrible world-changing incident like this one was going to be. She was torn between being grateful for the help and wanting to keep her secret safe a little longer.

She looked at him deeply in the eye. She was slightly taller than him in her heels and old enough to be his mother. Both good signs of authority. She told him that security and privacy were the most important issues right now, and that she would ensure he would be rewarded later if he kept quiet. The longer he kept quiet, the greater the reward.

He was ambitious. Instantly his mind swirled with all the possibilities that the rewards could end up being. He nodded, quickly and repeatedly. *Of course! Of course! You can count on me Ms Loughton.* They walked quickly to the armchairs and got Brandon and Drake to their feet. He was surprised that they were sitting there. How had they got there? What was wrong with them? He didn't dare ask, just followed her lead in getting them to their feet. They shuffled awkwardly as a group to the elevators and split into two groups to get up to the top floor suite. Amelia and the desk clerk installed the two men, childlike in their obedience, into chairs and left quickly.

Amelia reinforced her promises to the clerk as she hurried out of the hotel again. He glowed with greed and ambition. He was going to leap up the corporate ladder as soon as things got back to normal. He didn't even have to know why those two were catatonic like that. He had definitely smelled alcohol, but he figured - wisely - that he should probably stay ignorant of the details. He went back to staring out of the glass wall to the street with his colleagues and other hotel guests. Not much had changed outside. But a lot had changed for him. He suppressed a smile. That just wouldn't look right at the moment. Plenty of time to celebrate later.

Amelia, 18th May 2098

Amelia hurried back to the center of the action. She was grateful that no one was paying attention as she wasn't sure how much stamina she had left. The bed in that suite had looked tempting. She could just as easily lay down, fall asleep and forget what was swirling around her. Let someone else handle it. Eventually someone of authority would take over and she would just follow along. It was tempting, but she knew sleep wasn't in the cards for her right now. She was driven to reach her goal. She'd always been good at goals. One baby step at a time had been her strategy, and it had worked to get her through her life as the eldest sibling, as the daughter of great leaders, as the wife of a slimy, ambitious philanderer. One step at a time.

Charlotte was checking her face. Out of the bright lights for a few minutes. Maybe the newssites were figuring out that she didn't know anything and were getting tired of her repeating the same lines of shock and fear. Amelia didn't care. This was her chance. She slipped quietly next to her sister, looped her arm into hers, and pulled her firmly away from the crowd. Charlotte looked at her with instant irritation and started to pull away. Amelia tightened her grip, lowered her eyes, and insisted on striding calmly but forcefully away from the center of the chaos. Behind a tent, she loosened her grip on her sister's arm. She quickly told her about the hotel suite, Brandon and Drake, and her plan to contact Desmond for help. Charlotte didn't want to go to the room. Didn't want to be holed up there, out of the lights and possibilities that they held.

Ok, fine! The boys are too out of it to cause any trouble for now. We'll go together to find the chief. But you have to stick close to me. No more interviews right now. There'd be plenty of time for that later. We just had to have someone tell us what's happening and what we should do next. Charlotte agreed and linked arms tightly with Amelia. She knew that would play well on the vids, even if she wasn't going to stop and talk to anyone for now. The imagery was almost better than words anyway.

They took a few minutes to scan the scene. Each looking for the telltale signs of leadership and authority. There! Huddled over what looked like holographic maps under a camo, was the chief, some deputies, and other officials. The intrusive lenses being kept away, and the drones overheard masked by the camo tarp they had hastily constructed. The holomap was bright, a beacon in the grime and dust. They headed towards it, eyes down, conscious of the attention they were receiving and the whirring of drones and vids all around them. Not the time to stay in the shadows. Now was the time for action.

They reached the huddle quickly and dipped under the camo tarp. Uniformed men and women of authority turned to look at them. At first, the instinct was to shield them, but almost instantly Desmond stepped forward and hugged them both. He stepped back slightly to look at them up and down. Amelia was so relieved to see him. When had he arrived? Was he in charge? No, they weren't injured, physically, in any way. He took their arms and led them towards the holo.

It wasn't just a map after all. It had an overhead view, a live shot of the scene. One of the drones above was hovering and filming. Amelia leaned forward. She could see the outline of the hotel. She could even see the camo over their heads gently waving in the breeze. She widened her view and saw the tents, the crowds, the rescue teams, and just on the edge of the image, the Bergen Harbor Hotel where she had stashed the Brandon and Drake.

She asked the chief what he knew. He shook his head as he spoke, clearly not wanting to say anything definitive yet. He had been called in soon after the explosion and had arrived about 30 minutes ago. And yes, he was in charge. Amelia was visibly relieved and grateful that there was a friendly face and shoulder to lean on.

Besides the obvious explosion, the loss of the top floor of the building - no question resulting in loss of life - and the lack of survivors being discovered by the search teams, he could only say that they should prepare for the worst. It's unlikely their mother had survived, and it looked like an act of terror, although he wasn't prepared to announce either of these things publicly yet. Amelia shuddered hearing these words. An act of terror. A flash memory of watching her father and mother huddled over their porch table discussing backlash to their programs flooded her briefly. She swayed gently, supported by her grip on Charlotte's arm and a hand on Desmond's shoulder.

She took a breath. She asked when he could be free to come and speak to them and give them advice on what they should do next. She told him about the suite at the Bergen Harbor Hotel and the state that she had found Brandon and Drake. Desmond flashed a look of surprise, then relief. *Well done Amelia. You've done a good job in terrible circumstances.* At least there weren't more bodies to find.

Amelia confirmed what he had already known. The hotel staff had delivered Lynola's tea to her room around 21h30, and then followed her instructions to be left alone so she could get an early night. The chief glanced at the holo, then his watch. Give him an hour. He would come and debrief them. They should be ready for a long night of questions and statements. He would keep everything under tight security so that they could have

141

some privacy during this difficult time. They should get cleaned up and rest in the meantime.

Amelia breathed a sigh of relief. Nothing had significantly changed, except someone else was in charge. Someone who she could trust and who would figure out what happened and what they should do next. She tightened her grip on Charlotte's arm and they left the refuge of the camo tarp, eyes down, walking quickly towards the Bergen Harbor Hotel and away from the crowds and the vids. An officer trailed them, just to be sure. They slipped through the staring crowd in the lobby. It seemed smaller already. People became bored of staring at any unchanging scene and had retreated to their avatars to troll the cloud and see if there were any other viewpoints than from behind the wall of glass. Hundreds of tweets, fueling speculation and conspiracy theories. Even from the reputable newssites. But nothing beyond newstainment at this point. Even the Council hadn't released any information beyond the initial statement that an explosion had gone off at the Clarion Hotel and that the awards ceremony was postponed until further notice.

They strode quickly to the elevator and Amelia released the breath she had been holding as the doors closed on them giving them privacy for the first time. She and Charlotte almost hugged. But quickly regained their composure and their sanity and walked quietly into the suite not exactly sure what they would find.

Drake, 18th May 2098

Drake was spread-eagle on his stomach on the big bed, snoring loudly. Brandon was still on the chair where Amelia had left him, and he looked like he had been crying. His eyes were bloodshot and puffy. He stared out the window, at the grimy sky, still dark with night. Thankfully he hadn't thought to turn on the vidwall so there was very little noise besides Drake's regular snores. They were above the chaos below and could only barely see a faint glow of artificial light from across the harbor. The helipods and viddrones were far enough away that they didn't disturb the silence in the room.

Brandon turned and stared at the women entering the room, his eyes widening slightly in surprise or perhaps in fear. Amelia and Charlotte quickly surveyed the room and walked in opposite directions. Amelia went to Brandon, while Charlotte perched on the edge of the bed, almost like she was afraid of catching a disease, either from her brother or the bed itself. Amelia looked down at Brandon. She felt compassion at the man's crumpled face, but also anger at his weakness. He wasn't paid to be weak. He was paid to be invincible. She looked at him closely to see if she was still drunk or high or whatever he had been. He looked sober, smelled sober, but didn't look ready to do much else except stare at the darkened window.

Amelia sat down on the small chair by the desk and started writing notes on her vid. Key things to remember, key messages to send out, and keywords to set the tone. She needed to control the public view, entirely. For a moment, her eyes filled with tears again, with self-pity and fear. *Get a hold of yourself. Focus on the story, on your reputation and the messaging. We need to find out what's happened and control the narrative. That's gotta be the focus. No time for weakness now.*

Charlotte watched her sister frantically tapping on her vid. She smirked slightly at the desperate air of her sister and looked again at Brandon, who hadn't moved except to blink from time to time. Amelia stopped tapping and looked up. She went over and kneeled down beside Brandon taking his hand in hers. He didn't grasp back but let his hand simply rest, unfeeling, in hers. She asked how he was feeling. His eyes were so red. Maybe he needed medical help. He made the effort to look into her eyes briefly and then, almost immediately looked away, staring again at the blank window. She would ask Desmond when he arrived.

She stood up and looked around the room. It was important for the four of them to get their stories straight and make sure they all knew the details. They'd all been the bar. Brandon had left with booby-baby. Drake had puked in the bathroom. Charlotte and Amelia had run out into the crowd just after the explosion. Drake had trailed behind. No one had seen Lynola after she had left them to go to her room. Nothing untoward in their stories. It all made perfect sense and they were clearly above any suspicion in terms of their behavior.

Amelia, 18th May 2098

There was a sharp knock on the door that made everyone's eyes turn in that direction. Amelia strode quickly to the door and checked the peephole. Desmond and his detail were standing there, staring directly at the door. Amelia quickly opened in and fell into Desmond's arms. Then almost immediately, feeling embarrassed, ushered them into the room.

Desmond explained who everyone was, and the responders spread out among each person. Drake was awake now, sitting hunched over on the far side of the bed, staring quietly out the window. A responder went over to him, stood in front of him and took out his vid. He quickly and unemotionally read the disclaimer and asked Drake for his fingerprint authorization which Drake gave without meeting his eye. Then the questions started quietly and logically. Where had he been just before the explosion? What had he seen? Had he noticed any threatening behavior? Where had he been before coming to Bergen? Had he received any threats or notice of danger before coming to Norway? When was the last time he had seen his mother alive? This question made him flicker and raise his eyes to his questioner for the first time. It was at dinner? With everyone else. They had a nice time. Drake ignored the cramp in his stomach reminding him of his resentful feelings and suppressed anger at dinner. He wanted the memory on record to be of a nice, family dinner.

Amelia glanced over at Charlotte. She was performing perfectly. She wasn't even flirting with the responder too much. Just a flicker of a moistened eye once in a while. Perfectly appropriate. How did she do that?

Amelia looked back to Desmond and focused on his words. They didn't know anything, of course. It was completely unexpected. There hadn't been any overt threats, besides the usual nutcases. And Lynola wasn't working on anything too controversial at the moment, at least that she had shared with Amelia. She snickered without humor at the thought that Lynola would have shared any ideas with her. No, she didn't know the details of her speech for tomorrow. A speech was a speech – she didn't pay that much attention. She was sure there was a mirror and backup that could be checked.

There was no doubt that it had been an attack and not an accident. And that Lynola had likely been the target. Amelia swallowed hard. It was unsettling to hear those words out loud. Even though it wasn't the first time her family had been targets, it was the first time that anyone had succeeded. She asked the chief what they should do, glancing briefly around the room to her sorry band of charges. He said that the safest bet would be to stay here and keep a low profile. He would put a guard at the door and in the lobby. They should try and rest, stay calm, and above all, remain patient. This was going to take a while.

Brandon was describing the flowers. He was focused on every detail that he could summon in his fuzzy memory. They were dark pink and red, and there may have been a yellow or orange one too. They had those fake leaves that made them look slightly more real. The vase had been beige ceramic or maybe taupe, a sort of grey-brown. There were 8 or maybe 7 or even 6 of them in the vase. They'd been on the long table behind the couch. One of those tables that was hip high and the length of the couch, where you displayed knickknacks, or threw your keys when you got home. It made sense that he was so obsessed with the flowers, although he couldn't remember quite as much about booby-baby. Her eyes were brown, maybe. Her hair was red, for sure, but kind of a bright rusty red, and big, poofy, and curly. He didn't have the words to describe her hairdo. Her shape was...curvy. Yes, big boobs, spilling out of her green, like a sea-green, t-shirt. As he spoke, he knew he was providing completely useless information. In fact, he was probably digging himself a bigger and bigger hole. Everything about her had been fake - her hair, her boobs, her eyes, even her shape was probably artificially enhanced for the evening. He knew he had been a classic, clichéd stooge, and had been the perfect mark and dupe. He hung his head in shame, embarrassment, and a crisis of ego. What a fucking loser he was. Laughable to think that at any point in his pathetic, loser life, he had believed that he could keep this family safe. He walked into a classic trap, fell right into the hole dug especially for him, was taken in by a caricature, and had been completely oblivious the whole time. The hairs on his neck hadn't stood up. His gut hadn't cramped with suspicion or instinct. His defenses, if he ever truly had had any, had been completely unplugged. He had been the perfect victim in the perfect distraction. They were probably laughing at his stupidity, and marveling at their luck at finding such an easy mark. The responder's eyes were unsympathetic, even as she said words to let him know that this could of happen to anyone, and that he shouldn't blame himself. Her eyes were saying that he was a classic idiot and should have known better.

CHAPTER 4

Sean, 12th May 2098

Sean looked out of the window and took in every angle of the view. The plane was high, and he could see the curvature of the earth on the horizon. The dark abyss above him, split by the magenta line of the sunrise at the horizon, and the pale and misty landscape far below him. It all made him feel peaceful, for just a second. It was just a second. He wasn't at all fooled by the fact that he couldn't see the details from this height. The hunger, the abuse, the greed, and the egos. Those huge egos, which by all rights should fill up his entire view if they were visible. They thought they were gods. That they were invincible. That they were always right. Sean would show them the error of their ways. It wouldn't be hard to do, but it would take some coordination, determination, and a clear focus. Sean had all those qualities. The qualities that made him the perfect resistance fighter. The perfect leader of the underground. Even though his merry band was small, he knew that it would grow once he shattered the bubble of lies and showed everyone what was really at work here. How they just didn't care about the little people. How they lived their lives of luxury and comfort at the expense of everyone else. How this perfect utopia that they had created, was just an illusion. Sean knew that this was his calling, his fight, and his legacy to the world. This was going to change everything, and he was just the guy to get it done.

The meeting was in three hours. He wasn't stupid though, so he wouldn't be exactly on time. He would arrive early to scout the area, and then arrive late to the meeting like his plane had just landed. He was smart and calculating. He would make them see things his way, he would help them join his resistance, and walk away from their own family legacy. This would be the icing on the cake. Of course, he would move ahead with or without them, but the added credibility of just one of them being on board with his plan would be amazing. And he would control the conversation, the agenda, and every detail. His way or the highway. Forget equality for all and every man with a voice. The new future was being ushered in by him, and he intended to make it in his own image, giving himself the rights and privileges that he deserved. He was fulfilling his legacy, his destiny, and his future.

Sean, 12th May 2098

His eyes were a little too wide set and his hair had started thinning. He was on the short side for a man of his privilege and ethnicity. What was left of his hair was mousy brown and straight. Even when he was younger, he had never been able to keep any particular style going as his thin hair always fell back into straight wisps off his head.

It had been years now since he'd had any contact with Sienna, Dot or his younger half-brothers. He vaguely remembered that they'd been heading to Australia to plant new oxygen forests along the northwest coast. But he doubted they'd stayed for very long. A few months or a year at most. All that moving around, it was exhausting and dehumanizing. Always having to reinvent yourself and be interested in the new communities that you hoped would welcome you. He was glad to be rid of that pressure.

He had spent some time trying to be 'normal'. He had moved back to America after his time in Dublin had left him feeling even more impotent. He'd worked construction in northern Michigan, in the thriving cookie-cutter new northern suburbs of Detroit. He had made his way down to Chicago and had worked as a bartender for a while, but he just wasn't charming enough to make that work well. In northern Indiana, he'd slipped into factory work, where he could remain anonymous and still pull in a pay check. He rented the basement of an old lady's century-old split-level house and was able to benefit from the privacy and the hi-speed vid lines that she was hardly using. It was here that he first started properly developing his EF credentials and his delusions of grandeur. All those hours alone in the darkened basement, connected only to the rantings of extremists on the darkvid where Sean could shed his mediocrity and spout grandiose ideas in the privacy and safety of an old lady's basement.

Sean slipped into the community café where they had arranged to meet. He was early, just as he had planned. He looked around. There was the normal selection of families, groups of older retirees, one or two single business people dressed for work, and a group of loud giggling teenage girls in one corner. Nothing out of the ordinary here.

He walked over to the counter and took in the selection. No harm in grabbing a quick meal. This community was clearly into their grains. Bulgur, quinoa, corn, rice, wheat, barley and plenty of others with red, blue, brown, and yellow hues dominating the menu. Breads, salads, cakes, cooked dishes, and desserts were laid out in front of him. His stomach rumbled, and his mouth salivated at the sight - just as his head was screaming at the unfairness of the abundance and ignorance of the people seated around him. He'd have a quick bite and then keep going. It was good for him to act and seem 'normal'. He might be recognized when he came back in a few hours so no harm in testing the waters and creating a non-threatening persona.

The girl behind the counter cleared her throat in an attempt to speed him up. He ordered the vegetarian enchiladas in red corn tortillas with a side of spicy pepper, quinoa and bean salad. He drew the line at meat substitutes. He didn't have to go to those kinds of extremes to establish his persona. He wanted to blend in, not standout. And anyway, despite his resentful feelings, the food smelled and looked delicious. He used his fingerprint to pay. No reason to shield his identity at this point.

He sat at a table and nodded to the two grey haired ladies next to him. They were sitting on opposite sides of the long wooden table leading over their plates, deep in conversation. Sean tried to block them out. Who cares about a couple of octogenarians and their boring conversation? But his ears perked up when he heard one of them say 'Loughton'. Maybe he could learn something interesting after all.

Sean, 12th May 2098

Sean stood up and burped quietly. Damn, that was a good meal. He couldn't help but feel a tinge of nostalgia at the feeling of his belly being full and the nutrients racing through his body. He hadn't ventured out to a place like this for a long time. But now that his plan was in motion, he had no more reservations. He would fulfill his legacy and leave his mark loudly on the world. His vid held the entire record of every window, door and opening in the whole hotel. He knew the placement of every table, every chair, every barstool and other fixture and fitting in the place. He wouldn't be a victim of any surprises here.

He nodded to the bored girl behind the counter as he took his tray to the belt. He separated the bamboo utensils, plate, and mug from the rest of the waste and walked slowly out. No point calling an extra attention to himself by being rude and not clearing up after himself. Or making a fuss about the fact that the belt was mostly full and not being cleared up quick enough. Just go with the flow. As he walked out through the glass doors to the streets, he knew he was in control. He had all the power and was on track to realize his destiny.

He walked out and took a left turn, walking up the street to the small park on the corner. The weather was mild and sunny. The haze that was ever present, seemed a little thinner here. The sun's rays were diffused through the haze, making things warmer than they should be. The heat index was at 33C as was predicted, 3C higher than the average 10 years ago for this time of year, and 9C higher than the average 50 years ago. But people were adapting, as they always did. And the tourism industry in Norway was booming, especially the seaside resorts along the Atlantic side, with their mild breezes, tolerable ocean temperatures, reliably sunny days, and long summer nights. They'd certainly picked a nice place for the award ceremony. The irony of it almost made him gag.

He sat on a bench and watched the world go buy. 2 hours until his meeting. But 2 hours and 45 minutes until he planned to actually show up. He wanted to seem frazzled and out of breath, a bumbling do-gooder or idealist. He didn't want them to know about his cunning or his forethought. He couldn't reveal everything without making himself vulnerable. For a second, he wondered whether they would show up. Of course they would. He'd made sure they thought all this was their idea. They were completely wedded to it. It was their initiative, their plans, and their revenge, they thought. He smiled inside. He almost felt high with glee at the thought.

Brandon 12th May 2098

Brandon slipped into the booth at the diner a couple of minutes earlier than the planned time. He liked to be early, to get his bearings before anyone else arrived. He brought along a female colleague who he'd worked with in the past. She was versatile and discreet and worth the expense to drag her up here to Bergen and pay for her trip and accommodation. He felt sure the threat was minimal, but he wanted to have a second set of eyes on the situation, just as an extra precaution. Maybe Jolie could enjoy the beaches and go up the cable car to the mountains to see the views after they were done.

Jolie practiced her demeanor - the submissive, shy, docile persona that she and Brandon had decided on. She coyly straightened her skirt and readjusted her short hair behind one ear as she slipped into the booth next to Brandon. They'd rehearsed this a few times. Jolie was an attractive and petite woman, with rich dark brown skin and oversized black eyes and wavy black hair, giving her an air of someone much younger than her 40-something years. She was to be introduced as Lynola's longtime publicist's new assistant who had grown up in the refugee camps in east Africa. In reality, Jolie (not her real name) and knew no security or hope until she joined the jungle guerrilla fighters. She had been almost immediately recruited as a negotiator between them and the new non-elected government, mostly due to her naiveté which allowed her the open mind that the two sides desperately needed. She rose quickly through the ranks after a successful run at creating cooperation and compromise between the enemies and ended up with an enticing set of people skills which translated into valuable spy craft that made her an excellent choice for Brandon's mission today. Jolie knew that she was supposed to storm out at the right time, just after he had revealed the basics of his plan, pretending to be shaken, with her loyalties torn, while Brandon reassured him that she would come around. Instead, Jolie was to go directly to the responders, while vidding the lawyer to join them remotely. Then she was to come back into the diner, sit across from Brandon this time next to their guest, and pretend to have been convinced. And there they would listen to his detailed plan, stalling just long enough for the responders and the lawyers to join them.

They settled in and ordered food while they waited. The trays looked delicious and Brandon had worked up an appetite. Jolie had a tomato salad and a fruit pastry, in keeping with her persona, while Brandon had the daily special - a huge plate of salads and a meat-substitute sandwich, dripping with synthesized blood to make it smell, and taste like the real thing. They ate quietly, Brandon watching the time and repeatedly glancing out the window in between huge mouthfuls. Jolie stayed in character and nibbled at the edges of her pastry. Eventually, their appointment stepped through the door, made eye contact with Brandon who nodded imperceptibly, and slipped into the booth across from them.

Sean's heart was racing. This was his moment. His plan was working. He could hardly believe that they had both come. They were sitting in front of him, eating, of all things. He hunched his shoulders and leaned in. Brandon and Jolie did the same, convincingly playing the roles of co-conspirators wanting to believe him. They needed no introductions as Sean started in, explaining his plan. He was going to get the explosives in a few hours from a guy he'd knew on the darkvid. He had identified the doorman who he was going to bribe to let him into the hotel. The doorman who seemed most vulnerable was the one with a scar on his lip, obviously too poor to be able to afford the correction to get rid of it. Brandon nodded and smiled. *Smart thinking, you're good at this,* he said with a smile. Sean returned the smile and, on the inside, almost burst with pride at the compliment.

Brandon was to meet him on the top floor of the hotel while Jolie would be distracting Lynola with speech rehearsals and whatever else she would normally do. And Sean and Brandon would run the explosive wire along the edge of the carpeting and around the door frame, so it wouldn't be noticeable to anyone casually walking down the hallway.

But first, Sean had to test their loyalties. He asked Brandon why he had agreed to help him. Brandon repeated the words that he had rehearsed with Jolie. He was tired of being downtrodden and treated like a slave. He wanted the leadership to sit up and take notice. He wanted change and justice for the one percent. He had no loyalties to Lynola and her family. He had simply been a foot soldier to them for so many years. He had been invisible to them, barely noticeable considering their important daily lives. Sean smiled and nodded repeatedly at the words that were like music to his ears.

Jolie listened with a practiced small smile on her lips, while secretly horrified at the conversation, her diplomacy skills on full function. Were there really people who still believed this crap? Who were they, except for this clearly deranged madman? Everyone knew the one percent were not forgotten. There were dozens, probably hundreds, of programs all over the world working to help them. Even back in the camps where she grew up, life was improving for the majority of people. She felt her blood go cold at the words, even though she'd helped Brandon write and practice them.

Sean looked at her as she nodded along with him. He wanted to be convinced of her loyalties too. She started her speech. Telling him a story of her imaginary family members, suffering and needing help and justice. But, a few sentences in, she got choked up. Sean leaned over and laid his hand on her arm. It took practiced willpower not to flinch or pull her arm away. Instead she smiled wanly and said she needed some air, starting the next phase of their plan. But Sean was immediately on alert and pulled back his hand. He sat up straighter and was instantly wary and agitated.

Brandon turned to Jolie and put his arm around her protectively, reminding her of all the injustices she had endured. Jolie nodded appreciatively. She'd missed her window and the plan hadn't worked. She knew better to spook Sean, so she exchanged glances with Brandon and understood that she should stay in her seat. They'd find another way. Brandon kept his arm around her, comforting and reassuring her. Sean's shoulders relaxed a little as he watched the dynamic in front of him and felt back in control.

17-18th May 2098

17 MAY 2098 22:35:47
OMG my hotel's under attack. Fire and smoke everywhere. Gonna try and climb out.

17 MAY 2098 22:57:05
Lynola Loughton and her family are thought to
be victims of a powerful explosion at the
Clarion Hotel tonight in downtown Bergen. They
had checked-in earlier in the day and staff
cannot say if they were on the premises at the
time of the explosion. The search is underway
for survivors.

17 MAY 2098 23:42:48
Lynola Loughton, wife of former Global
President, Alfred Loughton, is thought to have
been killed at an explosion at the Clarion
Hotel in downtown Bergen this evening. Her
family are safe as they were not at the hotel
at the time of the explosion. Authorities are
not confirming whether it was a deliberate act
of terrorism. An investigation is underway.

17 MAY 2098 23:17:38
Mum, I was at the hotel that below up, but I'M
FINE. Am being treated for some smoke
inhalation but nothing serious. I'll call you
guys tomo.

17 MAY 2098 23:19:44
Dad?? Just heard about the explosion at your
hotel. Are you ok? Please vid us as soon as
you get this.

17 MAY 2098 23:27:31
Charlotte Loughton, daughter of the former
Global President Alfred Loughton and United
Peace Award recipient Lynola Loughton, has
just addressed the crowd. She says they don't
have any details yet about their mother, who
is thought to have been inside during the
explosion. We're being asked to wait for
further details.

17 MAY 2098 23:52:30
Charlotte Loughton, daughter of the former
Global President Alfred Loughton and United
Peace Award recipient Lynola Loughton has
confirmed that her mother perished in an
explosion at the Clarion Hotel in downtown
Bergen this evening. An investigation is
underway. Further announcements are expected
throughout the night.

17 MAY 2098 23:27:31
DAD??? OMG…where are you? Vid me ASAP!!

18 MAY 2098 00:04:49
Charlotte Loughton, socialite and daughter of
former Global President Alfred Loughton, has
confirmed tonight the death of her mother and
the safety of the rest of the Loughton family.
She has revealed that responders believe the
explosion was due to a bomb planted in or near
Ms Loughton's room. It is believed to be a

deliberate act of terrorism. The investigation
is underway.

18 MAY 2098 00:17:43
Baby, I'm fine. Was in the hotel when it blew,
but not near the blast. Scared, but fine. Will
vid when allowed to use line. Let everyone
know. Love you.

18 MAY 2098 00:44:16
Chief Responder Desmond Nkaya has been named
to head the investigation into the blast that
tonight killed Lynola Loughton, wife of former
Global President Alfred Loughton. Chief Nkaya
is a close friend of the family and worked
with the former President at the height of the
neo-agro movement back in the 60s. Chief Nkaya
announced that the rest of the Loughton family
are safe and well and have been secured at an
offsite location.

Desmond, 18th May 2098

Desmond had known each of Alfred's kids from their
childhood. As was his habit and talent, he remembered their
names, their ages and their particular likes and dislikes. He saw
that Lynola's method of childrearing was not always suited for
the personality of each of the children. He witnessed Charlotte's
desperate attempts to get her father's attention. And Amelia's
obsession about being self-sufficient and in charge. Drake's
problems with excesses of every kind. He noticed how
disengaged from his family Alfred was, but he always watched

from the outside, never overstepping his bounds, never interfering. He didn't even confide these details to his own wife, preferring to keep his opinions to himself. That was his way of being a friend, and more importantly, being trustworthy enough to deserve the next promotion or raise.

Now, he had to find a way to set aside some of the inflammatory behaviors he had witnessed over the years and investigate Lynola's death impartially. He was glad Alfred wasn't around to witness this. It would have been an overwhelming task for many, but it was a perfect position for Desmond. And he rose to the occasion with pride, with satisfaction, and with a faint feeling of excitement at the exposure and praise he would receive once he had solved the case.

After being debriefed and downloaded with all the details at the scene, he walked over to the hotel where the family was safely huddled. He nodded to the responders covering the front entrance, rode the elevator up to their floor, and knocked gently on their door. His detail stayed respectfully and silently a few centimeters behind him. Their faces neutral, their eyes forward. Amelia flew into his arms as soon as she opened the door, and then stepped aside to let them into the suite. Desmond walked her gently into the room as he and his team entered the suite and looked around. His team started their interrogations, gently according to his instruction. All three children were there with Brandon. Looking pale and somber. Without the vids as witness, they could each retreat into their natural behavior.

Desmond, 18th May 2098

First, Desmond expressed his regret for their loss and confirmed to them that he had officially been named to head the investigation. Amelia looked relieved and relaxed deeper into her chair. He walked over to the window and looked out. It was still night. The lights over the Clarion Hotel glowed across the harbor, probably visible from the whole city. The pain and fear and shock were palpable in the room. Desmond explained that they would each be spoken to individually, and then he and his team would head back to the site to catch up with the rest of the responders doing the onsite investigation. Just this little amount of information seemed to help all of them. At least now they knew what was needed from them over the next few hours.

After he was interviewed, Desmond sent Drake to go and take a shower and he gently took Amelia into the adjoining bedroom instructing her to lay down and close her eyes for a while. He then closed the sliding door and sat down opposite Charlotte in the armchair furthest from the window. Across the room, next to the darkened window, Brandon was engrossed in his quiet responses to the questions being posed by the responder in front him.

Charlotte looked surprisingly fresh and clean. It was her way of coping, he knew. He leaned over, touched her hand, and asked in his gentlest voice how she was doing. Her eyes welled up quietly as she looked Desmond in the eyes. She shook a little with emotion and he was silently stunned. This certainly wasn't like her. He hadn't expected to see much, if any, emotional reaction from her, at least away from the lenses. What she then said shocked him, although he didn't react in the slightest. *It's my fault*, she said, *I killed my own mother.*

Desmond calmly looked at Charlotte in the eye and told her to start from beginning. She took a tremulous breath and recounted what she knew. She told Desmond that three years before she'd met a man. A married man who was charming, wealthy, and not a big fan of her parents' policies. Charlotte didn't care about that last part, all she knew was that he made time for her, took her to the nicest restaurants, on the nicest trips, and treated her like a queen. It didn't hurt that he was tall, dark, and handsome, and amazing in bed.

Charlotte told Desmond how she bitched and moaned about her parents, about her childhood, and about her whole life in general – although not too much as she didn't want to bore him or scare him away. She knew he wasn't in love with her, but she was totally in love with his lifestyle. The yacht cruises, the weekends to tropical islands, the indulgences of fresh seafood, real chocolate, and lots of champagne. They didn't talk seriously too often, but she knew about his disdain for her parents. He was in favor in rolling back many of their directives, but he was powerless. He couldn't bribe an official, couldn't elect one, and couldn't influence one. He was just like everyone else, and he was frustrated and annoyed.

They had sometimes joked about making a statement – she about the destructive nature of neglectful parenting, and he about the impotence of un-influence-able political leaders. They had played with ideas like taking over the Brooklyn Bridge, or turning the moon green, or other absurdities like blowing up a building or taking over a small country to publicize their grievances.

Charlotte had seen this man on and off for more than three years. They both had other lives, but they would get together for weekends or evenings a few times a year. They had a similar routine each time and would often spend their pillow time thinking up more and more absurd ways to rid of her mother and her parents' policies. Charlotte got a lot of wicked glee from these conversations, but she never took them seriously and never thought much about them after their rendezvous had ended.

But it was obvious to her now that he had. She had just seen him 6 weeks ago and they had talked about the award and joked about how it would inflate her mother's ego even more and boost her perfect father's unblemished legacy. He had known exactly where they would all be, and when. Maybe he had done it out of an act of love for her – Charlotte's eyes softened for a moment. *Oh God! It was all my fault! This guy had the motive and the resources to get this done. You're the only person I can trust with this. What should I do?*

Desmond looked at her with kind eyes, like a father looks to a foolish child who has just broken her favorite toy. Of course, this wasn't her fault. Even if was her lover behind the violence tonight, it still wasn't her fault. All he needed was his contact details and he'd follow up to prove it wasn't her fault. Charlotte's face flooded with gratitude and relief at not being judged.

After a moment, she collected herself, visibly sitting up straighter, smiling a little and smoothing out her cheeks. She looked around the room a little nervously to see if anyone else had witnessed her little breakdown. Everyone seemed completely oblivious and engrossed in their own drama and guilt. Now that she had that off her chest she would reward herself with a few touch-ups, quietly of course.

Desmond, 18th May 2098

Desmond slid the door gently behind him as he walked into the darkened bedroom. Amelia was sobbing softly into her pillow. He walked over to the bed and sat on the edge beside her. She looked up at him with watery eyes and slowly sat up. She asked if he had any more news. He shook his head gently. She asked if he could find out whether her mother had suffered, and then the sobbing started again.

He put his hand on her back and she fell into his shoulder. After a few minutes, she had calmed enough to speak. He asked her to start from the beginning and tell him everything she knew. She took a shaky breath and he thought she was going to start crying again. Instead, she told him about her troubled marriage and her philandering husband. She told him that she had told her mother about her troubles and that her mother hadn't paid much attention. She told him how resentful she was towards her mother and how she had only wanted to come to Bergen to get away from her husband and didn't really care about the award. She hadn't even asked her mother about the speech or how she was feeling about the award.

Amelia started crying again. *Oh God! What a mess!* And now everyone was going to know about her failing marriage. She'd never be able to go out in public again. Did her mother suffer? She hoped it was quick. She hoped whoever did this would burn in hell forever. Desmond held her again as the sobbing started all over again. Then he gently smiled and said he was sure that her mother knew how much she loved and cared for her despite the distractions of her flawed marriage.

She looked at him gratefully through his tears. He handed her her vid and asked her to dictate all the details she could remember as anything could be helpful to the investigation. She lay back down on the bed and buried her head into the pillow again. He got up slowly, walking out and closed the door silently behind him.

Drake was walking out of the bathroom wearing a clean towel and rubbing his wet hair with another one. He looked, and smelled, a lot better. He glanced up at Desmond and asked if there was any news. Desmond shook his head. Charlotte walked past them into the bathroom and closed the door. Desmond took Drake's shoulders and looked down at him. He was almost a head taller than Drake and felt a mix of fatherly instinct and impatient revulsion towards this broken young man. Drake looked down to his feet. He was humiliated and ashamed and didn't want Desmond to see that in his face. Desmond asked Drake if he had any idea who had done this. He shook his head sadly and hung his head further. He turned to the armchair chair and sat down heavily.

Desmond asked Drake about his movements the night before. Drake recounted his sad story, barely able to look Desmond in the eye. When he was done, he had slouched even further into the chair. Desmond assured Drake that he would do everything necessary to find out who was responsible. He told Drake that he now had to step up and take care of his sisters while they tried to wrap their heads around their new reality and start to mourn their loss. He assured Drake that a security detail was posted outside their door, off their balcony, and around the public areas of the hotel. They were all safe.

Drake glanced out the window and saw the helipod hovering silently; its glass eye swiveling constantly. He closed the curtain and turned back to Desmond. He asked to be kept informed of the progress of the investigation and thanked Desmond for his support. Then he turned away to get dressed.

166

Desmond told him to try and get some sleep and that he was only a vid away. Then he quietly slipped out of the room and nodded to the responder who stood guard outside the door.

He spoke quietly to Amelia and told her that she and Charlotte would need to go to the station to register their statements. Drake's would be taken later when he was fully sober. He told her that he had ordered their suitcases from the Clarion Hotel to be delivered here as they had still been in the baggage storage area and were undamaged in the explosion. He advised her to get cleaned up a bit and wait for the responder to take them down to the car. He then relayed his instructions to the responder in the room and the juniors at the door, took a deep breath and headed back to the bombed hotel.

CHAPTER 5

Desmond, 2037-2051

Desmond Nkaya was a tall man. He was the color of a strong café-au-lait, had a shaved head, and a no-bullshit attitude. He'd seen it all. Corruption, perversion, cruelty, selfishness and selflessness, generosity, and immense kindness. He'd earned his way up through the ranks by working hard, keeping his nose clean and his ambition in the forefront of his every thought. He couldn't understand people who didn't have ambition. Why didn't they care about their future? The security of their family? The happiness of their children? To him, his ambition guaranteed that his kids would have security, and therefore happiness in their life long after he was gone.

Of course, this meant that he was never going to be selected as a candidate for government office, but that suited him just fine. He commanded a great deal of respect. He had resisted all the clichés and all of the corrupting temptations. To him, nothing was more valuable that the next promotion, the next raise, the next award, or the next newssite interview. Those were his goals; they represented his dreams and would facilitate his success. But he wouldn't cross the line to corruption to get there. That was a step too far and could easily backfire and ruin his plans. Nothing was worth that, especially as it put his ambitions at risk. He would raise the heights of his dreams, the only way that would guarantee his success. Work hard and honestly and exploit every relationship he could develop.

This attitude hadn't won him many friends. But he didn't really care, as friends were not his measure of success. His single-mindedness rubbed many of his colleagues the wrong way, and fear of exposure of their side-activities kept him at arm's length and excluded him from social activities and "team building" exercises. He didn't get invited to fight clubs, poker nights, vid exchanges, or life-event celebrations. Fewer distractions meant more time and energy towards the goals that mattered most to him.

He met Alfred during a networking event of the neo-agro movement in 2049. Alfred was double his age, almost old enough to be his father – if he had had one – but he was approachable and generous in his attention. Alfred was involved as a way to learn more about the shifting geography of raw materials production away from central regions of the world towards more north and south extremes. Desmond was involved purely as a networking opportunity, as he understood at an early age, the importance of being in the right places at the right times to meet influencers and future leaders. Alfred was 18 years his senior, but they were seated next to each other in the big auditorium and shared their reactions to the speakers and the presentations throughout the day. Desmond instinctively felt that Alfred was someone useful to know and made sure to ingratiate himself and not be easily forgotten long after the conference had ended.

Desmond had grown up as a normal inner-city kid. No father. No resources. Low quality schooling. No prospects. Friends and neighbors helped raise him, as was their tradition. The inner-city communities lived as the proverbial "village" to raise their children, as it was commonly understood as a necessity to raise strong and healthy children. And in doing so, Desmond benefitted from a strong sense of community even without many other resources at his disposal.

From a young age, Desmond had figured out that knowing the right people was important. Unlike many of his peers, he didn't shy away from the responders who came into the city from time to time. He was friendly – although managed to avoid becoming an official snitch – and learned who was in charge and therefore who was good to be the friendliest with, and who it was okay to ignore. He didn't suck up too much but kept out of trouble and earned the reputation of a clean kid who might have a future.

He jumped at every opportunity he could to meet people outside of the city. Field trips to farms, factories, other cities. Community programs to send inner-city kids to vacation camps at the lake, extra learning opportunities, meeting political leaders, anything to avoid sitting at home alone or being solicited by gang leaders looking to swell their ranks. If there was a writing competition to win a newssite interview, he entered. If there was a corporate-sponsored dance contest to win a trip to the regional sectionals, he gave it a shot. He didn't win everything, but he won or placed enough times to give him a taste of what life was like outside of the confines of his community and kept him motivated to find a way out.

He volunteered as a teenage responder but wasn't given a lot of responsibility. He would get to ride-along if it wasn't deemed to be too dangerous. From the back of the transport, through the thick bars, he could sometimes see a take-down. The stun guns. The gas. He sometimes heard the screams and crying and pleas for mercy, for drugs, or for exceptions to the rule. He saw faces devoid of emotion. He heard threats that made him shiver, and he saw great acts of courage and compassion that would stick with him for life.

Meeting people was his talent, even as a teenager. He could work a room like nobody's business. He could walk in knowing no one and walk out two hours later with a dozen new names in his contact list and leaving behind an impression of intelligence and compassion. He worked his contacts, smelling opportunities before they went on the wire, and capitalizing on his in-person meetings whenever possible. He asked for favors, but never beyond what was appropriate, and remembered enough key names, facts, and life event dates about the people he met to keep the relationships friendly and productive. By the time he met Alfred, he was only 19 years old, but his skills were honed, and he was able to integrate well and be of value, while maintaining an emotional distance that suited them both. Their relationship was mutually beneficial, and their friendship grew out of the respect they had for each other.

Desmond, 18th May 2098

When Desmond arrived back at the scene, he found that some progress had been made. An animation was already complete, recreating the explosion from all angles. He had the tech transfer the images to his vid so that he could view them later. He also saw that the digital recordings were already being used to eliminate the findings from the DNA sweep. Desmond let the techs take care of their work while he chased down the stories from the Loughton children. Nothing he had heard seemed like credible leads for the attack, but he had to do his homework nonetheless.

First, however, he assigned a deputy to recreate the children's alibis, track down the street footage and pull the recordings from the bar. And then he went to talk to Brandon before he headed to the station to set his eyeprints to his statement.

Brandon looked up as Desmond approached. Desmond felt that he should be interviewed at the station, away from the children, for protocol's sake. He had agreed without hesitation and was waiting on the quayside for his ride. The responder was about to put him into the car to take him to the station, but he waited until Desmond got to them. Brandon couldn't meet his eye. Desmond put a hand on his shoulder and gave it a little squeeze. He nodded to the responder and Brandon was loaded into the car. Desmond vidded the station chief that Brandon was on his way and that he should be given blood tests and guarded as closely as the children.

Now Desmond could think more clearly. He found a quiet spot and watched the recreation of the explosion on his vid. It was impressive how quickly the techs had figured out angle, thrust, and size of the explosion. It seemed to him that the bomb must have been stuck to the inside of the building, right above Lynola's balcony. When it blew, it took her room and rooms immediately below, to the left, and to the right of her. It also blew most of the windows on that entire side and some on the building opposite. It had been a big explosive, hard to carry around and store. That could be useful.

The vids had some tags already loaded and when he followed them they gave him the names and status of the people in the rooms on that side of the building. It also gave him an exact timeline, down to the second, of everyone's movements, the temperature in each room and outside the building, outside lighting, and passing traffic on the ground and in the air. It was a good compilation of a lot of the easiest to gather data, but nothing was very revealing. Desmond knew that this was only the start.

It certainly seemed like it was a targeted attack on Lynola. Whoever did this went to quite a bit of trouble to get to her without too much consideration of the collateral damage. And arranging it for the day before her award presentation meant a very high-profile case with a lot of newssite coverage and lots of exposure for the perp, or perps. It also meant that Lynola and her endless supply of new ideas, was forever silenced. These were motivations that Desmond could work with.

Desmond, 18th May 2098

As he sat there reviewing the vids and tags, another vid was wired to him from one of the responders. He had asked that all files be wired as soon as they were available, so he was getting what he wished for. He opened the file and watched it. It looked like footage from a stairwell. He glanced at the sender's name. It wasn't a name he recognized – probably one of the junior responders following instructions.

There were two people in the stairwell, obviously arguing. The man, or boy, it was hard to tell, was shouting at the woman, or girl. Desmond zoomed in and rotated the angle. They were adults, but young adults in their early twenties, or highly touched-up older adults. They were screaming at each other in whispers. The vid contained audio, but the audio had a lot of static and echo from the stairwell, and because they were whispering, it was hard to hear anything but a few words clearly. He would send this to the techs for cleanup. But first he needed to see it through.

The woman was yell-whispering at the man, gesturing wildly. The few words that were clearly audible didn't reveal too much, and despite Desmond's lip-reading skills, he couldn't pick up much else. He heard things like "but you said" and "she wasn't" and "that was before" but nothing strung together enough to make much sense. He watched it over and over again until he realized that he was just going around in circles. He wired a copy over to the techs and moved on.

After a couple of hours of watching more vids, animated and real, from every angle, he gave himself a break and stood up. The scene was considerably quieter now. Cleanup was well underway and most of the crowds had gone, taking their lenses and peering eyes with them. Most of the responders had left too, with their vids and witness statements filed and tagged. The hotel staff had been released and only a couple of managers were left to supervise the cleanup. The other hotel guests had been relocated, so Desmond was left staring at a mostly empty building, shattered on one side, and a whole lot of unanswered questions.

His vid buzzed with the arrival of another new witness statement. Charlotte's on-again-off-again married playboy lover had been located and had testified via vid and under oath that he barely remembered the things that he and Charlotte spoke about. It was all a bit of a laugh to him at the time, as he was mostly high when he was with her. Besides, he had a pretty good alibi as he had been caught on vid with another part-time lover on a boat near the old Seychelles, diving to see the preserved underwater villages with his rich and privileged friends.

There was also a statement from Amelia's husband who had been in touch with her to make sure she was safe. Since they were technically "on a break" he didn't want to assume she wanted him with her, however given the traumatic incident, he at least offered to fly out to be with her. She was touched but declined and asked him to talk to Desmond. He had given vidded testimony and admitted he had been having an affair, but it was mostly for harmless adrenalin fun but really nothing serious and he was going to end it. His lover wasn't a threat as she was married too and certainly didn't want her rich and influential husband to find out about her indiscretions.

More serious and unsettling was Brandon's story. Who was this woman he'd hooked up with? Had he been drunk or drugged and was there any truth to his theory that she'd lured him away to get him out of the picture when the bomb exploded. The timeline, which was measured to the millisecond and rarely inaccurate, had him leaving the bar almost immediately after the explosion, which didn't make any sense. In fact, Brandon seemed to vaguely remember the sounds of the sirens as he was leaving the bar with the redhead.

Desmond reviewed the vids from the bar again. He saw Brandon approach the girl and he fast forwarded through the inane and drunken flirting, hair-flicking, and tattoo and scar-comparing stages. Then, as they left, he switched to the vid re-creation from behind the bar. They walked up the alley, around a corner and across a street, moving away from the blast site, and up the fire escape of a tired-looking building. Brandon looked tipsy and lustful, but definitely not drop-down drunk. They climbed up three floors and went inside.

Desmond called a couple of junior responders to take a walk and re-create the route that Brandon and his companion had taken. When they reached the building, they climbed up the same fire escape and went through the same door. On the vid, it was the woman who opened the door, so Desmond tagged the handle for DNA screening, knowing however, that it had probably captured hundreds of smudged prints. Inside the hallway, they were faced with two doors. One had a name on the doorbell, so they started there. And old lady came to the door and asked in Norwegian what they wanted. Desmond had the junior take her details and have a quick look around her bleak space. They turned to the unnamed door and rang.

On the vid, he could hear the echo of the bell inside but no footsteps. The junior ended the vid and set the laser borders around the door to warn any visitors that this was part of the crime scene and ongoing investigation. Desmond was going to have to see this for himself.

He put away his notes and told a junior that he would be back in half an hour. He walked past the harbor to the bar and followed the same route that Brandon and the redhead had taken behind the bar and down the alley. Following the report from his junior, he crossed the same street and climbed up the same fire escape. It was all a little dingy, that was for sure. This neighborhood hadn't yet benefited from the newest city revitalization efforts, but it was still quite quaint and had an air of respectability.

Desmond took his responder-issued swiper and laid it on the lock. He typed his name, badge number, incident code, and the name and code of a judge that he knew wouldn't be hesitant about authorizing the opening. A few seconds later, he got his response and the door clicked open.

Inside, it was neat and quite bare. The couch that Brandon had described was there and was a little rumpled. But there were no beer bottles on the table, no photographs on the wall, and no vase with flowers. The view from the window was of the back alley, so it wasn't surprising that Brandon didn't know what was going on just a few blocks away. The kitchenette was empty, and the bedroom and bathroom were too.

Desmond went back to the old lady's apartment and asked about her neighbors. She said she had a longtime neighbor who had been there for a number of years. A banker, she thought. They didn't know each other well, just as neighbors. She thought perhaps he'd recently got married and moved away. A young single man didn't share many details of his life with the old lady next door. She thought the apartment was still empty. She hadn't heard or seen anyone move in.

Desmond showed her pictures of Brandon, the busty redhead, and, on a whim, the couple who had been whisper-arguing in the stairwell of the hotel. She didn't recognize any of them. By habit, more than hope of finding anything useful, he ordered a complete DNA sweep, took another round of vids, thanked the lady and left. He wired everything to the techs and sent the responders back to the scene. Then he went to the bar.

Brandon, 18th May 2098

Brandon sat in front of the terminal piecing together her face. She had definitely had a high brow. He knew because her hair had been tied back. In a ponytail. Or maybe a bun or a braid. Her hair was red, or at least it had been for that night. He was under no illusion that it had been red earlier in the day, or the same color the next day. She was tall, almost as tall as he was. She was probably wearing heels, but honestly, he hadn't noticed. She hadn't stumbled or walked awkwardly, that he would have remembered. So, either she was practiced on heels, or she was just tall. She had broad shoulders, a strong body all around.

He remembered her having a formidable, well-defined body and he felt ashamed at the memory of his lust. That obviously what had made her attractive to him. Her face was oval with wide set eyes and a long, thin nose. Her lips were shapely, nothing unusual that he could tell. He couldn't remember any identifying marks or really anything useful at all. He stopped and looked at the composite. It could be anyone of ten million people. She could even have been a feminine-looking man for all he really knew. Although he felt he would have known, deep down, if she wasn't a woman. Oh, who was he kidding? He had been played, very well-played. She could have been part horse for all he had noticed through his lustful gazes at her ample chest, made especially for him, he was sure. He had taken the bait, hook, line, and sinker. He was one of those suckers born every minute. The ones he had always hated for their weakness.

He hung his head in his hands and felt the wave of nausea run through him. Nausea, mixed with shame, mixed with guilt, mixed with a deep sense of loss and grief. He looked through the glass at the entrance area and waiting room. People bustling backwards and forwards, some in uniform, some in plain clothes, some with tablets and vids in front of them, others staring at a vidwall and manipulating the images. It seemed like he was looking through a fog. Or from another dimension. Nothing felt real, but everything felt too real, at the same time. God, he was completely useless to them, and to the family. How had he ended up sinking so damn low? He wanted to crawl into a deep hole, lay down, and never get up again.

He wondered how the children were doing and though about the kindness that Amelia had shown him when he was still coming down off his high. He was grateful. At least she didn't hate him. Or maybe that came later. One of the stages of grief was anger, he was sure. That's when he would feel the full force of all their rage. Maybe he could be gone by then. He looked back to the composite. Completely useless. He'll leave it as is. It wouldn't be of any help anyway.

Amelia, 18th May 2098

Amelia turned back to the responder. *Yes, I'm sure I didn't notice anything. Of course, I saw the redhead that Brandon left with, but why was that important. No, I didn't see anything of real substance. I was chatting with my brother and sister - we were relaxing and drinking like everyone else. Mother was safely in bed, behind the wall of security.* She paused as her lip quivered, then took a breath and continued. *We were all taking a breather in the bar before the big event.* She felt defensive and angry. Didn't she have the right to a night off once in a while? No, she hadn't noticed anything suspicious. No, nothing had caught her eye. No, she didn't know the details of the damage. No, she hadn't seen anything except the rubble afterwards. *No! No! No!*

Charlotte wasn't faring much better. She was repeatedly answering the same questions, this time to an older female responder who clearly had no interest or patience with her flirtatious attitude. She huffed a little, pouted a little, and then resigned herself to get through the list as quickly as possible. As soon as the responder acknowledged that they had come to the last of the questions, Charlotte got up quickly and went to stand next to Amelia who was slowly standing up too.

One at a time they stared into the eyeprint scanner to sign their statements and prepared to leave this horrid place. Amelia stood up quickly and caught her balance. Too much alcohol, no sleep, an almost empty stomach, and the overwhelming series of competing emotions battling inside her were starting to take their toll. She asked for a lift back to the hotel for her and Charlotte. They would lie down and try to sleep for a few hours. The responder checked in with Desmond who authorized it, and a patrol car took them back to the Bergen Harbor Hotel, deliberately avoiding the smoky ruins along the quayside.

As they walked into the hotel, Amelia didn't feel like she had the strength to go to the same room and be with her brother and sister right now. She told Charlotte to go up alone and she sat on one of the armchairs and hung her head looking at her feet and shoes. They were black with grime and dust from the rubble, the tents, and the station. She thought about the bathroom that still had the towels on the floor that had comforted Drake as he worshipped the porcelain god. Yuk!

She got up and asked at the front desk if they had another clean room available. She was grateful that many of the hotel guests had checked out quickly after explosion. The hotel was cleaning them for – what they hoped would be – new guests. They had one ready on the top floor, two doors down from the suite that they already occupied. She went up quickly to a room that was clean and fresh, and empty. She immediately slipped off her shoes, climbed out of her clothes and stepped into the warm shower. She used the free mini shampoo to wash her hair three times, and the shower gel to scrub at every crevice she could reach. The body lotion softened her red skin after she dried off and she wrapped her hair in a separate clean towel.

The room was smaller than the suite, but the bed was just as comfortable. As soon as her head hit the pillow, she felt like she was sinking into a black sea. Sleep overcame her quickly, but she woke up with a start just forty minutes later. She was immediately alert and on edge. Her heart was racing. Her ears were burning with effort. Her eyes darted around the room. But the room was empty. Everything was silent. The sun was starting to go down and the room was turning a soft dusty pink. The shadows were soft and gentle. There was nothing there to be afraid of.

She lay back down and closed her eyes. Sleep didn't come again. Now her brain was awake and wired. She was composing grams and vid messages. The public statement. A statement about Brandon. What about Lynola's acceptance speech? She had never even asked her mother what she was going to say. Probably the same old drivel. She felt guilty at that thought. Should she try to get a copy? Maybe publish it posthumously as a tribute? Might work well for the public communications plan.

She tried to push all her thoughts out of her head. She had learned a trick a few years ago where she could visualize a white wall that covered all her thoughts. Her job was to keep the white wall - which somehow was on wheels - in front of her thoughts that kept trying to barge through.

But even as she fought the thoughts, she kept coming to the realization that she was losing the fight and focusing on a new thought, and she would need to readjust the wall in front of them again. But it didn't work. She wasn't going to sleep again today. She slipped on the bathrobe and hotel slippers and padded down the hall to the suite, nodding and smiling as gracefully as she could in a hotel bathrobe and slippers to the responders standing guard in the hallway.

18th May 2098

The world lost a true leader yesterday in a horrific and bold terrorist attack in Bergen, Norway. Lynola Loughton, wife of Alfred Loughton (Global President from '61 to '75) was killed along with another guest, a security guard and a hotel employee. Seven other guests were injured when a bomb was detonated above Ms. Loughton's hotel room on the top floor of the Clarion Hotel. Ms Loughton is survived by her 3 children and 1 granddaughter. The world mourns today as responders and investigators start the long process of figuring out who perpetrated this callous and frightful attack.

Amelia & Charlotte, 18th May 2098

When she entered the suite, Amelia heard Charlotte in the bathroom humming as she filled up the bath. Thank God for her sister. She never thought she would need to lean on her, but truth be told Amelia wouldn't have gotten this far if Charlotte hadn't been there to keep her walking. She sat down heavily in the armchair and waited. After a few minutes she realized how hungry she was, how they all probably were. She called down to room service and ordered some dried fruit salads, breads and coffee for everyone. Ever the sensible thinker and planner.

Charlotte lay in the bath and played with the bubbles. Wasn't it interesting how so much can change in such a short amount of time? She was an orphan now. Granted one with an older sister, younger brother, and a dedicated staff. But officially an orphan, nonetheless. She had to figure out the best way to play this story. It was big, and she wanted it to be drawn out and last a while. She could ride this for a few months, maybe even a year.

First things first, she would strategize with her agent and closest friend, Miriam. Miriam was a brilliant media strategist and knew how to spread messages far and wide. She and Miriam had been scheming and riding the wave that was Lynola and Alfie Loughton for a couple of decades now. Her instinct was to lay low. Build the suspense and then do an exclusive with one of the biggest newstainment shows which could be hyped for weeks in advance building the story and teasing things out. She'll call Miriam in the morning and together they'd figure out the plan. Meanwhile, she should think about touch-ups. Did she need anything done? Or maybe a slightly tired, slightly saggy look was a good idea. Miriam would know.

Charlotte, 18th May 2098

Amelia's eyes were drooping. She couldn't believe she could feel this tired, but she wasn't going to last much longer. After she'd eaten a little, drowsiness overcame her, and she curled up in the armchair in her oversized robe and still wet hair. Her mind swam for a short while and then she was asleep, quietly snoring through her opened mouth.

Charlotte came out of the bathroom wrapped in the thick white hotel towels and bathrobe. She felt clean and fresh and invigorated. Her mind was racing, and she was dying to get started on her plans. She saw Amelia sleeping in the chair and felt a wave of pity, mixed with disgust at her sister's weakness.

She saw the food tray and realized how hungry she was. She ate a dried fruit salad and enjoyed a strong cup of unsweetened coffee. Then she went back into the bathroom and changed into a one-piece lounge suit. Stylish in khaki silk and bamboo, with an elastic waist and a loose fit. She curled her legs under her as she sat in the other armchair next to Amelia and started surfing on her vid. Her instinct told her to not post anything right now. She cloaked her identity, so she would remain anonymous as she got a good look around. Keep the silence - and suspense - going for a while. She planned to release things a little at a time. Too much too soon would speed up the passage of this moment and she preferred to keep people hanging on and wanting more details. Charlotte had to tread lightly.

She knew that she and Miriam would come up with a good plan to milk this for all they could, and she wasn't going to spoil anything by rushing blindly into posting simply out of reflex. This was going to be fun.

18th May 2098

Our beloved mother and mentor, Lynola Loughton, died yesterday. A victim of an apparent terrorist attack. She is survived by her three children, Amelia, Charlotte, and Drake, and her loyal staff of many years. She will be greatly missed.

Ms Loughton was born in 2023, as the worldwide climate and food crises were growing around the world and as the Purple Revolution was ending and launching our new world order of governance. After graduating from Southhead University with a bachelor's degree in Behavioral Science, she went onto get her master's Degree in Psychology from Yale University. It was during her time at Yale that she met the great love of her life, Alfred P Loughton, the future two-term Global President.

Over the decades, Alfred and Lynola shaped our world so dramatically that almost all of us now live in peace and prosperity largely because of their work. Lynola's contribution to these policies went mostly unnoticed until Alfred's tragic death 16 years ago. But today, even the youngest school children around the world are aware of her profound influence on so many of the benefits and societal innovations that we take for granted.

Lynola was immensely proud of the work she and Alfred did to adapt to climate change, to alleviate poverty through revenue distribution programs, to eliminate inequalities in the tax system, and their most first and most controversial program – the elimination of industrial subsidies. Throughout it all, Lynola kept cool and poised and allowed Alfred to be the front-man and take the glory. The global community will forever be indebted to Lynola's intelligence, compassion, and quiet determination to leave the world a better place than she found it.

The family and staff will announce the time and place for the upcoming memorial service and celebration of Lynola's life. The committee will present Lynola's Universal Peace Award posthumously to representatives of her family in the coming weeks. We invite everyone to add their comments and personal stories about Lynola to this article. #lynola #worldpeace #alfred #loughton #stopterrorism

18th May 2098

@sandrasmith: What a loss. We will miss her so. Why do people do these hateful things? #stopterrorism #lovelynola

@sthfork: goodbye Lynola. You will always be our hero. #lynola #lovelynola #stopterrorism.

@ruinedinalabama: These people shouldn't be celebrated, they should be condemned for what they did. They got no idea what they did to our family. Our fishing business is dead because of them. #hatelynola

@trunews: Click here to see authentic pictures of Lynola & Alfred naked on the beach in Thailand in 2041. #sexonthebeach #Thaisex #loughtonsex

@ashleyintx: Lynola's my idol. What a woman. Controlled her man, controlled her kids, made a fortune off her name, and is still celebrated as a peacemaker #myidolislynola #wonderwoman

@alfredfan: Lynola claimed all the glory after Alfred was gone. Where was she when farmers were striking and throwing food at his convoy? She should have kept behind the scenes where she belonged. #alfredismyhero #loughton #hatelynola

@lghtnheros: We are forever grateful for the work Lynola and Alfred did for this planet and the people on it. #nowordsareenough #loveloughton

@nomorelies: Oh please!! Look around. People are still starving. Climate change has devastated us. They didn't do anything but line their own pockets and revel in the glory. #theonepercent

@erth1st: The Earth First movement is grateful for the elimination of one of the world's most corrupt individuals. Now we can rebuild together. #theonepercent

@islandgurl: We love you Lynola. You will be missed. #lovelynola

Brandon, 18th May 2098

Brandon was spent. He could barely keep his eyes open and he had nothing more to say. He'd told the same story at least five times and the responders were fairly sure there wasn't much more to tell. The composite was pretty useless - a generic female face, obviously highly touched up and enhanced. It wouldn't help to capture anyone, or even to confirm their identity if and when they did catch her. There wasn't any reason to keep him talking.

The cruiser dropped him off in front of The Bergen Harbor Hotel. The streets were quiet after all the excitement of last night. He walked to the reception and asked for a room. He didn't want to be with the family and wasn't even sure if anyone was here. The receptionist confirmed that the family were still at the hotel, they had two rooms on the top floor. There was any empty suite available on the 2nd floor if he wanted it. It was way outside of his normal budget for a bed, but who cared at his point. He took the keycard and dragged himself to the elevator.

He planned to take a shower and shave when he got to the room, but the minute he saw the bed, he lost any strength that was propelling him, and slumped down, headfirst into the pillow. He was asleep in under a minute.

Desmond, 18th May 2098

Desmond took a booth in the back of the bar and ordered a drink and a smoke. He didn't care that he was on duty. It was a difficult day for many people, including him. He inhaled deeply and sat back looking around. It was an ordinary place, served mediocre food, drinks, and smokes to mediocre people. The Loughton family must have shaken the place up a bit by their presence alone. The redhead had targeted Brandon here, so either she knew he was coming or had followed him here. For a fleeting minute Desmond quietly entertained the thought that somehow Brandon was involved, but the notion didn't last long. No motive, no opportunity, and while means were always possible, the likelihood was extremely slim.

He stared at the bartender and the barflies in turn. None of them seemed very concerned by his presence, but he needed to make the rounds anyway. The responders had already been and collected vids and DNA, now it was Desmond's turn to look around, with all the human instincts that a computer program or bot would never be able to replicate.

The bartender's name was Raul Ortega, originally from Havana, moved to Bergen in his early twenties mostly for the economic possibilities thanks to the changing climate. He made a decent living, had a wife and three children. His DNA came back mostly clean. Desmond moved on.

The three barflies were as uninteresting as the bartender, but Desmond reviewed their DNA history anyway. None remembered much about the Loughtons except that they all drank a lot, were loud, and blocked access to the bar. This group was so wrapped up in their own misery that anyone having a good time would seem disruptive to their daily routine. He checked the bathroom. No need to sweep in here – too much data would require too many resources, with no usable returns. He downloaded the bar vids, just to have an original copy, thanked the bartender and left. Nothing much there – no surprise. Seemed like there were only two real leads to follow – the couple in the stairwell and Brandon's girlfriend. He walked back to the scene to check in, downloaded the latest reports, and went home. It was time to sleep on it.

CHAPTER 6

19th May 2098

Less than 48 hours after a massive explosion
hit the Clarion Hotel in Bergen, Norway,
killing Lynola Loughton and 3 other people,
and injuring 7, Chief Responder Desmond Nkaya
has released an update of the investigation.
He confirmed that the explosion was deliberate
and caused by a man-made device. The
responders believe it was a crude device, not
built by any sophisticated organization. The
device was embedded in the eave of the roof
above Lynola's window, ensuring she would be
killed in the blast. The explosive device was
triggered by a crude timer, similar to an old-
fashioned timer switch on a garden light. And
it seemed to be placed there a few days prior
to Ms Loughton's check-in. The room in
question had not been occupied for more than a
week but the room had been cleaned and
inspected the day before Ms Loughton's
arrival. The room had been renovated over the
winter break and had been occupied over the
busy spring and Easter holiday season with
tourists and families. The hotel management
refused to release the names of the cleaning
staff who had access to the room, but the
responders have the information and are
investigating. Chief Responder Desmond Nkaya
thanked the public for their cooperation and
support and asked for patience as they worked
through the details of this crime.

Sean, 19th May 2098

Oh my god! Oh my god! Oh my god! Sean's heart was pumping, and his eyes were darting around under the peak of his cap that he had pulled down low to the bridge of his nose. He still couldn't believe it. It was like someone had read his mind. Where he had failed, his guardian angel had succeeded. And somehow, he still felt proud.

Were they looking at him? He was sitting on a bench at the back of the train station, just getting his bearings. He hadn't decided on his next move. In all truthfulness, he hadn't planned on getting this far. He had always assumed he would get caught or somehow die from the explosives, but now it seemed that he was free and clear, and somehow his plan had worked! It was a miracle! He was both ecstatic and terrified. He didn't want to get caught. He wanted to revel in his accomplishment, not that he really understood how he could be responsible. It was just too much of a coincidence to not be caused by him. He must have somehow willed this to happen.

The responders patrol stood at the main entrance of the train station glancing around. Sean dipped his head and stared at his shoes until he was sure they'd passed. There was no point drawing attention to himself now. He just wanted to leave town. The responders were monitoring all the transport options out of town and IDing everyone. Sean wasn't sure which option would be the most anonymous. He finally decided on the magtrain and bought a ticket to Copenhagen. It was only a two and a half hour journey, but it would give him time to think and figure out what he was going to do next. Next, was such a strange concept. He never believed he'd get so far in his life. What could possibly be next?

On the train, he sat against the window in the last row by the luggage rack. The rack was pretty empty so only a few people even glanced in his direction as they walked through the train car. He stared out of the window at the blurred landscape moving too fast for the human eye. A stripe of white was the sky, and a stripe of green was the fields. Every once in a while, a stripe of brown that lasted a few seconds was a town that they whizzed by. Sean's eyes relaxed into the blur leaving his brain clear to think.

It was really confusing. The bomb blast obviously was not what he had planned. He hadn't planned for it to go off late at night and he hadn't planned to take out most of the hotel. Maybe he has miscalculated the explosives and this was the result? Maybe Brandon or the girl had a made a change to something at the last minute because they knew this would be the better outcome? He'd probably never know because it wasn't like he could contact Brandon and talk about it. The explosives had been his. But the timing was all off.

Sean had thought the detonator was broken or the software was defective. He couldn't get it to stay turned on and connected remotely with the bomb. He had tried for hours turning it off and on and trying to figure out how to keep the connection live long enough to adjust the setting to activate the bomb. He'd finally gone to sleep, hoping that in the morning he would have a clearer head, or it would just magically turn on in time for him to complete his plan. He had wanted her to be getting ready to go out to the award ceremony. For her to believe that this was her day to be celebrated and lauded for all her "achievements". But in fact, it would be her day of reckoning and of punishment for all her misdeeds. But he couldn't get the damn detonator to connect remotely. But somehow, miraculously, the bomb had blown up anyway and killed Lynola anyway. So, other than the timing issue, it had worked exactly as he had planned.

Was he in the clear? He couldn't be sure. After leaving the explosives in the room with Brandon and Jolie, he had been racked with doubt and indecision. Maybe they were tricking him. Maybe it was a trap and he was going to be picked up at any minute. But, on the other hand maybe everything he had planned has been perfect. It had always been hard for him to feel that confident in himself, but the proof was there, all around him, on the newssites, and in everyone's consciousness, forever. He had been successful and now Earth First would have their day in the sun. The one percenters would be heard and Sean's name would be the first word on their lips. He would be revered for his courage and strength. For his creativity and foresight. He would be their hero. He WAS their hero, but they just didn't realize it yet.

These days he really didn't have much contact with the larger Earth First community. He had tried to build a strong and close following. He liked the idea of having a loyal band of disciples around him. But as he lay in his bed at night, his thoughts always turned to the bible story of Judas, and his paranoia prevented him from trusting anyone. Even the Earth Firsters, who were loyal to the cause, were not above his suspicion. Why did they follow him? What did they really want? Were they really loyal to the cause? Now they would all know him. They would fear him and revere him. This was HIS day to shine!

He would have to reach out to his followers soon - in real life, not online? He had talked and talked to hundreds of them online about the cause, just in the past year. But now he wanted to look them in the eye. He wanted them to see him in person, to know he was real, and witness what he accomplished in their name. Sean felt giddy at the thought. He would organize an event, with his name in lights as the headliner and big draw. It would be a revolutionary event. For sure he'd have to wait a little bit until things died down. He didn't want to give any excuse to the authorities to come after him, or EF. He was pumped up at the thought of his future, but he had to maintain his calm and unassuming demeanor for a little longer.

Sean, 12th May 2098

Jolie kept glancing nervously out of the window. What the hell was she looking at, or waiting for? Sean didn't like the smell of this. He had come today ready to trust them, and he wanted - with all his heart he wanted - to believe that they were Firsters. Lynola and Alfie had ruined this planet and ignored so many people. Couldn't Brandon and Jolie see that?

Brandon was still talking to him earnestly, convincingly. Jolie seemed nervous, but actually, he realized, that was normal too. *Of course, she's nervous. She's about to betray her employer. Duh, Sean, stop being so paranoid. Take a leap of faith, for once in your life!*

He leaned into Brandon and started laying out the details of his plan. At the same time, he gently touched Jolie's hand and gave her a soft smile. It will all be okay. He's thought through every detail. He was in control, and all they had to do was follow along. She gave him a weak smile, glanced at Brandon and seemed to calm down and focus on the conversation at hand.

Sean had the explosives. All he needed was access. Either to her room or the one next door. The device was rigged with a remote detonator that he could set up when he decided the time was right. All Brandon and Jolie had to do was get him into the hotel. He'd brought his fake plumbers' outfit and would bring "the package" and the wiring. Brandon was going to say that, because of security reasons, they couldn't let the hotel staff into Lynola's room, and so he'd brought a plumber he could vouch for to check the leak in Lynola's bathroom. What could be easier or more believable? Brandon nodded his agreement and looked admiringly at Sean. The plan was good, solid, well-thought through. Nicely done!

Sean tried not to be flattered, but Brandon was clearly impressed at his ideas and planning and was definitely on board. Jolie would be fine once she got over her jitters. Brandon looked directly at Jolie and told her that this was the right move that Sean had clearly got all the details taken care of, and that he, Brandon, and Jolie could easily handle the last hurdle. Brandon's deep voice and piercing eye contact with Jolie seems to do the trick. She smiled and nodded and calmed down even more. Sean was ecstatic. He almost couldn't believe it, but here they were, the three of them working out the last details of his plan. This was going to put Earth First on the global map and help the one percent be vindicated. This was his destiny.

Brandon, 12th May 2098

Brandon slowly squeezed Jolie thigh twice under the table. That was their signal that he knew what he was doing and was in control. She took a shaky breath to reinforce her nervous, but committed persona, and stared intently nodding gently at

Sean as he spewed the Earth First doctrine into her face. Sean smiled. The operation was a go.

Brandon agreed with everything Sean said. He wanted Sean to keep thinking that he was in control and that everything he said and thought was genius. Narcissists were easy to manipulate with flattery and false agreement. Brandon was sure that Sean bought their story and believed in their betrayed of Lynola and Alfie's legacy. What an easy mark this kid was. It was incredible he hadn't been blown up by his own explosives or double-crossed by his own side before now. It was like taking candy from a baby.

They agreed on the time to meet in the hotel lobby. Brandon was going to take him to the largest suite on the top floor - on the opposite side of Lynola's actual room. And Sean could set the device and the wiring. Sean would bring all his tools and the equipment. Everything was in place. Sean left the diner with a skip in his step.

As soon as he was out of sight, Jolie sat up straighter and looked at Brandon. *Really? Is this what you brought be all the way up here for? This guy's pathetic. How come you needed me?* Brandon reassured her that he had needed a female persona that seemed weak and submissive to convince Sean of their commitment. If it had just been Brandon alone, Sean might have felt skittish and not in a position of power and control. Now he was certain that Sean was convinced of their loyalty to him and EF. They needed to make sure his DNA would be left on the device if he was going to get the full punishment that the law allowed. The most important thing was to get those explosives off Sean and render him impotent. Jolie agreed, anxious to get her hands on the explosives to be done with this mission and get back to her life.

Sean, 13th May 2098

At five minutes to 0800, Sean was in place. It didn't pay to be there too early as he was supposed to be a plumber, not a hit man. He sent a vid to Brandon, in the coded language they had agreed upon. "Plumber from Sorensen Plumbing arriving to address leak in Ms Loughton's suite at 0800". Brandon replied "copy that" almost immediately. Sean walked towards the hotel, keeping his eye on the security guards and the hotel concierge. It was unlikely any of them were armed with anything more than a stun pistol, not in this day and age, but he couldn't be a hundred percent sure. As he started across the street to the hotel's side entrance, he saw Brandon poke his head out of the service door. All's set, he nodded and propped the door open for Sean to walk through.

His 'tool box' felt immensely heavy in his hand. It was all in his head, as he knew the device was no bigger than an old-fashioned tablet with some extra bells and whistles. The wiring and other tools were carefully arranged on top, hiding the device, but being careful not to damage the protective outer casing. He gently moved his tool box from one hand to the other as he came through the door, being sure not to let it touch the door or walls. He couldn't be sure if its stability, even though he'd paid top dollar for it.

Brandon led the way through the narrow hallway to the service elevator. They didn't speak. It was all very professional, just as Sean had imagined it would be. He felt taut. Every muscle and tendon in his body was stretched and on alert. His moment of glory was just moments away - figuratively speaking, as the plan was obviously to wait until Lynola was getting ready to leave for the award ceremony. That was the day that Sean's name would finally be known around the world.

They got to the top floor and Brandon motioned Sean to wait for a second while he poked his head out. All was clear and together they walked to the end of the hallway and rapped quietly on the door. Jolie opened it and nodded silently to them, opening the door wider to let them through. She glanced at the 'tool box' immediately understanding the power that laid within in. She flushed a little as her eyes widened slightly and she smiled at Sean. She was clearly over her jitters.

Brandon directed Sean to the bathroom and the towels closet that they had decided was the perfect spot. Brandon and Jolie stood at each of Sean's shoulders as he carefully lifted out the device and placed it between two towels. Brandon nodded his agreement and Sean quickly took the extra wiring from his tool box and gave it to Brandon with the glue gun. Brandon ran the wire as discretely as possible along the baseboards of the room until reaching the central control panel next to the bed. The panel controlled everything in the room. The lighting, the curtains, the color of the windows, the comms, including the vidwalls in the main room, the one in the side office and the one in the bathroom. All he had to do was connect the wires, and as soon as Lynola turned on a vid or a light, boom, the whole thing would blow. But of course, it wouldn't. Because Lynola would never be in this room, and the device would never be connected.

Brandon, 13th May 2098

He was happy to go along with the charade. He was rather enjoying it, truth be told. It was rare that anyone in his industry had his leg up so completely on a potential attack, days before it was going to happen. This guy was such a narcissistic hack, that Brandon couldn't help but be amused by it all.

They could have arrested Sean in the instant that he arrived at the hotel with the explosives, but Brandon was enjoying the power and control he had over this too much to have it end so quickly. Brandon knew there was no real danger as the explosives were deactivated as soon as Sean had left the building. And he knew that Sean was totally fooled by his and Jolie's performance. Why end it all so quickly when Sean could be strung along for a few more days. Besides, his real punishment would be when he saw Lynola up on that stage, accepting the award that she so deserved, and making history with her newest ideas – which Brandon was sure would be both controversial and also inspirational, as usual.

Jolie had played her role to perfection. Vulnerable, nervous, but committed. He couldn't have asked for it to be done any better. She was worth her weight in gold, and because of her petite size, that wasn't even that much gold. He smiled at the irony. Oh, he loved his job. This trip was going to be fun and relaxing. He would make the most of his free time, letting his proverbial hair down. He deserved a break, especially after taking this guy's plan down with him.

Alice, 19th May 2098

Alice had blond hair and dark blue eyes. The name on her travel card was Alice Silva. She had to remember that. Her amble breasts had been reduced to an unremarkable size and she was largely undistinguishable from the other commuters on the magtrain. She kept her eyes and ears on high alert, but her outward appearance was nonchalant and casual. She was feeling quite confident that she was not being followed or watched. It was that easy.

She couldn't believe it really. All that planning, the old-fashioned spy trade of coded messages and false identities. The changing details of when, where and how, were all over and done with. The plan had worked. The whole thing had gone off without a hitch. It was hard to get her head around it. She had played her role to perfection. She should win an Oscar for her performance. She was puzzled why she felt so blah, let down, even empty and pointless. Everything had been perfect. Why didn't she feel elated? She was finally free. She hadn't inquired about anything beyond her assignment. She had followed her instructions to the letter and everything had worked out perfectly. She was on her way to reaching the pinnacle of all her dreams, her success. The only thing she had to decide was whether she want to stay as Alice?

Maybe, when she could start spending some of her hard-earned rewards, maybe then she'd feel more fulfilled. Of course, she wouldn't be part of the headlines and her name would never be associated with the events of the past two days. She had no idea what her role had to do with the attack on Lynola, and she didn't really want to know. She had to lay low for a long while. She couldn't be sure that any number of touchups would disguise her enough to fool an old pro like Brandon. She had to fall off the grid for a long while. She would miss Norway. It had been her adopted country for a while now. So green, prosperous, fertile and fair. She'd lived in luxury and freedom there. She hoped she hadn't got too soft living there for that long.

She reached the terminal and took a deep breath. This was the last hurdle. She tucked her short blond hair behind her ear and walked through to security. Tensions were high. You could feel it in the eyes of the guards. She half-smiled at one as she went through the scanner. Nothing to see. She'd made doubly, triply sure of that. As she stepped on to the shuttle, she risked one quick glance behind her. Nothing. She'd done it. He would be pleased.

She took her seat in the middle of the row in the middle of the ship. Nothing to make her stand out, not even now. Unlike many, she'd never aspired to live in the Tri-Cities. She had visited last year, after years of hearing about it and dreaming about its possibilities, but her dreams had turned to dust when she learned that some of the worst rumors were largely true. In large part, it was cramped with low gravity and recycled air, and lots of menial labor jobs. Luxury, as defined by the TriCities, wasn't nearly as luxurious as the life she had once been used to. But she knew she'd be pretty impossible to track from then on and could reinvent herself completely. She had an anonymous janitorial job waiting for her – she'd done a lot worse - and she'd found a generic hotel where should could rent a room for a while. It was just a short while, then she'd be allowed to come back and live the life that she had earned. She indulged a small smile and then a wobbly sigh. The flight was full. The doors closed. The ship's staff did their checks. The ship tilted ready for ready for lift off and then whoosh. Her head was pinned to her headrest as the rocket surged them far into the atmosphere. She closed her eyes and took slow, deep breaths. She had made it.

Desmond, 19th May 2098

After a fitful night of sleep, Desmond spent a few hours alone with his vid. A bunch of new wires had come through. Mostly DNA sweep results. As was expected, the hotel had hundreds of potential culprits, dozens with some sort of violation on their record. But nothing stood out to Desmond as a match with what he expected to see as a motive. Motive was definitely the key here. All these people had the potential means and opportunity, but who had the motive to kill Lynola, especially in this kind of spectacular fashion?

As he browsed through the list of names and faces and skimmed through all the tags, he continually tried to imagine a motive big enough to pull this off. Someone with a personal grudge, a passionate personal grudge. That much was clear. Going through these records was like searching for a needle in a haystack.

He switched gears and moved over to the couple who were caught on vid arguing in the stairwell. At least the file on these two was considerably shorter. The techs had cleaned up the audio. Desmond played it as it auto synced to the vid. The boy/man was whisper-yelling at the girl/woman. "But you said it was over." And she replied, "It was, then. But it started up again." Then she continued, "It's not like I don't love you, I do. But I have so much more in common with her. She wasn't sure if she wanted to be with me, but now she does. We both do. We're both women. It's a better match." He replied, throwing his arms up in the air, "How can I compete with that? I gave you everything. I have nothing more to give you." And she looked down at her feet and said, "I know, and we were happy for a while. But that was before. Now I must follow what's practical. For me, for my kids, for our future. I'm so sorry."

Desmond rolled his eyes and sighed. Obviously, this was completely irrelevant to the investigation. What a waste of public resources. It was just the same old discussion. More women opting to live among women, shutting men out, using them as sperm donors. He sneered sarcastically to himself. Back in his grandfather's day, some men had been happy to be relieved of their parenting duties. Be careful what you wish for.

Desmond opened the file from the apartment that Brandon had been in with his girlfriend. The techs hadn't found much of use. No useful DNA. Nothing on the couch, except from Brandon. For another fleeting second, he entertained the thought of not believing Brandon. But he knew him too well. Luckily for Brandon. And also, there was enough vid evidence to prove his story, at least up until they'd walked into the apartment together.

The techs had found a partial blond hair in the drainage pipe. Brandon had brown hair and the woman had bright red hair, so he wasn't sure what the blond hair would tell them, but he tagged it for a full DNA re-creation and scan anyway. It would take a few hours, but you never know. They had also found some skin molecules on the stool she had been sitting on at the bar. They were fairly degraded, but again, nothing should be overlooked at this point.

Desmond was still trying to put together a reason for her to have distracted Brandon after the explosion. He could see why she would have had motive before the bomb went off, or even earlier in the day when someone probably had planted the bomb. But why after? Then it struck him. What would Brandon have done if he hadn't been distracted and drugged? Likely he would have run into the building to try and save Lynola. Possibly he would have donned responder gear and gone searching for victims and survivors elsewhere in the building. He definitely would have gotten in the way, and possibly made quite a scene.

But except for the long shot of trying to save Lynola, what other goals could Brandon have obstructed? The bomb had taken off half the side of the building, so trying to save Lynola would have been extremely unlikely. But what if the bomber wasn't sure that the bomb would do the job? What if he/she/they needed reassurance that the bomb wouldn't just kill Lynola, but also destroy her entire room? Why would that matter? What was in her room that needed destroying? What couldn't be recreated or replaced?

Her vid. And everything on it. Desmond knew that Lynola disabled her autobackup right before a big speech. It was common practice. Most speakers, especially the exceptionally famous ones like Lynola, didn't want unfinished drafts of their speech notes floating around to be discovered. Hackers could get into almost anything these days, so Lynola, like her contemporaries, always disabled the autobackup for a few hours or even days. That was the only thing that Desmond could think of that made any sense. Not that any of this really made sense. Everyone loved Lynola and Alfred. Their legacy was secure and positive, and filled the hearts of most of the world's population with love. He needed to talk to Amelia.

Desmond, 19th May 2098

Brandon and the children had got through a difficult night fairly intact. And they had a plan. Charlotte was going to organize a charity ball in the name of her mother, calling on the privileged classes to memorialize her mother's legacy through anonymous donations that would be used as an endowment to her future foundation. Drake would publicly admit his additions and check himself into the best rehab facility for as long as it took to get completely clean. When he got out, he would work at the foundation. And Brandon would volunteer his services to the Responder Corps and see if Desmond could pull some strings to get him into an appropriate unit. Their plans were neat and tidy, and decided. This all constituted a nice first public statement from the family and they were ready to put it out there.

They were ready to leave and get started on each of their plans. He told them they had to wait another 24 hours, just so he could be sure there were no other credible threats against them, and he then gave preauthorization for their release the next morning. Amelia asked if he had any idea why someone would do this to them, to their mother? Why would someone deliberately want to kill her? After all she's done. Was it an accident maybe? He took her hands in his, deliberately looked at each of them in turn and said – honestly – that he had no idea. Except that it looked like it wasn't an accident. He said the investigation had turned up very little, but that they were still sifting through everything.

Brandon looked at Desmond, with a defeated puppy-like expression, and asked quietly if they had tracked down the woman. He shook his head and told them not to worry. The best minds and best tech were working on it, and they would figure it all out. They'd be the first to know once he knew something definitive.

Charlotte asked about her lover, and he shook his head again gently and smiled, saying there was nothing to worry about there. She then asked if it was okay if she used the spa and salon in the hotel. He nodded and looked around again, saying that as long as they told the responders on duty where they were inside the hotel, it was fine. Charlotte nodded and smiled again. He asked them all to continue to stay off their vids and the newssites until things settled down a little more and he could be more certain that there would not be any more trouble. He then asked for some private time with Amelia.

Desmond and Amelia went down the hall to her room. They went in and sat in two corner chairs, near the window. Amelia had kept the curtains drawn tightly. The room was simple and clean, and except for the rumpled sheets and towels piled on the bathroom floor, looked unused. Desmond leaned in and looked at Amelia. How was she doing? She was going to be the face of the family, in a much different way now. It was clear to Desmond that she was steeling herself against her emotions. He supposed that was a natural emotion and it was serving her well at the moment. He needed her to be in control and resilient at the moment. She could face her grief and mourn later.

She had decided that she was going to go home, find her husband, and try to cleanse, and then revive, her marriage. Desmond nodded and agreed that this was the best course of action for her. But that's not what he wanted to all to her about.

He asked Amelia if she had a copy of Lynola's speech or her speech notes. She was surprised by his question and asked why. He shrugged his shoulders casually and said he was following up on all leads and random ideas. Amelia told him that, as far as she knew, Lynola turned off her autobackup while she was preparing her speeches, just as he had already suspected. Then she looked him, wide-eyed, and asked if this was important. He shrugged again and said he wasn't sure, but that he had to consider everything.

Amelia fell back into her chair and stared off into the room. She told him that Lynola always drafted her own speeches and she hadn't asked for Amelia's opinion or feedback in a long time. Lynola was quite particular about her speeches, as most people were, and she insisted on as much control as possible. It was unlikely that she was going to say anything too controversial or inflammatory. Mostly stuff about Dad and the programs they'd started together. She'd figured Lynola would stick to standard rhetoric about her gratitude and maybe some positive and hopeful forecasts for humanity. That sort of thing. Amelia couldn't see how any of that would be controversial or motive for murder.

Desmond agreed and thanked her. As they were standing up, he casually asked if Amelia knew of any other backups or notetakers that Lynola had used. Amelia shook her head and apologized that she couldn't be more helpful. But she couldn't really see the relevance. She didn't believe that Lynola was planning anything particularly world-shaking.

He thanked her as he left the room, reminding her to keep everyone close, and definitely within the confines of the hotel. She nodded and sat down in the chair by the window. She was staring at her feet as he closed the door behind him.

Desmond, 19th May 2098

Desmond went back to sifting through reports as the cruiser took him back to the scene. His mind kept wandering and he couldn't focus on the banalities of people's lives that he was reading about. To help him focus, he decided to go to the squad module. The module had been placed near the front of the hotel and was bustling inside. Responders of every stripe and purpose were walking around, speaking into notetakers, standing in groups of two or three comparing notes and findings.

The vidwalls had been sectioned, and different portions were displaying different updates. Information on the other victims and the wounded were included, but Desmond didn't pay that much attention to them. They had just been in the wrong place at the wrong time, unfortunately for them. Results from DNA sweeps with tags highlighting anything of interest. Images and vids from outside the building, inside the hotel, across the harbor and around the neighborhood. Suspects from the DNA sweep were being checked against other vids and submitted alibis. Everything was being eliminated, step by step.

Desmond walked over to the tech team area and spoke to the responder in charge. She was a veteran and he had worked with her several times over the years. Reliable, accurate, dispassionate – just as he liked it.

She nodded to him as he approached and launched into her report. He let her go on for a while – it was only polite – before cutting her off and asking if anyone had recovered any vids or notetakers from Lynola's room. She barked a sarcastic laugh before realizing that he was serious. Nothing had been recovered, absolutely nothing. The implication was that everything had been reduced to dust, even Lynola. Desmond nodded soberly, thanked her, and walked away.

He had an instinctive feeling that this was the missing link. Nothing else had even come close to an appropriate motive.

Even that loser that Brandon had played a few days earlier, who had handed over all his cheap – and ultimately defective "explosives" - was a close candidate for means, motive and opportunity. Desmond made a mental note to pick him up. No good could come out of leaving that guy out in the world loose to spread his stupid ideas.

Neglected kids with grudges, irritated employees, or random acts of violence. Nothing made sense except a targeted attack to silence Lynola, in a spectacularly public way, on the eve of one of the biggest speeches of her life and career. It certainly explained the timing. It explained the oversized scope of the explosion area. And, most importantly, it explained why Brandon had been lured away and drugged. The only remaining mystery was the theme. What could Lynola have been planning on talking about - that none of her kids knew about, but someone else did – that could have required this level of violent intervention. It was hard to imagine anything. But something was there. He was going to have to dig deeper.

CHAPTER 7

Celia, 2086

Sometimes she went by Alice. It made her inwardly smile as it was simply an anagram of her real name, but it made her feel a lot different on the outside. She wore herself differently as Alice. Charlotte loved the idea of Alice, and helped Celia build the Alice persona into one that she could use professionally and personally, when she was in the mood. Ironically, her Alice persona much more accurately reflected her biological mother's profile. Serena had always been beautiful and poised, and Celia was unknowingly channeling Serena's instinctive sophistication through Alice.

Charlotte took her on as a little project. As a successful socialite herself, it fed her ego to take an ugly duckling and turn it into a swan. It was almost like playing with dolls, but a live one with great potential. Charlotte encouraged her to stand up straighter and act more confidently as Alice. She taught her that the world treats you how you see yourself, so if you see yourself as a victim, so will everyone else. When she wanted to project meekness and submissiveness, she went by Celia. But when she wanted to project strength, independence, and confidence, she went by Alice.

Charlotte was amazing. She had built a life for herself that gave her security and freedom, and she didn't have to rely on anyone but her own wits. True, she had come from a life of privilege, but she could have chosen a much more conventional path. Instead she chose to live – really live – as she wanted, with independence and confidence. Things that had escaped Celia so far, and that she desperately yearned for. Charlotte lived her life with luxury and security. She didn't have a "proper" job, she didn't have a "proper" husband or wife, and she didn't have a regular source of income, but things just fell into place for her. She could have just lived off the Loughton name, but she created her own image and her own character apart from the Loughton legacy. She lived on boats, in plush hotels, in penthouse apartments, and on private yachts. She knew lots of people with wealth, with power, with influence, and with ambition. That was the world that Celia – and Celia, as Alice – wanted to belong to.

After she and Charlotte had first met, she had returned to Newfoundland with her and been introduced to a brand-new lifestyle. One of decadence and luxury and fake boredom. Who could be really bored among these people who flew off wherever they wanted, whenever they wanted. Who could order anything their hearts desired on a whim, and within a moment's notice. Who had drugs, and alcohol, and synthetics, not to mention real meat and fish, endless sugary treats, and clean and fresh water at their fingertips? The rich and famous, and not-so-famous, privileged set. The ones who took up so much of normal people's fantasy world. She was now a part of it.

Celia, as Alice, fell in easily with the men just as Charlotte knew she would. She'd had a lot of experience reading people's interest and matching their desires. Alice was slim and petite, but strong-willed and confident. Over a few months, and then years, Alice honed her skills to become one of the most sought-after dominatrix in the right company. She could be both sweet and shy, almost like a school-girl, and then turn into a strong, assertive, and domineering teacher. A certain type of men, and women, were attracted to her. The ones who needed to be domineered in private but wanted the air of strength and power out in public. Celia – with Alice in her back pocket – fit the bill to perfection. She couldn't thank Charlotte enough for the introduction and the tips. This was the life she had always dreamed off and Charlotte had showed her the way.

Celia, 2096

Sometimes Celia got bored with her life. The men and women were all the same after a while. It had been 10 years now and her life as a dominatrix was stable, her reputation was impeccable, and she lacked for nothing. She had hundreds of thousands of credits squirreled away in several accounts across several continents and even off-world. She had security like she had never had before. She had adoration and a social life and a couple of little private spaces that no one else knew about. An apartment in Greenland, where development hadn't quite reached yet. And a beach house in northern Australia that was safe in its anonymity among thousands of beach houses.

She still counted Charlotte as among one of her closest friends. She didn't see her very often, but when she did, she felt she could be real, as it was only Charlotte who had known her as the original Celia, before she had donned Alice and started her new life. It was Charlotte who had paid for her touch-ups and adjustments to look half her age. It was Charlotte who had brought her to Newfoundland and introduced her to the in-crowd. And it was Charlotte who had encouraged her to consciously define Alice as her alter-ego and build her reputation among the privileged set. Charlotte was her true inspiration.

Celia was happily partnered up with Jorgio III for now although she was starting to get bored. Jorgio III – who went by Trey - was the son of Jorgio Jr and the grandson of Jorgio Sr, a multi-zillionaire. Trey's grandfather had made it big in agriculture, long before the industry had been shackled by the policies of the past 30 years. He had invested well and had been smart about buying property in places that were going to be – and now were – hotbeds of development and tourism. The family owned property all over the world. They had an island in Central America – between what used to be Panama and Costa Rica. They had another island off Vancouver. They owned a big resort on the coast of the Monument Valley Lake with amazing views along the border of Arizona. And many more places besides.

Trey was a typical spoiled-brat inheritor. He hadn't taken his studies seriously as a kid and really didn't give a shit about anything except his next high. He hadn't worked a proper day in his life. He was indulged at every turn by his parents. His father, the only son of Jorgio Sr., was so submissive to his father and his father's estate, that he took his frustrations out on his children, Trey and his sister, Bianca. He tried to control their every movement and every thought and ended up ruining them as much as he had been ruined before them. Bianca married well and followed her father, and grandfather's wishes, to every letter. Trey found his own life and eventually became tolerated as the playboy who wasn't going to make much of himself. His trust funds were secured against complete destruction, but he was given enough to live on, and live on well, and the freedom to use much of the properties owned by the family, as long as he didn't embarrass them on the newssites.

Celia and Trey had no illusions about their life together. It was a life of convenience and mutual need. Alice helped Trey fulfill his fantasies, sexual and otherwise. Trey gave Celia a life of luxury and ambivalence. Alice had other "friends" besides Trey, including Jorgio Jr, Trey's father. They met discretely as Celia didn't want to shove it in Trey's face. JJ wanted Alice to be her strongest, her most domineering. He wanted the black leather outfits, the whips, and the chains. The whole deal. He wanted to feel powerless and helpless, completely at her mercy. He wanted her in high heels and with a black mask, stun whips, and handcuffs. And she was happy to oblige. It was good credits for her and it kept her in favor with the whole family.

Celia, 2097

It didn't come as much of a surprise to Celia that JJ had his fingers in lot of shady pies. Yes, he had inherited his father's fortune, but with it, he also had a lot frustration that he couldn't prove himself in his father's eyes. He wanted to grow the business, experiment with new business models, find creative and profitable ways to adjust to the climate changing. But he couldn't. His hands were tied by the legislation imposed by the Global Council. The agro-industry was cut off at the knees by the unleashing of open source seeds, by the prohibition of all chemical farming products, and by the labor laws that made their workforce as expensive as local and legal workers.

Supermarkets were also obliged to price their products so that they could cover the full cost of fair market labor wages, full benefits for every worker, even part-time workers, and a healthy profit margin for their investors. This served to raise the cost of food over 100%, which in turn served to considerably reduce food waste by consumers and restaurants, influence the value of food in the eyes of the public and reducing obesity across the entire population, and ensure fair market wages for all laborers in the fields. But they shackled JJ's business to regulation and impotence.

It was a win-win-win situation for global populations and the climate, but not for JJ and his family's legacy. His frustration was palpable. It wasn't that they need more money. The family had plenty of resources to last several lifetimes. It was that he was unable to prove himself and show how clever, manipulative and devious he was. He felt that he was in a straitjacket and his frustration made his behavior ugly and often cruel. His only release was with Alice. She could get him to his knees and make him feel like he was receiving the punishment he deserved. She could hurt him and make him beg and cry. Alice was his savior.

He adored her beyond a reasonable amount. She was his only outlet, where he could act like a meek weakling and she wouldn't laugh or mock him. She would flick her stun whip at him and put her stiletto heel sharply into his abdomen. God, he loved it. He loved her. She was a genius. She was his lifeline to sanity. He wasn't sure how Trey had got so lucky in finding her, but JJ was going to be sure that neither of them would lose her.

JJ, 2097

He was so aroused. On his knees, blindfolded, shackled, pain radiating from the most recent lash of the stun whip against his spine. But his brain was sharply focused on one thing – his swollen dick. He had no thought in his head for anything else. None of his deep-seated frustrations were present in his mind. None of his feelings of impotence, of weakness, or of humiliation had room in his brain. Only his hard-on. He listened for her. His ears sharp and singularly focused. He could hear the click of her heels as she moved slowly around him. The low growl in her throat and the ticking of her whip lightly tapping the floor.

He wasn't going to last much longer. She knew that. She could see all of him in his nakedness. His knees were throbbing from his own weight. But she wasn't going to satisfy him. He knew that. She would follow his instructions to the letter and leave him, just before the moment of climax, to fend for himself. She brushed against him, letting her whip trail behind her and tickle his dick. That was it. He heard the door click gently as it closed behind her and realized that his wrists were unshackled. He hadn't even noticed her doing that. She was so good. The very best. He fell forward onto his knees and removed his blindfold.

He finished himself off under the shower, in his private humiliation. The perfect end to the session. The hot water was strong against his small, weak body. He scrubbed himself with the oatmeal paste that she made for him. It made his skin throb with pain, with pleasure, and a cleanliness that was revitalizing. His mind was clear. A plan was forming. A plan to give voice to his frustrations and his impotence. A plan that would wake up the world and change its rotten trajectory.

The collective mind was weak and ineffectual. Cut-throat competition made the world a better and stronger place. Collaboration and compromise, catering to the lowest common need was foolish, shortsighted, and doomed to failure. The world needed people like him to rise up and take charge again. Ambitious men who had vision and influence, and who could manipulate the masses to behave in their own self-interest. The world needed him, and he was up to the task.

He left the bathroom in his robe and sat at his desk. He started talking fast into his vid, watching the words jump up and organize themselves into paragraph after paragraph. He was high on his clarity. He would get his revenge and prevent any further damage by those people. He would make sure that whatever "great ideas" were brewing, would be forever disappeared and forgotten. He would stop the hemorrhage and rebuild his family's foothold and influence in the agricultural world. That was the future. That was his mission.

He would work only with the people he trusted. He could count them on just one hand. Not his foolish son who was spoiled and ruined. Not his wife, his sister, or his business partners. Alice, first and foremost. She could be trusted to know his darkest secrets and all his fears. His father, his personal assistant, and two other men he knew from the industry, would all have roles to play. This would be his posse and he would lead them to glory.

Celia, 2097

Trey was boring. He always wanted the same thing. To get drunk, to get high, to fuck her upside down or inside out. To fall asleep snoring and start again the next day. It made her think about her life. She was about to turn 50, although it was impossible to know that from her looks, her behavior, or her energy levels. She could pass as a 30-year-old in almost any situation. She loved to celebrate her birthday, with friends and fun in exotic locations. This year she wanted to go off-world, see the TriCities. Trey said it was a dump and he wouldn't take her. She could afford to go by herself, of course, but what was the fun in that.

She looked over at Trey. He was drooling slightly. His paunch belly was growing and starting to protrude. She was going to have to get him touched up this weekend. He was still too young and had too much potential to go slack on her just yet. She'd make a game of it and maybe take JJ along for giggles too.

He could always use a little firming around the edges. She had no idea of his age but judging by Trey's age and JJ's family legacy, she would guess he was pushing 70. Not bad for an old geezer. The supplements, synthetics, and regular touch ups were keeping him young in looks and in everything else. She smiled at herself. Who would have guessed that she'd end up here? Life was good, she was comfortable, and the worst thing she had to deal with was boredom on her birthday. She giggled quietly to herself, sat up, and padded over to the picture window. The Greenland landscape was lush and beautiful. The blue sky was deep and vivid. And she knew the beaches, just over the dunes, were filling up with young and energetic revelers. She was going to get dressed and join them.

On her way back from the beach, her vid signaled JJ's tone. She glanced at the screen and saw he'd put in a location and time for lunch. Great – anything to avoid watching Trey snoring all afternoon long. She acknowledged and agreed to the invitation, cleaned up quickly and squeezed into a red dress. A strong color she knew JJ liked. The dress was skintight, but still modest by some of her other standards, and it accentuated all her curves in all the right places. She slipped into the matching red heels, brushed out her long dark curls, and added some subtle eye makeup and lipstick. She couldn't know how much she looked like a brunette version of her mother, Serena, at that very moment.

JJ was waiting for her on the patio deck overlooking the beach. The breeze was perfect, the waves were far enough away to not be loud and disturbing to the low hum of conversation around the restaurant, the sun was warm but not oppressive, and the champagne in her glass was chilled and bubbling. She smiled and pecked him on the cheek as she sat gracefully down in her chair. Charlotte had taught her that every move counted. Every body movement was a chance to seduce. She leaned gently forward, her chest covered modestly by the round cut of her dress, but the shape of her under the dress was evident. He looked at her and smiled. He had bought and paid for everything about her, and he regretted none of it. It was the best money he had ever spent. By pure luck – as it couldn't have been his judgement – Trey had brought him a masterpiece.

Throughout the meal, she behaved perfectly. It wasn't often that JJ took her out in public. He was usually happy to have their interludes in a suite at his club or a hotel. This was a rare treat. The fish was exquisite, delicate, and obviously fresh from the depths of the sea. The vegetables were fresh from the soil and lightly sautéed. The champagne, of course, was excellent, a Moet from the late 90s she would guess. And JJ was charming as always, looking deep into her eyes and gently holding her hand between visits from the waiter.

Celia was the submissive. Eyes lowered with small smiles and a soft laugh. Often sweeping her hair behind one ear and tilting her head to one side. She tittered at his jokes and agreed with his opinions. She leaned into the table with her legs crossed modestly under the table. When she left the table to powder her nose, she swayed gently with a feminine swing of her hips, without effort or exaggeration. And when she returned, she sat gracefully, touching her napkin to the corners of her newly reddened lips and drying her fingertips.

JJ pulled away from the table and held out his hand. She grasped his fingertips and walked next to him as they left the patio and went towards the elevator bank. They went up to the penthouse suite with stunning balconies overlooking the forest on one side, the dunes and the ocean on the other. The view was glorious. JJ sat on one the lounge chairs and invited her to sit next to him. This was unusual. Typically, he went straight to the bathroom to undress and she prepared herself by changing into her leathers and turning into Alice. She sat next to him shyly, trying to read his intent, staying in character as Celia. And he started talking.

Celia, 2098

She was trying on different looks, under the close watch of JJ. He liked the skinny Asian look. But he wasn't sure it would attract the right target. She went for blond and busty. But, ironically, he hated the blond with her pale skin tone. She darkened the tone, but he still didn't like the blond. She tried a curvier look with thicker thighs, a round ass, and broad shoulders. He liked it but still wasn't convinced about the coloring. They settled on a trashy red color, tattoos, big bust and ass, green eyes, and a sharp nose. She was glad the look had been decided as she was sick of doing more alterations. They took a toll on her and she was always afraid that something would go wrong leaving her with permanent damage. They split up as planned. She had 3 weeks now of being alone, traveling, doing anything she wanted, far away from him and their collaborators.

She decided to go to London. It had been ages since she'd visited, and she could get lost in the crowds and try out reactions to her new look. Trey was still somewhere in Greenland or maybe he'd gone to their ranch on the shores of the Monument Valley Lake, she didn't much care. They were on a break and she was eager for some brainless excitement. The pressure of the last 6 months and the intensity of JJ's convictions were weighing on her. He didn't want to spend time with Alice, only Celia, which made her more uncomfortable. As Alice, she knew how to behave with him and she was in control. With Celia, her repertoire was more limited.

London was hot and sticky. Anyone who could afford it was already up in Scotland, on the beaches or at the golf resorts. The streets were fairly empty, and the clubs were relatively quiet. She was happy for the break. She danced the nights away to rhythms that pounded in her ears for hours and hours. She hung out with nameless, unremarkable people who lived on synthetics and the good life without thinking or questioning. They experimented with their bodies and their brains while Celia watched. She wanted the anonymity of it, but she didn't want the out-of-body experiences. She was happy to stay in the shadows and repair herself. She ran into people she knew now and then, but no one special and no one who questioned her. With JJ's allowance, she rented the roof apartment at the Dorchester and ate freshly grown food, drank fresh mineral water, and indulged in fresh fruit juices and real eggs every morning. Her body was renewing, and she could feel her own power emerging.

Once in a while she would reflect on the details of the plan. She wasn't political. She didn't care about the cause or about anyone being targeted. She was enjoying the excitement of it, the meaningfulness of having a plan of action – any plan beyond just sleeping, doing drugs, and fucking like Trey wanted – and having all the resources that JJ was giving her. She was going to be set for life. All she had to do now was figure out what life she wanted. This was a new idea to her. She could be free of Alice forever. Who was Celia and what life did she want? It was like a blank canvas and she didn't really know where to start. A puzzle, but a wonderful puzzle. A freedom that she had never had, and a future that she could design for herself. To her, this was the pinnacle of her career, her life, her goals, and her success. This was it!

Alice, February 2098

Her adrenaline was pumping. She had checked out of her hostel, and she had wandered around the neighborhood and stepped into the bar. She had kept a low profile as she didn't want to be recognized when she came back again in a few weeks. Her hair was dark for now, and her nose was wider, softer. She walked a little hunched over and kept her sleeves and pant legs covered with nondescript jeans and t-shirts. Nothing that would stand out in anyone's memory.

She took the magtrain back to Bodo where she had been living for more than 4 months now. The tourism industry was up and coming there, and holiday resorts for every budget had been popping up along the coastline. Yacht clubs, water sports, family resorts, luxury spas, and all the trimmings that come with tourism were proving ample opportunities for enjoyment.

Celia had a small but comfortable condo near the harbor. She kept a low profile and was enjoying life on her own. She still hadn't settled on her future persona, but she was spending time getting to know herself, for the first time in her life. She knew she liked the comforts of a luxurious lifestyle, but she surprised herself by realizing that she didn't really like to be around people all that much. She preferred her own company to a large crowd and started to enjoy hiking and even camping once in a while. She found that sleeping out under the open spring sky gave her an added sense of freedom, of independence, and of hope.

She had spent so much of her life in survival mode, this time of self-discovery was both thrilling and unsettling. What was her favorite food? What was her favorite color? How did she like to spend her free time? What clothes did she feel most comfortable in? She had every choice open to her now. Her resources were soon going to be endless. She could design a life for herself that met her every need. But what were her needs. That's what she wanted to find out.

The bar was one of several in the city, but it was the closest to the Clarion Hotel and the one where JJ said she would likely meet her target. She had already rented the apartment around the corner for the next 6 weeks. She'd paid in cash of course, no credit trail to lead back to her or eventually Jr. He had sent her everything she needed, including the flowers. All she had to do was be seductive – no problem there – and activate them at the right moment. Then, her role was done, and she could catch the magtrain out. She would miss her condo in Bodo. She would always have fond memories of that town, although it was clear that tourism was probably going to ruin it over the next 20 years.

Alice, April 2098

The package arrived. It was pretty heavy. She knew what her instructions were. She was supposed to take it to her apartment in Bergen, leaving it wrapped up. She didn't need to know what was in it, and she didn't need to do anything else. She was grateful for the ignorance and, although she sensed that there was some danger in what she was doing, she was completely fine with the fact that she didn't know all the details and couldn't implicate anyone else in the plan. She kept her mind completely focused on the few responsibilities she had, and the freedom that was waiting for her in a few short weeks.

A couple of weeks later, the flowers arrived. Again, she took the magtrain to Bergen and placed them in a vase on the shelf. The box that she had left on the couch was gone. She was grateful for that as she suspected there was danger there. She left the flowers wrapped up and went back to Bodo the same day. She didn't want to have her face be familiar to anyone in Bergen, even though she knew that the alterations she had planned would make it fairly unlikely that she could be recognized.

Celia, 9th May 2098

She packed her last box and looked around the room. She sighed. In many ways, this little condo with a view of the harbor was the gateway to her freedom. Her first taste of who she was. The first time in her adult life that she was alone, in control of herself, her time, her tastes, her dreams, and her hopes. She would always have fond memories of this place. She put the last box on the pallet and checked the mailing address. All her belongings were going to an orphanage in Northern Italy. She knew that they wouldn't be DNA-checked as places like that were desperate for any supplies they could get. They would be happy for the hats, t-shirts, shoes, and even toiletries that she'd packed up. All her possessions would be untraceable as soon as the pallet arrived on their doorstep. She swung her backpack onto her shoulders, took one last look around and stepped out the door and into her future.

Desmond, 19th May 2098

Desmond had fairly given up on identifying the busty redhead who had seduced Brandon. The only theory he had that didn't seem to be full of holes was that she had been paid to lure Brandon away from the scene so that he wouldn't rush to the hotel to try and save Lynola just before or just after the explosion. Desmond was convinced that the only reasonable explanation was that her vid, with Lynola's draft speech with the auto-syncing turned off, held something special that the killer – or killers – didn't want to have released. Why else would they bother to remove Brandon from the scene? He was the only real threat to their plans, assuming that there was something they were trying to hide after the explosion. Desmond was convinced, at this point, that the redhead was going to get away with whatever her role had been, as she had been careful and hadn't left any trace of herself anywhere. Whatever she had been paid, it had obviously been worth it as she had played her role to perfection. He had to admire that, even while he was revolted by the terrorist attack and the loss of a beautiful and intelligent woman.

He decided to return to Amelia and the others to see if any of them had any idea what Lynola was going to say that would merit such a violent reaction. They were still in the hotel, in various rooms at this point. Each of them had generally composed themselves, washed, eaten, and even slept a little if he had to guess. Ironically, they each seemed to feel some level of guilt at the recent events, although Desmond was sure that none of them – even Brandon, despite his lack of judgement – had any personal involvement in the attack. But nonetheless, they were each, individually, wallowing in self-pity and a sense of responsibility, and an eagerness to get acknowledged. Desmond knew that none of them could hold a candle to the achievements and integrity that Lynola and Alfie had displayed over the years.

Overall, nothing very impressive in this bunch, Desmond concluded, as he drove back to the station and decided to close the files on the children and Brandon. He was convinced now that the motive was the key. What was in Lynola's upcoming speech that had triggered this attack? It had to be something impressive and hurtful to someone, or some group of people. He would focus his efforts there.

JJ, 19th May 2098

Damn, he was going to miss Alice. He'd visiting her in Bodo a few times, staying at the offshoot of his club in the center of town. She'd revived her dominatrix persona especially for him, but he felt that her heart wasn't in it anymore. He'd given her hope for a different future and she had already moved on, emotionally anyway. He'd enjoyed the few sessions they'd had – as always. The pain mixing with arousal providing him with a huge release and a renewed sense of power and clarity. His glory moment was coming soon, and she was playing an important role – even if she didn't know it. Ah, Alice. What an amazing woman she had been. He wouldn't be able to replace her. He would really miss her.

CHAPTER 8

Lynola Loughton, 18th May 2098

Ladies and Gentlemen, people of the world. I am honored, beyond words, to receive this award that recognizes the achievements that I, and my beloved Alfred, worked on throughout our life together. I stand here today, humbled by your acknowledgement and grateful that our work has been able to raise up so many people out of poverty and despair, and create a better world for everyone.

Today, I want to take this opportunity to review the programs that we have built together and to present ideas and proposals for how we can continue to evolve together in collaboration and community. For starters, we have a brand-new healthcare system that supports everyone in every corner of the world, no matter their heritage, their economics, their social status, or their nationality. We have a tax system that enforces a fairness that the world has never seen before, redistributing wealth across communities and societies. We have an agricultural system that feeds everyone and takes advantage of innovations and technologies that are open-source and shared by all. And we have dignity, respect, and equality on a scale never seen before in recorded human history.

To be sure, the world is still not perfect. It will never be perfect. Humans aren't perfect, and we will always suffer the consequences of greed and envy and all the other human failings that lie within each of us. But despite the overwhelming calamities that we have faced as a species over the past hundred years, the world is a better, healthier, wealthier, and more equitable place for us all to thrive in.

If you would indulge me, I will take this opportunity to recount some of the untold back stories behind many of our breakthrough policies that led to our new world order.

After the flu pandemics in the sixties, Alfred and I knew that the healthcare insurance system that was so unjust and inequitable had to change. There was no reason for people to die of the common flu or dehydration. There was no fairness in rich people surviving and poor people dying from superbugs or avian flu. Collectively, we have the resources and ingenuity to heal our fellow men and women and provide the preventative systems of care that reduce all our costs - both in financial and in human terms. We found this system infuriating and as Global President, Alfred had the opportunity to tackle it.

During his travels in his youth, Alfred learned about the success of the healthcare coverage pyramid in Asia, and we brought the model to the WHO for study. Younger, healthier people supporting older, sicker people, with an understanding that eventually everyone will need proper care. The pyramid scheme – a tongue-in-cheek term that we used to refer back to financial scandals of the 20th century – was a way to get everyone involved and feel responsible. The theory behind this system had been implemented in a lot of different countries throughout the 20th Century, but it was doomed to failure because of the corruption of the capitalist economy that it was restrained by. The only way the model could work, was if the healthcare industry itself was decapitalized. It was controversial to take an industry that had built such capital wealth – prescription drug research and sales, the insurance industry, private clinics, and the booming healthcare tourism sector – and turn them into nonprofit entities where wealth was prohibited. The common wisdom at the time was the pharmaceutical companies – to name one sector inside the healthcare industry – would be dis-incentivized to spend the billions necessary to do research to find cures if they couldn't eventually make a profit. Rubbish, we thought. Cures for diseases shouldn't be part of a capitalist system. Cures and treatments were for everyone and should be supported by a global system of funding and equitable distribution.

The WHO became the entity to oversee the transformation of the whole sector. And, as most of you no doubt recall, it took years and it was painful. We regulated salaries, we regulated profit structures, and we regulated organizational hierarchies. We impounded whole sectors of the industry and paid off their corporate owners. Instead of nationalizing healthcare, we internationalized it.

Alfred and I – especially Alfred – endured open hatred in many circles because of this initiative, but today, people in every community – poor, rich, and everything in-between - have access to globally-supported healthcare treatments with affordable medicine and access to new technologies and cutting-edge treatments. We couldn't have lived with ourselves had we allowed only the rich to benefit from gene therapy treatments and cures for cancer and HIV immunization. We were so grateful when the new system started to take its shape and we started to witness a renewed industry that was itself healthy and thriving and able to benefit so many.

Desmond, 19th May 2098

Desmond had watched the vids so many times, he could run through them in his dreams. Normal and everyday people going through their normal and everyday lives. He couldn't pinpoint anything out of the ordinary. People entering the hotel with suitcases and shopping bags. The same people leaving the hotel to explore the city or go out for dinner. A few suspicious-looking women, too dressed up for normal life, entering the main doors, and leaving a few hours later. Nothing unusual about that. The world's oldest profession was legal, regulated, and still in high demand.

He closed his vid and laid his head back in his chair. He was at a dead-end. What was he going to tell the children, the public, and his bosses? There were just no leads to follow. The only motive he could even imagine was the potential of controversy in a future speech that Lynola would never give. And the only loose thread was Brandon's strange redhead. She was the only incongruous thing that he could find. But it helped support his theory of motive, which may or may not be simply a self-fulfilling prophecy.

He pulled up the vid of them walking through the back alley. Brandon's following, a little unsure of his step. She was striding confidently ahead of him, making sure he was close behind. When they got to the corner of the next street, they stopped for a few seconds while she checked the road, and then crossed over to continue down the alley. She was leading him away from the hotel and the bar. Desmond knew all this. He had watched it dozens of times already. There just wasn't anything there. He had enhanced the video with infrared and with a crispness that only the newest vids could accomplish in a dark alley. He studied her clothes, her shoes, her hair, her hands, and even her boobs and her curves. He didn't have a full-on view of her face, but he could see her eyes were lighter than Brandon's and her chin was a little pointy with her full lips painted red for

Brandon's sake. He could see the individual hairs on her head and her neck under her hair. Damn! He just wasn't getting anywhere.

He watched it one more time and then closed his vid. He'd pick it up again in the morning. He would check in with the family and feed them some line about the ongoing investigation taking time but going well and try to look at this with fresh eyes in the morning. The tips his team were bringing him were all dead ends so far, and the ones he hadn't looked at yet could wait. It wasn't like him to give up hope, but it was hard to see where this was going to end up. Maybe something would show up tomorrow. He didn't feel optimistic, but he certainly wasn't ready to throw in the towel, especially with the potential recognition of this case could bring him. He packed up his desk and headed out into the night.

Lynola Loughton, 18th May 2098

Our next true achievement and one we were particularly excited about, what the universal savings plan, also known as The Giving Circle or just The Circle as the younger kids call it. This idea wasn't really ours. Alfred and I came across examples of giving circles when we were travelling through Central America one summer and learned about a quilting group in what had once been a traditional community in Old El Salvador. The women used scraps of fabric from their children's old clothes to sew quilts that would be given to each of the members, one at a time. Each woman ended up with a beautiful, warm, and useful quilt, while nothing was left to waste and no one was left out of the circle. Once one woman got her quilt, she left a place in the circle for another. This is how we saw savings plans working. Each person gives when they can, and each person gets when they need. Everyone needs at some point in their lives, and everyone has a chance to give. By mandating this as policy, we were able to level the playing field globally and today, there are healthy retirement funds in almost every community around the world.

Of course, we encountered resistance to this plan, just as we had for the healthcare insurance restructuring project. But in this instance, we weren't prohibiting personal investment or eliminating private funds, we were just mandating a certain behavior. And we wanted it to be a natural behavior that made sense for everyone, in every culture and every community, which is why the messaging was rooted in indigenous languages and traditional symbolism.

In many ways, our ancestors understood community so much better than we do in the modern world. Alfred and I felt that going back to these roots was such a wonderful way to honor the indigenous ancestors that we all share. When traced all the way back to our common progenitors who lived in caves and hunted woolly mammoths, a human's primal instinct was to collaborate in order to survive. It was only in the modern era, when certain individuals accumulated more wealth than they could possibly use, that we started to understand the sociological source of empathy and of community. When a person has all their needs taken care of, they have no reason to rely on their neighbors and their community. Their empathy towards their neighbors starts to disappear. This has been proven with behavioral and psychological studies, and Alfred and I felt strongly that the need for community had to be preserved, no matter what the individual's wealth status.

The Giving Circles are rooted in our youth today just as the need for collectivity and empathy was rooted in our ancestral communities hundreds and thousands of years ago. Even our grandchildren put in a penny or two from their pocket money each week. I am so grateful to hear the stories of families who have survived difficulties due to their share of The Circle, and retirees who live out their years comfortably surrounded by community and support, thanks to their share. This was Alfred's special vision – a global community of empathy and support – and I am especially gratified to meet the people that have benefited from his foresight.

Desmond, 20th May 2098

Desmond felt refreshed. A good night's sleep, even though it had been enhanced and hadn't come naturally, had done him wonders. He resolved to watch all the vids again, from start to finish and in chronological order. And he started going through the leads being sent into his vid with a renewed sense of optimism. But it didn't last. He was briefed by two of his sub-commanders and had read through about thirty dead-end leads before dejection started to set in again.

He set aside his inbox and started in again on the vids, from the top. He watched people coming and going from the hotel. He watched the activity around the hotel. Inside the bar. Outside the bar. And in the streets around the bar and the hotel. He watched the redhead lead Brandon down the alley. He saw her stop at the crossing and look both ways before leading Brandon across to continue the alley. He watched when, a few seconds later, a car came down the street just after they had crossed. And something struck him. The street was small, only wide enough for one car. An old street in the center of the old town of Bergen. Why then, did the redhead look both ways before leading them across? It could be habit, but Desmond had a feeling that she knew those streets like the back of her hand. It niggled at him. It was something. He felt a spark of excitement. Such a small thing, but it felt like an oasis in the desert. He watched again and again, as she looked both ways before leading Brandon across. Why did she do that? It didn't make a lot of sense to look both ways on a dark, quiet one-way street, when she was pulling a big drunk guy behind her. Why did she look up and down the street when it was obvious there were no cars moving? She would have heard the silence. Was it a signal to someone? To whom? There wasn't anyone there?

He called the tech team. Could they pull vids from that street on both ends for the timestamp that matched when Brandon and the redhead crossed? Send them to him right away. Within a few minutes his inbox bounced, and the vids were in. He started watching. They were dark, unenhanced. Just dark and mostly empty streets. He watched one all the way through. Nothing interesting. Just the rear view of the car that passed just after Brandon and the redhead had crossed to the alley. On the other vid, the one that showed the car coming down, Desmond was surprised to see that there were actually two cars that turned into the street, even though he'd only seen one pass and that was confirmed by the rear lights passing in the first vid he'd watched.

But there had been two cars. The first car turned slowly into the street and pulled into a parking spot before the crossing. It powered down and the lights went out. No one got out. Dennis jumped up from his seat, freezing the vid on his screen. He stared closely at the vid, expanding the image until the pixels blurred all its features. He immediately replied to tech and told them to enhance the clip in every way possible. Light, infrared, and heat signatures. He needed a clear view.

He finished watching the vid. Brandon and the redhead crossed, as usual. She looked both ways up and down the street before crossing. Nothing happened with the parked car. It just sat there. No one got out. No one turned on a light. Nothing moved. The second car turned into the street and passed by the crossing continuing to the end of the street. The first car didn't move. Nothing else stirred on the street. It remained dark until the vid ended 30 seconds later. Desmond called tech again. He needed more. He needed more vid from the street, for the next 5, 10 even 30 minutes.

Desmond started the vid again. He watched the whole sequence. The first car parking. Brandon and the redhead crossing. And the car sitting there in the dark, not moving. His heart was beating fast. This must be it. The lead he had been searching for. The only thing in any of the vids that want logical or explainable. Something that tied the redhead to something else. He didn't want to jump to any conclusions, but he could feel it in his gut. He had just busted the case.

Desmond, 20th May 2098

Desmond watched the enhanced vid. Nothing much was revealed. The street was still dark, and the car was still parked. No one moved, and no one got out. The car was silver, nondescript, and blended right in. The edge of the license that was visible was fairly useless as it only showed 2 of the 14 numbers. It would take his team ages to follow all those leads. Was it worth it? Desmond couldn't be sure.

He watched the lightened version and the infrared version with anticipation, but nothing much was revealed. There just wasn't anything there. But then, his inbox bounced as he received the version with heat signatures. Bingo! Now he had something. There was a heat signature in the parked car. It just sat there. In the parked car. Doing nothing. Desmond slowed the vid, frame by frame, and as the redhead crossed the street and looked first left, and then right, he saw a barely imperceptible movement of the top of the heat signature. Some kind of acknowledgement. A nod. That was it. He had his lead.

Desmond grabbed his jacket and ran over to tech. He told them what he wanted. He needed every detail of that car, of that heat signature. He wanted to know when it left the parking spot and where it went. He wanted to know everything about that heat signature. Trace the car backwards. Where did it originate? Who was in that car? Age, gender, height, and above all a face. He needed the full license plate. He needed all of it NOW. Tech started working immediately as Desmond went back to his desk and replayed the vid over and over again. This was it. He sat back in his chair and smiled to himself. He'd done it. This was his final career-making win. He was overjoyed with a sense of accomplishment.

Lynola Loughton, 18th May 2098

After Alfred was nominated for his second term, he knew that he had been empowered to tackle something truly revolutionary. He figured that after a seven-year term of positive change, he was clearly doing something right if the Global Council on Leadership wanted him to continue. So, he decided to try something riskier, but which had the potential for a much bigger change that could help so many people.

As we all knew long before Alfred's second term, that local community, federal, and global taxation systems were incredibly corrupt and no matter what small fixes were put in place, the wealthy and big business always benefitted from loopholes that were built-in especially for them by their friends with power and influence. We knew that this policy, the third big hurdle that Alfred decided to pour his energy into, was going to be a big one. Alfred felt that the time was right to tackle it. He was obviously doing something right and so he decided to dedicate his efforts to fighting the tax battle.

The first thing to do was to get re-commitments from all the nation-state parties that they would follow the Global Council on this one. As the policy was going to affect the wealth of national councils, and that they were going to feel the wrath of important people in their countries, this was going to be an important one. Alfred worked himself to the bone, even before any policies were announced. He travelled to almost every country on earth, and even went off-world to prepare the TriCities for what was coming. We knew that the policy was going to benefit most countries and most communities, but we also knew that a large and powerful interests would receive the short end of the stick and not be happy about it.

The system of nominating even the lowest non-civilian positions worked in Alfred's favor. Most people that he met had true intentions and were as close as possible to being incorruptible as was humanly possible. It helped that special interest groups and the super-wealthy and already been neutered compared to their compatriots 30 years before. But of course, powerful factions still existed in the corners of society and Alfred had to make sure that everyone was on board.

The most common reaction he got from his meetings was surprise, and then admiration that he was going to take this on. Most people already knew what the solution should be. It wasn't complicated. A simple tax system that favored wealth redistribution, higher taxes on activities that didn't contribute to the positive productivity of society – like algorithm-generated investments, sports betting, and the leisure activities of the very wealthy – and the elimination of taxes on the basic needs of society, including shelter, heating and cooling, and of course, water and food.

Alfred was a star when it came to building rapport and trust amongst colleagues. He was immensely trustworthy because he was immensely honest. You could read his every thought on his face and he was never ashamed of his thoughts, even if they went against the common wisdom. He was always right, because he was always just and fair. He only concern was peace, harmony, justice, and equity for all. And his tax proposals were a reflection of everything good that he was. It was a risky fight, and one that could have broken him, but he was strong enough to take it on, and he was humble enough to compromise when necessary and when it served the common good. Signing the Tax Fairness Act (TFA) of 2072 was one of Alfred's proudest moments as Global President. He closed loopholes and imposed a level of global equitable wealth distribution that had never been seen in human societies. The world we live in today is better because of Alfred and TFA.

Desmond, 20th May 2098

Two hours later he had the full report from tech and about 15 minutes of vid compilations bouncing in his inbox. He started with the vid. He watched the car as it crossed the bridge into Bergen, and the vids followed it as it weaved through the smaller streets, in a seeming random pattern, until it ended up parked in the street where the redhead and Brandon crossed. Desmond watched as it pulled out of the parking spot, about 3 minutes after the signal from the redhead. He had been patient. The vids followed the car to the street behind the hotel. The blast had obviously just happened. The responders were arriving, and the crowds were starting to appear. The car parked in the alley behind the hotel hidden by the garbage chutes. The heat signature stepped out of the car and Desmond leaned in. It was mostly obscured by the chutes and he slammed his hand against the desk. Come on! Gimme something here! The heat signature was almost completely obscured by the angle of the vid, the crowds, the dust and debris, and the garbage chutes. It stepped through the back door of the hotel and disappeared.

Desmond ran back out to tech and asked about the hotel security vids. He was told that they went only up until the blast and then cut. The explosion had disabled their systems. There was nothing there. Dammit! He wasn't going to find out this way.

Okay, back to his desk. He opened the report and searched for the license plate. The car had been traced to the helipod rental office. The company were sending over the rental agreement details. He should have them soon. He sat back in his chair again. His heart was pounding. He was getting so close. He tapped his feet on the floor. Tapped his fingers on the desk. Waiting. He watched the vid again. He slowed the vid as the heat signature got out of the car. Could he discern anything about its shape or size to be helpful? It was big, but not big enough to rule out being female. It wasn't fat or unusual in shape. Just an average person.

His inbox bounced. He opened up the rental agreement document. Here it was, in black and white. Nils Freeman, from Seattle, rented the car for 2 days – a day before until the day after the explosion. But he hadn't flown out on any transport after dropping off the car. Where had he gone? Desmond searched all the hotel and private rental manifests. He didn't find his name, but he did find his vid reference signature on a private personal rental just out of town. A cabin just north along the river with its back against the cliffs. He had him!

Desmond, 20th May 2098

Desmond and the team of responders drove up quietly in their electric cruisers and surrounded the cabin. It was a beautiful day, the sun was reflecting off the water sparkling through the trees, and Desmond could hear sounds of children laughing and families splashing along the rocky embankment a few dozen meters from where they stood. A line of trees shielded them, so he didn't have to worry about attracting too much attention.

It was an old-fashioned wooden-style house. It was small enough for easy maintenance and large enough for a young family to enjoy weekends by the water. Desmond's detector was showing signs of heat inside the building, but they were faded. The signature was lying down in the middle of the house. He or she might be on the couch or in the bath, Desmond thought. A strange activity for the middle of the day, one day after your involvement in the most infamous terrorist attack of the year.

Clearly, he, or she, was relaxed and not on the lookout for any danger. This was going to work in his favor.

Desmond signaled the team to approach the building cautiously. Nothing stirred. Desmond tested the front door, but it was locked. He used his police override code that had been preauthorized by a judge - as he didn't want anything to derail this person's conviction in a court of law - and turned the handle quietly. As he peeked around the door, he could hear the sound of water running. He or she must be taking a bath. His team entered simultaneously through both the back and front doors and made their way quietly to the center, meeting outside the bathroom door.

Desmond held up his detector and saw the heat signature through the door, still lying down. He nodded to the team and stepped back. Two responders hit the door in unison with their shoulders and the door fell instantly forward in a cloud of dust. They stepped inside and stopped. The body was lying in the bathtub, with the water running over it. Steam was coming off the water as it trickled slowly onto the body and then down the drain. Desmond stepped in between the two responders and stared down at the face. It was puffed and bloated from being in water for more than a day, and the bullet hole between the eyes was glaring and red.

Desmond almost fell to his knees. He felt like all the air had gone out of the room. It was as if someone had punched him in the gut. His one and only lead was dead in a tub, likely under a false name, and probably with enhancements and DNA blockers that would make him untraceable. He stared down at the body and then looked away in disgust. He left his team to do what they knew how to do and stepped out of the house. He walked through the trees and looked down at the rocky embankment just below them. Two children were playing in the shallow water while their parents were watching and smiling. A dog was sniffing alongside a pile of rocks and the gulls circled and screamed overhead. A normal day.

CHAPTER 9

Lynola Loughton, 18th May 2098

Ladies and Gentlemen. Today I am so immensely proud to accept this award on behalf of myself and my beloved Alfred. We were so honored and humbled to work towards the greater good, and we did it together out of love, common respect, and a desire to leave this world a better place than we came into.

As you know, the issues we tackled were tough ones. I believe we made a difference in people's lives and that communities around the world are thriving because of the work we did. We have eliminated 90% of world poverty and we have successfully fought and cured diseases that had ravaged human societies for decades. We have adjusted to a disrupted and changing global climate, and we have ensured that almost every man, woman, and child is fed, clothed, immunized, educated, free from fear, has basic shelter and clean water, and has an opportunity to build whatever life they choose for themselves.

Today, I am pleased to announce two important initiatives. First, after months of personal reflection, I have decided to release selections from Alfred's journals. As some of you may not know, he kept a journal for most of his life and he recorded his most conflicting experiences in them. Experiences when he had the most trouble deciding which the right path, and where he found himself up against the strongest forces fighting against change and positive evolution. It was during these times that Alfred turned to his journals to help organize his thoughts and express his innermost frustrations. I believe the world has a right to understand his thought processes and learn the details and arguments behind some of his most controversial policies. I am therefore proud to release relevant selections of his journals and to be able to share them with you.

Second, there is one more policy that Alfred and I worked on before he unexpectedly left this world. It took me a few years to get back to this project and gather the inputs necessary to make clear decisions on the best way to implement this new policy. Alfred was so passionate about this and felt so strongly about it that I could not give up. It took a few more years to rebuild the alliances that Alfred had established to be able to support such an initiative.

I am honored and humbled today to have achieved that milestone, and today, I am taking the opportunity of this global stage to present the model that I, and of course Alfred, designed for the Global Council on Leadership. This initiative will forever eliminate the need for commercial industrial agriculture and will ensure a new and healthy way of life for people across the globe. It wasn't easy, and it may not be very popular with some of our most powerful members of society, but we all know in our heart of hearts that it is necessary for humanity's survival, and I believe that Alfred and I have designed a way to get it done.

This is the final stage of the agricultural revolution that we started during Alfred's first term in office. We have laid out a plan that the Global Council on Leadership will be examining in the coming months, to eliminate all forms of commercial agriculture and replace it with cooperative agriculture around the world. Unlike the communist models that failed so badly in the early last century, we now understand how to organize collective agriculture so that everyone benefits, and no one is exploited. We know how to stay motivated and grow and process food beyond our individual consumption which is beneficial for everyone along the supply chain. And we know how to organize our local farms to feed our communities. We must leave behind the inefficient and inequitable system of industrial farming that exploits the land and benefits only a few.

I have worked closely with behavioral scientists, land managers, and industrial agriculturalists, who have all reached the same conclusion. We are perfectly capable, as the human race, to cultivate enough food to feed ourselves and future generations, without creating further destruction to the environment and without compromising nutritional quality.

Many decades ago, when I was raising my children in the inner city, we started a community garden in an empty urban lot. My neighbors thought I was crazy. They were happy to live on processed foods and meals from boxes, and not get their hands dirty. I let my kids play in the dirt, plant seeds, water the seedlings, pull out the weeds, and reap their own harvests. We juiced carrots and ginger. We made jams and preserves. We experimented with bamboo shoots, pumpkins, Marsala spices, and cloves. We julienned vegetables and made chop-suey from scratch. We made disgusting combinations that the kids called their "potions", and we made delicious and nutritious meals for ourselves. We raised chickens and ate fresh eggs on a regular basis. It wasn't hard, but it took work and we faced ridicule and lacked community support.

Gradually, as my kids grew up and left home, I was determined to keep the garden going and I started getting more interest from the community. As food stocks got tighter and rationing hit the inner cities, especially after a quake or a hurricane, people got more interested in my little urban farm. The experience opened my eyes to how necessity was truly the motivator to change. And even though, in the decades since, the world has learned how to feed itself with meat substitutes and nutritional supplements, I never got over the simplicity and satisfaction of farming one's own food.

Of course, I am aware that it is not a possibility for everyone, but it is a possibility for most. Therefore, my recommendations to the Global Council on Leadership include a mandate for a one-acre community garden for every 100 citizens around the world. We will open-source all agricultural research to help people learn which foods will grow well in their environment, and how to maximize production without expensive supplements or wasteful fertilizers. And mandate a few hours a month for each and every able-bodied person from age 8 to age 88 to work in the community garden. We will no longer have a need for the monoculture that has destroyed 90% of all our species of fruits and vegetables. And the agricultural speculation and commodities trading that has ruined our food industry for the past 250 years, and which continues to this day, will be undermined and eliminated.

We will be able to grow our own wheat and sell it to a local cooperative that will grind it, process it, bake it into bread and sell it back to us, at a reasonable price – as there'll be no need to make a profit, only cover the costs of labor, production equipment and distribution. We will be able to grow grapes and sell to a co-op to process into wine. We will be able to raise goats and sheep, pigs and chickens. If we live close to water, we can raise fish and other sea life. And if we do it on a small scale, rather than the mega-sized industrial farms that we have been slaves to over the past 100 years, we can manage the waste by composting and creating natural fertilizers to feed back into the next generation of seedlings. I've done this. It works. Alfred and our family were self-sufficient for those years. It didn't take a scientist to tell me how to grow carrots or broccoli or raise chickens to feed my kids. And we didn't generate excessive waste, we didn't ruin our land, our children weren't malnourished, and we didn't go hungry.

This is the vision that Alfred and I have for the global community. Tonight, I will be submitting my detailed proposal to the Global Council on Leadership. It relies on the cooperation of dozens of disparate industries and sectors, with whom I've had extensive conversations over the past few months. For the first time, they will be able to see how each of them will play a vital role in the reinvention of our global food production and our evolution to truly end world hunger and become a self-sufficient race that doesn't destroy this planet as we feed ourselves.

I am immensely grateful to the United Peace Award Committee for giving me this platform to tell Alfred and my stories, and to announce these two initiatives. I feel sure that Alfred's journals will illuminate and inspire many, and that our recommendations for eliminating industrial agriculture will make the world a better place. I have no doubt that future generations will be better off even if our path to that future is a little challenging to navigate.

Today I must thank you, our family, and everyone who has supported Alfred and me over these decades. Our service to you was the greatest achievement of our lives and your confidence and trust in us made us humble and immensely grateful. Thank you all.

CHAPTER 10

Alfred, 2069

Jesus, these people are monsters. It almost hurts to know that people like this exist in the world. Of course, I know it intellectually. There have always been monsters in the world. Genghis Khan, Attila the Hun, Hitler, Putin, and even those who didn't obviously murder numbers of people but had evil in their hearts anyway and were powerful in a different way. In just the 50 years at the turn of the last century, we could list Nixon, Cheney, Bannon, Trump, Stevens, and Blackman as the modern equivalent of evil monsters. They caused the same amount of destruction and devastation, but from behind a desk instead of on a horse with a gun or a sword in hand.

Sometimes I forget that human nature has this evil side. Sometimes I get lost in all the good we are doing. All the change we are making that helps so many people. Sometimes I make the assumption that everyone is with us, everyone is on board, and no one is fighting this change to line their own pockets or wallow in their own selfishness. I shouldn't be this stupid, I know, but it's easier to think this way.

Today I met with the Global Agroforum. Jesus, talk about a whole bunch of old white men clinging to an outdated, unfair system of exploitation. They really couldn't give a shit about making the world a better place. They just want bigger houses, fancier cars, and a bigger yacht at the end of their dock. These guys are the epitome of selfish and egotistical.

It's hard for me to believe that they actually accept that what they are advocating for is right for the world, or whether they're so caught up in their own lies that they've convinced themselves as well. Maybe I'm too idealistic, but I have to believe it's the latter. They wholeheartedly believe their own deceptions and they're being truthful in their passions based on the lies they now consider as truth. They couldn't be this persuasive if they didn't believe their own arguments.

I don't think we have any chance of changing their minds. There are so many things we could be doing but aren't. There are so many obstacles in the way. The elimination of the commercial agro sector is still decades away, and we will have to build the path slowly. We will have to chip away at their power and have more wins under our belt before we can affect the kind of change that the world needs. I'm going to have to be patient.

Lynola and I had a dinner with some of the big players. Having them in our home was kind of disgusting. There was this one guy who was looking at Charlotte with such a lustful gaze that I wanted to punch his lights out. She's a big girl now and can easily deal with any unwanted advances, but the leer in the guy's face was disgusting. His name was Jose or Jesus or Jorge. I can't remember. His dad runs one of the biggest industrial agrofirms so I guess I'm going to have to get to know him a little better. Sometimes I hate my job, even while I'm still so honored to have it. Lynola's excitement over this one is palpable. I'll have to keep my eye on the prize.

Alfred, 2069

Lynola and I are just back from Jorgio's estate in Guatemala. Such a beautiful spot, but so decadent. His father, Jorgio Sr was the one who earned most of this wealth. Jorgio Jr, aka JJ, is just living in his father's shadow and his frustrations are obvious. It was billed as "negotiations", but honestly, I don't think he was very interested in negotiating anything. He's as slimy in person as he is by reputation. Lynola spent most of her time with his business team, while I had to play snooker with him in front of the cameras in the open-air game room overlooking his bay. It's so hard to have a straight-laced discussion with someone you know has evil in their hearts.

Lynola was flushed when she came to the room before dinner. I asked her what was going on, but she said she wanted to just take a bath and relax. I could tell she wanted to be left alone and organize her thoughts. By the time it was ready to go to dinner she had calmed down and reassured me that she would tell me what had happened. It must have been something she'd figured out when talking to the business team. Maybe she found a way to convince them to change their exploitive ways. Unlikely.

Alfie, 2069

She secretly recorded it on her vid. A conversation between the business manager and Jorgio where he was being updated on the numbers of deaths and dismemberments in his fields over the past month.

*Deaths were mostly due to heatstroke and malnutrition.
Not his problem, he's heard to say on the recording.
Followed by laughter as they joked about how many
fewer mouths they were going to have to feed that
month. Immediately followed by a brisk order to recruit
more people to work the southern harvest. This time
find stronger and younger ones. My stomach turned.
These people are disgusting. Even if it takes me the rest
of my life, Lynola and I have to find a solution.*

"Niels Freeman", 18th May 2098

The smoke was thick and suffocating, but he wasn't
worried. He had one mission. To make sure that Lynola's vid was
destroyed and that no drafts were ever found. Then he could
move on with his life, pay off his debts, and live forever with
money in his pockets. He knew that the blast had already
disabled the hotel's security system and he went directly to the
basement tech room to make sure that it was destroyed as well.
Every building with multiple residents, workers, or guests, like
this hotel, provided free backup systems for their guests. They
worked off remote transmission and were useful to business
people whose vids got corrupted, or hotel staff who needed to
calculate their tips at the end of their shift. They were always on
and always there. But their data remained local, unless the guest
or an authority requested it. Usually they were deleted after 30
days and served just as a precautionary service to the guests in a

hotel like this one. His mission was to destroy the backup and make it look like a casualty of the blast.

As he stepped into the kitchen, he found debris among the remnants of dinner cleanup. Broken plates of food were strewn over the floor. One wall was cracked, and chunks of plaster were mingled with broken crockery and raw vegetables. Bags of meat substitutes had exploded against another wall, leaving a grey-green splatter that made his stomach churn. He moved through the mess quickly, knowing exactly where he would find the stairs to the basement. He had memorized every nook and cranny of this place and didn't expect to encounter too many surprises. As he stepped into the side hallway, he could see through the glass into lobby area. Guests, covered by plaster dust and huddled together into groups, were being shepherded by employees out through the main doors where responders were meeting them and taking them to the treatment tents that had sprung up in front of the hotel. He looked like any one of them. Medium build, medium hair, no remarkable facial or body features. Anonymity was paramount to his success and he was pleased to see that he would fit in well with this crowd.

But first, he had to finish his mission and he wanted to be sure that he would go unseen. He saw that the responders were not entering the hotel yet and he relaxed a little knowing that he still had some time. He glanced up through the center of the hotel building. He could see the stars peeking weakly through the dust cloud of the ruptured structure. He checked the sensor on his vid. Dozens of vids were active in the immediate area, but none had Lynola's signature. He searched again. Nothing related to Lynola or any of the Loughtons. Nothing that even came close to her known synonyms. He relaxed a little more. Two of out three of his missions were complete. One left, and then he could go to the beach house he had rented and lay low for a while before reinventing himself yet again. Maybe this time was the last time.

He padded silently down the concrete steps to the basement, pausing every few steps to listen for the sounds of people. He could hear the cries and conversations above him on the street, but nothing closer. He stopped again, his acute hearing picking up a noise nearby. He barely breathed as he listened harder. Plaster and gravel were jolted down a crevice. Nothing else. He waited another two heartbeats before continuing down the stairs. He turned on his vid light and scanned the basement. No one was down here. No bodies, no carnage. A few cracks in the walls which probably went through to the foundation, dooming the whole building, but nothing that put him in immediate danger.

He moved quickly down the hallway to the fourth door on the left and tried the door. As he expected, it was locked. He removed a small hammer from his back pocket and smashed the identification pad. He had 15 seconds before the alarm would sound. He quickly reversed the hammer and used the strong magnetic element hidden in the handle to disable the hinges on the door. They sagged when their magnetic force was incapacitated, and the door fell forward into the room. The alarm was disabled. He stepped onto the door and walked in.

Inside, most of the towers were still functional. Lights were blinking, and the fresh air of the controlled environment was uncontaminated by the dust floating in the rest of the building. Well, until now anyway. He had let in all the contaminants and that certainly wouldn't be good for the towers. Not that he cared anyway. He stepped over to the last monitor and hit the keyboard. It lit up with the log. He saw all the transmissions that had gone out in the last few minutes. People telling their loved ones that they were fine. Others asking for news of their family. He scrolled backwards up the screen.

It was clear when the blast had happened. Just before the blast, there was minimal activity. A few room service orders, a couple of messages to personal assistants and family members. The hotel manager's log just before shift change. A late guest checking-in. Then, just seconds after the blast, a furious amount of messaging outwards and inwards. Messages to the responders, to family members. Hotel employees to each other, to their managers. And managers to their employees. Get the guests out. Secure the floors. Identify the wounded and dead. Check on Lynola Loughton!

He read through the messages with a sense of voyeurism. He hadn't been involved in the blast, per se. His role was limited to the verification of the demise of Lynola, and the destruction of her vid and its backups. Clearly the first item was a check. The fact that her vid wasn't registering was a good sign for item number two. He'd keep an eye on it over the next few days, but he felt fairly confident that it was lost in the explosion.

He had to take care of item number three. He scrolled backwards to before the blast and slowed down, scanning each entry. Standard stuff. Autobackups of vids and the entries he'd already seen. He scrolled back slowly. There! He'd found it. An autobackup of Lynola's vid. About 40 minutes before the blast. She had likely gone to bed early in anticipation of the big day. That means that she had probably died in her sleep and hadn't even known what was going on. Not that he cared either way. A job was a job. The rest was none of his business.

He could see from the parameters of the backup that she wasn't doing any mirroring. The intel was good. As most leaders and private speakers were doing these days to avoid leaks and hacks, she had the habit of turning off the mirroring when she was drafting a big speech. This was the only copy of what had been on her vid at the time of the explosion. His heart was pounding. The last trace of Lynola and her speech. She'd clearly been happy in its final version and had set the backup before she turned in for the night. His mission was complete. He would retire in luxury, in one of the Fjords up north, where the mild weather and soft winds would sweep over his front porch in the early evenings as he watched the sunset. Maybe he'd get a dog or a horse. He could almost feel the breeze in his hair.

He touched the screen and highlighted her backup. Store, Copy, Send, Delete, Save. His finger hovered over the Delete button and his eyes wandered over to the Copy icon. Should he? Would he dare? Curiosity almost got the better of him, but he shook it off and pressed Delete. He pressed it and it confirmed again. Yes, again. Absolutely sure. Delete it from the face of the earth. Whatever it said, whoever it was going to threaten, whatever it was going to launch was gone forever. Not even he knew what was in it. No one would ever know the details. That was his mission and it was complete.

He walked out of the room, stepping over the broken door. He padded silently up the stairs and kept to the darkened hallway back through the kitchen. Then he took a handful of plaster dust and rubbed it into his hair and onto his clothes. He tore his shirt at the shoulder and threw more plaster down his back. He rubbed his shirtsleeves and pants into some of the food scraps and other trash on the floor. He then took another handful of dust and rubbed it onto his face, in his eyes, and deliberately inhaled a little.

He started coughing violently as he pushed through the kitchen's swinging doors into the hallway and stumbled into the hotel lobby. Almost immediately one of the hotel employees ran to his side. He doubled over as he coughed and grabbed onto the man's arm, giving him a grateful look. The employee supported him as he walked out of the main hotel entrance doors and into the care of the responders. He blended anonymously into the crowd and let them take care of his injuries.

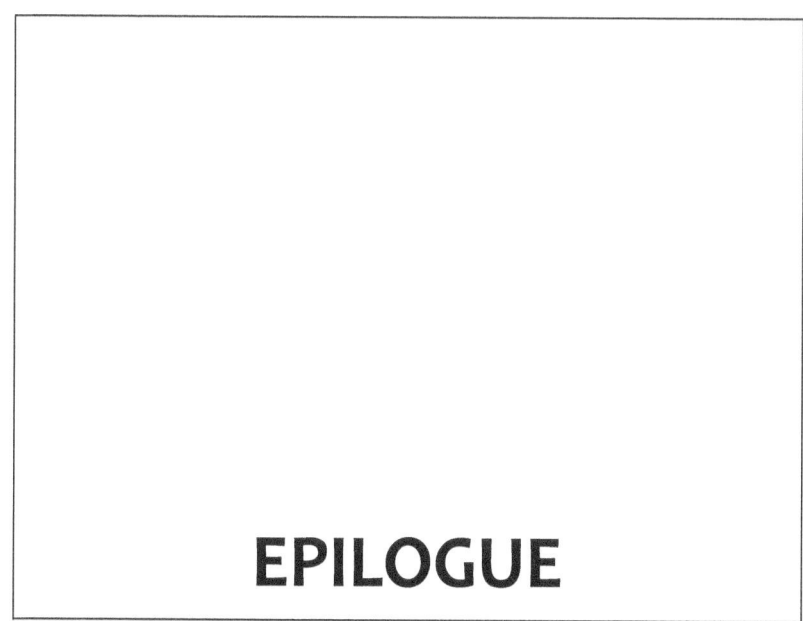

EPILOGUE

United Nations  A/RES/101/392

General Assembly

Distr.: General
11 October 2027

Hundred and first session
Agenda item 92

Resolution adopted by the General Assembly on 29 August 2027

101/392. Follow-up to the Conference of African Nations on Voting Rights and Leadership

The General Assembly

Recalling its resolution 101/303 of 9 July 2027 in which it endorsed the Outcome of the Conference of African Nations on Voting Rights and Leadership, held in Accra, Ghana from 24 to 30 June 2027,

Recalling also its resolution 101/305 of 31 July 2027 in which it decided to establish an ad-hoc open-ended working group of the General Assembly to follow up on the issues contained in the Outcome of the Conference of African Nations on Voting Rights and Leadership,

Recalling further its decision of 13 September 2027 to take note of the progress report of the Ad Hoc Open-Ended Working Group of the General Assembly to follow up on the issues contained in the Outcome of the Conferences of African Nations on Voting Rights and Leadership,

Expressing great enthusiasm for the short-term positive impact on local and national economies and social development in the countries that have adopted a new model of leadership nomination,

Taking note of the important concerns and opposition to the new model of leadership nomination being adopted in the west African nations,

Recognizing the need to ensure proper follow-up and study of the long-term impacts of the new model of leadership nomination being advocated in the Outcome of the Conferences of African Nations on Voting Rights and Leadership,

Decides to explore further, in its hundred and second session, the most efficient modalities for intergovernmental follow-up to the Outcome of the Conferences of African Nations on Voting Rights and Leadership, and in this regard requests the President of the General Assembly to hold open, inclusive, timely and transparent consultations with all Member States.

222nd plenary meeting
11 October 2027

United Nations

 **General Assembly**

Distr.: General
31 March 2028

Hundred and second session
Agenda item 07

Resolution adopted by the General Assembly on 5 March 2028

106/307. Towards an incorruptible and equitable model of regional, national and international leadership

The General Assembly

Recalling its resolution 101/392 of 29 August 2027 in which it decided to explore further the most efficient modalities for intergovernmental follow-up to the Outcome of the Conferences of African Nations on Voting Rights and Leadership,

Conscious that development in west African countries that have adopted the new model of leadership election has dramatically and significantly improved in the past 5 years with measurable and significant decreases in hunger, disease, corruption, and poverty,

Recognizing that the African model may not be applicable to every society around the world, and that significant opposition to such changes in leadership election may cause local and regional short-term upheaval,

Acknowledging that climate change is causing significant distress to large regions of the world who are ill-equipped to handle the long-term negative effects on their populations,

Taking note of the important concerns and opposition to the new model of leadership nomination being adopted in the West African nations,

Decides to establish a new Global Council on Leadership apart from this body's General Assembly or Security Council, to examine and, where appropriate, help implement the new leadership model at the local and regional level to be organized as follows:

To commence with a plenary meeting and two interactive round tables, to be chaired by states from the west African nations who have adopted the new model of leadership, at the invitation of the President of the General Assembly and to address the following themes:

> Round Table 1: Present the process by which each country transformed their leadership structure and adopted the new election model.

> Round Table 2: Describe the challenges they faced, their methods of resolving each one, and their lessons learned that can be passed on to other members.

The opening plenary meeting will feature statements by the President of the General Assembly, the Secretary-General and representatives from the African Council on Leadership.

The meeting should be organized and held in a neutral location within the following 12 months.

The closing plenary meeting will feature statements from individual states detailing their action plans to implement a non-election model and join the Global Council on Leadership.

Global Council

On Leadership

EQUAL TAX RE-DISTRIBUTION AND ACCOMMODATION PLAN

A CITIZEN PROTECTION AND WEALTH REDISTRIBUTION MODEL

ADOPTED BY THE GLOBAL COUNCIL ON LEADERSHIP IN REPRESENTATION OF ITS GLOBAL CITIZENRY

MAY 2064

ETRAP ensures equitable access to income and social services for global citizens of every age, race, economic level, and other sub-group. It is unlawful for individuals to hide, horde, or exploit their wealth to avoid ETRAP.

An equitable income tax rate is hereby imposed upon all individuals who earn hourly or monthly revenue, or any compensation from work performed or investments earned. According to the Global Council's annual assessment of the value of a Basket of Goods, each citizen will pay a 19% tax on every unit of currency earned above 11 times of the value of a Basket of Goods on a monthly basis. There are no exceptions, waivers, offsets, or deductions. Consumer product, state and local taxes are eliminated.

All corporations will pay a flat rate of 17% of every unit of currency earned, no matter their positive or negative profit margins. Corporations are prohibited from offering any compensation package to any employee, board member, advisor or consultant that

269

is valued at more than 300 times the lowest employee hourly wage or salary. Corporations are prohibited from raising any sales prices more than 100% in a given 12-month period without the consent of the Fiscal Board of the Global Council on Leadership.

Revenue from income and corporate tax will be used by the Fiscal Board to fund all governmental and social activities. All global citizens will have equal access to fair housing, healthcare, childcare services, clean water, food distribution, primary and secondary education, technical training, legal services, climate change refugee services, and disaster relief.

About the Author

Sara Pax is an entrepreneur, wife and mother. She was born in London, UK and has lived in Chicago, IL, Washington, DC, Geneva, Switzerland, and Albuquerque, NM. She currently lives in Paris, France with her family and works as Associate Dean at The American Business School of Paris. She also runs a consulting company helping women launch and grow their small businesses, and she occasionally works as a business mentor and coach.

She has a degree in International Relations from The American University in Washington DC and an MBA in Marketing Research from the University of Illinois at Chicago. She is currently pursuing her Doctorate of Professional Studies in Instructional Design from Franklin University.

Sara intensely follows politics on both sides of the Atlantic. She moved from the UK to the US when she was 15 years old, and still holds a permanent residence status in the US. As such, she has never been eligible to vote in any local or national election.

This is her first novel.